"Someone's coming."

Alexa's eyes widened, and some of the blood drained from her face. The unmistakable sound of footsteps echoed down the hallway, approaching the office, and Zack did the only thing he could think of to keep Alexa safe.

He pulled her against him and kissed her.

As Zack's mouth closed over hers, Alexa gasped and then melted into him almost instantly. His lips were firm but gentle, warm and sweet as they moved against hers. His hands stroked her back, and as his tongue slipped into her mouth, she slid her hands up his chest, over his broad shoulders, and into his thick, soft hair. His tongue caressed hers, and a sparkling heat exploded over her skin. He groaned softly, and she opened more for him.

Never in her life had a kiss felt like this…

ALSO BY TARA WYATT

Necessary Risk
Primal Instinct

CHAIN
REACTION

Tara Wyatt

FOREVER

NEW YORK BOSTON

Copyright © 2017 by Tara Wyatt
Excerpt from *Necessary Risk* © 2016 by Tara Wyatt
Cover design by Christine Foltzer
Cover illustration by Tony Mauro

Forever
Hachette Book Group
1290 Avenue of the Americas, New York, NY 10104
forever-romance.com
twitter.com/foreverromance

First Edition: February 2017

Forever is an imprint of Grand Central Publishing. The Forever name and logo are trademarks of Hachette Book Group, Inc.

The publisher is not responsible for websites (or their content) that are not owned by the publisher.

The Hachette Speakers Bureau provides a wide range of authors for speaking events. To find out more, go to www.hachettespeakersbureau.com or call (866) 376-6591.

ISBN 978-1-4555-9031-5 (mass market), 978-1-4555-9030-8 (ebook)

Printed in the United States of America

OPM

10 9 8 7 6 5 4 3 2 1

To the Thursday girls, Amanda, Robin,
and Sarah. Thank you for not forgetting
I existed while I wrote this book.

ACKNOWLEDGMENTS

Thank you to my friends and family, especially my husband, Graham, and my parents, Gerry and Catherine, for your ongoing support and love. I think it's important to note that while these books have featured some pretty horrific examples of parenting, none of those examples bear any resemblance to my own parents, who are wonderful and awesome. I'd also like to thank my fantastic critique partners, Harper St. George and Erin Moore. You ladies are wonderful, and I'd be lost without you. Thank you to Julie B. for beta reading a draft of this book. Your feedback was so helpful (G loop!).

Thank you to my editor, Alex Logan, for all your hard work on this book. Thank you as well to my HPL coworkers Stacy, Gina, Joe, and Janette. I'm lucky to work with such wonderful people.

Writing is a solitary profession, and I feel very fortunate to have found a wonderful group of writer friends who get my crazy. Thank you to Shannon Richard, Nicki Pau Preto (my bae), Morgan Rhodes, Juliana Stone, Molly O'Keefe, Maureen McGowan, Jenn Burke, Kelly Jensen, Kelly Siskind, Amanda Heger, Jessica Lemmon, Eve Silver, Elly

Blake, Samantha Joyce, Elle Wright, Rachel Lacey, Colleen Halverson, Heather Van Fleet, and Anise Eden. There are probably more, and I'm sorry if there are any names I've forgotten. Chalk it up to deadline brain and know that if you've supported me or cheered me on in any way, I'm grateful.

Finally, and most importantly, thank you to my readers! I wouldn't be doing this without you.

Special shout-outs: wine (always), Sarah Younger, my puppy Schroeder, the gratuitous shirtlessness of MMA, and Nick Bateman.

CHAPTER 1

Gilded cages were deceptive things. People tended to focus only on the "gilded" part, the glitz and the glamour, and gloss over the fact that even though the bars were made of gold, they were still bars. And now that she was out of that cage, Alexa Fairfax was certain that she never wanted back in.

The opulent dining table sparkled in the dim light from the chandelier above, the Carpathian elm gleaming, the edges of the black-and-gold serving ware shining. All around her, conversations buzzed through the air, mingling with the jazz floating from an invisible speaker in the ceiling. Her father sat at the head of the long table in the Fairfax mansion's dining room, smiling as he talked with the directors and producers flanking him, all hanging on his every word. And although he was laughing, there was a hardness in his eyes, a sharpness in the set of his jaw, that had her on edge. She'd seen that look enough to know that he was scheming, plotting something with his cronies. *Cronies* felt like such an old-fashioned word, but it completely suited the men surrounding her father, with their expensive cigars and hungry grins.

She just hoped that this particular scheme, whatever it was, didn't involve her. She couldn't do that again. She wouldn't. She fought the urge to nibble at a fingernail or play with her hair, knowing she'd catch hell from the well-preserved woman sitting across from her.

"I'm so glad you were free for dinner, honey," said her mother, leaning forward slightly. "You know how your father likes so much for you to make appearances at these parties."

Alexa took a deep breath and smoothed her hands over her black-and-white strapless silk dress, bracing herself.

"He's still upset about you moving out, you know."

She'd moved out of her parents' Malibu mansion two months ago now, and it was one of the best decisions she'd ever made. For the first time in her twenty-five years, she was out from under their thumb. Feeling free. Happy. And realizing that the life she'd led up to that point wasn't what she wanted for her future. She hadn't fully realized just how much she hated being in this house until she'd moved out. As soon as she'd walked in earlier that evening, a weight had settled over her.

"It was time, Mom. Besides, aren't most parents desperate for their kids to leave?"

As a response, her mother murmured something unintelligible that sounded a lot like "ungrateful, spoiled brat."

Alexa refused to take the bait, although the words still stung. "I can't stay long. I have another party to go to."

"That would explain the dress," said her mother, taking a tiny sip of her wine, one perfect eyebrow arched in disdain.

Alexa clamped her teeth together and clenched her hand

into a fist under the table. All the things she wanted to say danced on the tip of her tongue, but as tempting as it was to spew some of her mother's nastiness back at her, she knew it wouldn't accomplish anything. It would only feed the beast, when all she really wanted was to get this dinner party over with and leave as soon as possible.

If Alexa hadn't looked so startlingly like her mother, with the same blond hair so light it was nearly white, the same silvery blue eyes, the same button nose crafted by the same plastic surgeon, she'd have wondered if she was adopted. But she wasn't. The only child of Jonathan and Melanie, destined—or so she'd always been told—to carry on the Hollywood dynasty started by her great-grandparents back in the days of silent film. Fonda, Barrymore, Huston, Fairfax—all were names synonymous with glamour, with Hollywood, with fame. With talent, success, and power.

And she wanted nothing to do with it, because she knew the cost of that success and power. Knew the ugly truth behind them.

Gordon Kramer, a producer in his early sixties, sat down beside her mother. He swooped a hand over his short salt-and-pepper hair and smiled at Alexa, his eyes traveling from her face down to her breasts, leaving an imaginary trail of slime in the wake of his gaze. She suppressed a shudder and took a sip of her water, trying to hide the revulsion crawling over her skin.

"Alexa, darling, you look lovely this evening," said Kramer, taking a healthy sip of wine and then settling his hands on his protruding stomach. "And you're here alone, I see. No young man with you this evening?"

Her mother jumped in. "I've been trying and trying to set her up with someone, but she won't let me." She stuck out her bottom lip in a fake pout. "And I know so many men—powerful, rich, successful men—who'd love the chance to date her."

Kramer's eyes once again slid over Alexa's body, and she managed a thin smile, not wanting to participate in the conversation. She checked her watch, wondering how much longer until they ate and she could leave for the party at her friend Sierra's, when a server appeared silently at her elbow and placed a salad down in front of her.

"Could I please have a glass of wine?" she asked, picking up her fork to dig into the salad.

"Of course." The server nodded and continued down the table.

"You know, if you'd asked for a vodka soda, you could've saved thirty calories." Her mother shot her a pointed glare from across the table.

"I don't like vodka." She looked down at herself, keeping her hands on the table and not giving in to the urge to adjust her size-six dress. And it was a six only because she couldn't fit her 34C's in a four.

Another server came down the table. "Prime rib or salmon, miss?"

Before she could open her mouth to say, "Prime rib," her mother shooed the server away. "She's fine with the salad."

Anger and humiliation prickled through her, leaving her feeling hot and itchy. She tugged at her dress, smoothing it over her stomach and then letting her hands rest for a moment on her thighs, digging her fingers into the flesh hard enough to make dimples pop up. An ache settled right in the center of her chest, and she swallowed, hard, pushing it down.

Her mother leaned toward Kramer and spoke in a stage

whisper. "She's such a pretty girl, but her figure is a bit challenging."

Alexa didn't ask, already knowing exactly what her mother meant by *challenging*. Short, with boobs and hips. Feminine, but not "skinny." At least not by Hollywood standards. She worked her butt off—literally—to keep her stomach flat and her thighs slender, but there wasn't much she could do about the rest of her curves. They weren't going anywhere, and she was fine with it, most of the time, even if her mother wasn't. Her mother, on the other hand, had that willowy slenderness that often came with height and borderline starvation.

That was the thing about Hollywood. Everyone was always hungry, in one way or another, and that hunger dictated *everything*.

And Alexa knew, better than most, that starving people did desperate things.

So she sipped her wine, ate her salad, smiled and nodded politely at those around her, and silently counted down the seconds until she could get in her car and get the hell out of here. Mindless chatter filled the space around her, and she zoned out, focused on the lettuce at the end of her fork. As she'd done so often as a kid, she slipped into a fantasy that both amused and soothed her, and she imagined her mother's reaction if she told her to fuck off, threw the salad in her face, and stormed out of the house, middle finger held high. It was an incredibly appealing image, given her mother's nonstop passive-aggressive barbs.

"So, Alexa, what are you working on these days?" asked Kramer, pulling her from her reverie as the server cleared her empty salad plate away. He smiled at her, not even trying to hide the fact that he was staring at her boobs. He wiped at his mouth with his napkin, his prime rib having disappeared in record time.

"Actually, I'm taking some time off," she said. "Trying to figure out what I want to do."

"I have a project that might be right up your alley. You know my studio's making an Aquagirl movie?"

Her mother bit out a sharp scoff. "Alexa's not exactly superhero material, Gordon." She eyed Alexa skeptically, one eyebrow arched as she sipped her drink.

"I'm not looking for a new acting project right now," Alexa bit out, watching as the servers circulated with luscious-looking slabs of chocolate cake. She didn't take one, knowing she wouldn't be able to enjoy it in peace. "I'm taking some time away from acting, and I've been doing volunteer work with UNICEF."

Her mother rolled her eyes. "Honestly, Alexa. You're so strange. You don't want to act, but waste your time volunteering. You don't want to date anyone. Your fashion sense is…interesting. Sometimes I wonder if you're actually my daughter." She shot Kramer a smile. "We couldn't be more different," she said, as though she was embarrassed by Alexa while assuring Kramer that none of Alexa's perceived shortcomings were her fault.

Despite the fact that she was sitting in a crowded room having dinner with her family, a sense of loneliness wrapped itself around Alexa, thickening her throat.

"You are *so* right, Mother." Something hot and dangerous clawed at Alexa's insides, begging to be set loose, and she nearly snapped. She stood and tossed her cloth napkin down on the table, more forcefully than she'd intended. Her hands trembled slightly. "Excuse me."

"What?" Her mother looked up, her eyebrows raised in question.

Alexa forced herself to take a deep breath. She seemed to be forcing herself to do a lot of things tonight. "Bathroom." She didn't need to pee, but she did need some space. A few minutes to get it together, to rein in the anger pounding through her veins. But it wasn't just anger. No, there was something smaller and darker there too, thrumming right along with it. Something desperate and inadequate and fucking miserable. She pasted a small smile on her face as she strode through the massive house, nearly running toward the swooping marble staircase in the foyer.

The scent of roses hit her as she reached the first landing, and she slowed. She leaned a hip against the banister, glancing first left and then right at the curved staircases branching off the main one, leading to the west and east wings of the house. The sounds of the party had faded into a soft, gentle murmur of voices, clinking dishes, and music. A burst of laughter erupted, her father's booming laugh at the center, and she plucked one of the white roses from the giant urn on the heavy wooden table and took the stairs toward the east wing two at a time, wanting to spend a few minutes alone in her favorite spot.

Growing up, she'd been terribly lonely. Her only real friends had been the staff—her nanny, the cook, the maids. They'd all been kind to her, and as a young girl, she'd taken to using the servants' passageways to get from one part of the house to another, and she'd discovered all sorts of nooks and crannies throughout the mansion. Her absolute favorite one was just off the library. One of the bookshelves was actually a narrow door in disguise, and behind it was a small room with a dusty window, an old leather couch, piles of books, and a small, broken table. If her dad had ever known about the room, he'd apparently long since forgotten about it. Although she had a lavish bedroom, Alexa had claimed this space for her own, because she could hide there in a way she couldn't in her bedroom, and the staff had kept her secret.

She stepped into the dark library and pulled the door shut behind her. The room was one of her favorites in the house, the walls lined with bookshelves stuffed to the gills with books. A fireplace—dark and cold—sat nestled in one of the walls, plush leather armchairs arranged around it. Huge floor-to-ceiling windows lined the far wall, facing the backyard with its fountain, sculpted gardens, and infinity pool. Silvery moonlight streamed in, slanting across the Oriental rug that covered much of the gleaming hardwood floor. After striding quickly across the room to the far corner, she pulled open the bookcase door and shut it quietly behind her, then paced to the window.

"Breathe. Just breathe," she whispered, but as she tried to take a deep breath in, it turned into a shuddering gasp and she felt her throat thicken with tears. She pressed her forehead against the cool glass of the window and scrunched her eyes shut, trying to prevent the tears from falling. She lifted the rose to her face and inhaled deeply, pulling the scent into her lungs, trying to focus on something besides how much she *hurt*.

She looked up at the ceiling, and she let out a choked half sob, half laugh. Twenty-five years old and she was hiding, crying because of something her mother had said to her. She suddenly felt fourteen again, and the ridiculousness of it—she was a grown-ass woman, and it was time to start acting like one—gave her the strength to fight back most of the tears, despite the tangled ache welling up inside her. She pulled one of the petals free and worried the velvety softness between her fingers, letting the texture soothe her. She swallowed thickly and swiped a thumb under her eye.

She spent a few more minutes alone, relishing the peace and quiet, collecting herself, watching dust motes float through the pale moonlight.

Screw this. She had friends to go see—friends who loved her. She was done wasting her time here when she had a celebration to go to.

She began to push open the narrow door to head back into the library when the library's main door swung open, and light from the hallway cut a swath across the floor. Her father entered with Kramer, and, not wanting to deal with either of them right now, she quickly eased the door shut again, sealing herself away.

"It's done?" she heard her father ask on the other side of the wall.

"Yes. Jeff Astor's dead," said Kramer, his voice low but still audible.

Alexa gasped and pressed a hand to her mouth, her other hand curling around the rose's petals. Jeff Astor was the president of one of the largest film studios in Hollywood, and he'd gone missing over a week ago. The story had been all over the news. Before his disappearance he'd made a play to buy Innkeeper Films, the production company her father had a large stake in. She'd thought the deal had simply fallen through.

"You saw to it yourself?" Her father's voice was tense, urgent.

"Bullet to the forehead, point-blank. Burned and ashes dumped, just like you asked."

"Good. That motherfucker was a pain in my side."

Alexa's heart pounded in her ears as she tried to wrap her mind around what she was hearing. Because it sounded an awful lot as if her father had ordered Kramer to murder Jeff Astor. A tremor coursed through her, and she closed her eyes, trying to center herself against a wave of dizziness.

"Have you made a decision about Morales yet?" asked Kramer.

Her father hesitated, making a low humming noise she recognized as his "I'm thinking" sound. "Not yet. Morales knows a lot, maybe too much. But killing a cop is the last resort."

"Understood."

"And what about Crosby?" asked her father. Alexa racked her brain, trying to figure out if she knew who Crosby was. She licked her lips, her mouth dry as fear and panic worked themselves into a tight, cold knot right in the center of her chest.

This couldn't be happening. This couldn't be real.

"Still on the list. It's in the works."

"Make it happen, and soon. He knows too much about us."

"And what about me?" Kramer's tone shifted slightly, and his voice took on an edge. There was a pause that stretched out for several seconds before her father spoke.

"If you kill Crosby, you can have Alexa."

She crushed the rose until crumpled petals littered the floor around her feet. Sweat prickled along her hairline, and her stomach churned.

Oh God. Please, no. You can't do this to me again.

"You promise she'll cooperate?"

Her father snorted derisively. "Alexa will do what I tell her."

CHAPTER 2

Zack De Luca walked into his boss's house, late for the party that was already in full swing. A few dozen people mingled throughout the spacious Mediterranean-style mansion that Sean shared with his fiancée, Sierra, and classic rock thumped through the speakers. Sean had been cryptic about the occasion, saying only that Zack, along with all the other Virtus Security guys, should come, and that there'd be plenty of free food and beer.

And hey, free beer was free beer. Considering how much of Zack's paycheck went toward training, he was all about the freebies.

He shrugged out of his jacket and tossed it onto the bench in the foyer with the others, running a hand over his hair, still damp from his quick shower. His training session at Take Down, the MMA gym downtown, had gone longer than he'd anticipated. He had a major fight coming up soon, and his trainers were pushing him hard. Big things could happen if he won that fight and the local championship title that went with it. Chances were high he'd be offered a contract from a major international fight promotion, like the UFC or Bellator. It was everything he'd been working toward for years now. And so his team of coaches drilled him, beat the hell out of him, yelled at him, whatever it took for Zack to push through each barrier and hit harder, move faster, and fight smarter than anyone else. He both hated and loved them for it.

Right now he mostly hated them as his tired muscles screamed at him, his empty stomach growling dangerously. He strode forward through the house, smiling and nodding at the people around him as he made his way to the kitchen. White and silver balloons and black streamers hung in swoops from the ceiling in the living room, and Zack wondered what the party was for. Sean and Sierra had already had an engagement party, and as far as he knew, it wasn't anyone's birthday. He stepped into the kitchen, his mouth practically watering at the sight of pizza, chicken wings, and coolers full of beer covering all the available counter space. He grabbed a paper plate and loaded himself up, knowing he'd have to make up for this cheat meal tomorrow.

Whatever. The extra time on the treadmill was future Zack's problem. Because right now he was going to massacre the pizza and wings on his plate, and fuck, was he going to enjoy it.

He chuckled at himself, shaking his head slightly, as he moved into the living room and sank down onto one of the chairs set up around the perimeter of the room. He couldn't remember the last time he'd been so excited about a damn slice of pizza, but that was what happened when he cut all the fun stuff out of his life—junk food, beer, sex, anything that could be a distraction, really—in order to chase his dream.

A dream that was finally within reach, and once it came true, all the sacrifice would be worth it.

"Hey, everyone!" called out Sierra, her hands cupped around her mouth. The music died, and conversations dropped away as everyone turned their attention toward the front of the living room, where she stood on an ottoman. Once all eyes were on her, she smiled. "Thanks for coming. I know it was really short notice, and you're probably wondering what this little shindig's all about. Well…" She glanced over her shoulder at her best friend, Taylor, who was also Zack's ex-girlfriend. She stood nearby, holding hands with her boyfriend, Colt Priestley, who worked with Zack as a bodyguard at Virtus. "This party is for Colt and Taylor."

"We got married!" Taylor shouted, a huge smile on her face as Colt pulled her into him, kissing her in front of everyone. Zack nearly choked on his beer, pulling the bottle hastily away from his lips as a wave of pure shock slammed into him.

Married?

Everyone erupted around Zack, clapping and cheering and laughing, and a weird sense of loneliness wrapped itself around him like a cold, wet blanket. Not because of Taylor; he wanted her to be happy. He'd cared about her but hadn't been in love with her by any stretch, which was why they'd broken up in the first place. He didn't really understand the reason for the sudden wave of loneliness, just knew that it was there. Or that something that felt a hell of a lot like loneliness was there, which was probably just fatigue, more than anything. He'd been putting in long hours at the gym as well as working his regular shifts as a bodyguard.

And even if he *was* lonely, it was just the way things had to be right now.

"When?" someone from the crowd called out.

Colt flashed a smile, taking his eyes away from Taylor for only a second. "We went to Vegas last weekend."

"You guys are crazy!" Chloe Carmichael, another friend of Sierra and Taylor, called out, and everyone laughed.

Taylor and Colt looked at each other, wordless communication passing between them in a way that had that damn wet blanket pressing harder around Zack's shoulders.

"When you know, you know," said Taylor, and Colt slipped his arms around her waist, pulling her in for another kiss. Everyone cheered again, and the party resumed, guests moving toward Taylor and Colt to congratulate them. Zack grabbed a napkin from a nearby table and wiped his hands and mouth, waiting until the initial rush died off before making his way toward them.

Despite the hard knot sitting in the center of his chest at the sight of Taylor smiling wide and practically vibrating with happiness, he couldn't help but return her smile. He'd hurt her when they'd broken up because he hadn't been able to give her what she'd needed, what she'd deserved. Zack wasn't at a place in his life where he could be that man for anyone, and he'd been stupid to get involved with Taylor in the first place. The guilt over how things had gone down between them still ate at him, but seeing her so happy, with a man who clearly adored her, helped take some of the bite out of it.

Zack shoved one hand into his pocket, holding his beer with the other. "You guys are nuts." Something tugged in his chest when he noticed the matching ink—Roman numerals, probably their wedding date—on Taylor's and Colt's inner left wrists.

Colt tipped his head and shrugged, smiling. "Pretty much."

Zack clinked his beer bottle against the ex–Army Ranger's. "Congrats, man. Seriously." He stepped forward and pulled Taylor in for a brief hug. "I'm really happy for you, Taylor."

She pulled back, and her eyes, so full of happiness, met his. She rested a hand on his cheek and smiled warmly at him. "I know you are."

Tipping his head at the happy couple, Zack moved out of the way so other guests could talk to them, and he sank down onto the couch beside his boss. Sean sat with his long legs extended in front of him, a beer in one hand.

Zack glanced back at Taylor and Colt, not really wanting to untangle the knot of emotion their announcement had lodged in the center of his chest. He didn't feel like pulling at its threads tonight. He was too damn tired. "I can't believe they got married. They've known each other, what? A month?"

Sean nodded and took a sip of his beer. "Something like that." He glanced at Zack, one eyebrow raised. "It bother you?"

"Nah. I'm happy for her, as long as she's happy. Does it bother you?" Zack asked. There had been tension between Sean and Colt in the past, but it seemed to be resolved now. A couple of years ago, Colt had worked for Virtus, and he'd ended up getting himself fired, and it had been Sean who'd done the firing. Now Colt was back in Sean's good graces and was once again working for Virtus. Given that Taylor and Sierra were best friends, and given Sean's natural inclination to protect everyone around him, Zack had to wonder how Sean felt about Colt and Taylor together.

Not just together. Married.

Sean tilted his head, considering. "I'm surprised, but no.

It doesn't bother me." He took a sip of his beer. "Besides, Priestley knows I'll hurt him—badly—if he fucks this up."

Zack didn't doubt it, and as Sean's eyes tracked Sierra as she moved through the party, Zack couldn't help but wonder what it would feel like to be so...*much* for someone. Protective, and possessive, and everything that went along with it. It wasn't that he didn't care about the safety of his clients, because he definitely did, but there was a clear line where the job ended and his personal life started. Yeah, he'd had some clients come on to him—some of the other guys on the team referred to it as the "Costner effect"—but he'd never been tempted.

The music got louder, and several guests, under Sierra's direction, started moving furniture out of the way, making room for an impromptu dance floor. Zack nodded at Sean before making his way back to the kitchen for more pizza.

As he passed by the foyer again, the front door opened, and Alexa Fairfax, another friend of Sierra and Taylor, stepped in, shutting it quietly behind her. His steps slowed as he watched her.

God, Alexa. So fucking pretty. So damn sweet. Truth be told, *she'd* been the one he'd first noticed when he'd met Sierra's group of friends over a year ago now. But he hadn't made a move, because he'd known that Alexa wasn't the type of woman you started something casual with. She deserved so much more than a casual, no-strings-attached hookup. And casual, no strings attached was all he'd been able to offer. Was still all he could offer.

So Alexa was completely not for him.

She leaned her back against the door and shut her eyes, her face ghostly white. Her hands shook as she adjusted the strap of her purse on her shoulder.

Frowning, Zack shoved his hands into the pockets of his

jeans and headed toward her. She smiled weakly when she saw him, her lips twitching up for a second, but the smile didn't reach her eyes. Her fingers curled around the strap of her purse, her knuckles going the same shade of white as her face. Something hot and protective tightened his chest, and for a crazy second, he wanted to reach out and pull her into his arms, to promise her that, whatever it was, she'd be okay.

Instead he stopped a few feet in front of her, his hands still in his pockets. "Alexa? You okay?"

Her eyes met his, and she sucked in a shaky breath. "I…Oh God." She pressed her hands to her face and let out a soft sob, her shoulders trembling.

Zack yanked his hands from his pockets and pulled Alexa into his arms, cradling her against his chest. She felt so tiny, so vulnerable. She barely reached his shoulder despite the fact that she had heels on.

"What happened? Did someone hurt you?" he whispered into her light-blond hair, so fine and soft under his fingers as he stroked the back of her head. So help him God, if someone had hurt her, he would make them bleed.

She pulled back, just enough to look up at him, and he noticed the mascara smudged under her eye. He left his arms around her. It would've felt wrong to take them away.

She shook her head slowly, her bottom lip caught between her teeth. "I…don't think…I can't."

"Do you want to go outside? Get some fresh air?" Maybe if she calmed down a little, she'd be able to tell him what the hell had her so…It was more than upset.

The poor girl was fucking spooked.

She hesitated a second before nodding. Without a word he tucked her under his arm, shielding her from the view of the other party guests. He led her down a hallway off the foyer and into the garage, where a side door led into the quiet, dark backyard. The noise from the party filtered out through the open windows, mingling with the soft gurgle of water from the pool. A cool spring breeze rustled the palm fronds and teased Alexa's shoulder-length hair around her jaw. She brushed it aside as he led her to a stone bench off to the right, their backs to the house.

For several moments they just sat, Alexa sniffling and staring blankly at the still water of the pool. Zack stroked a hand up and down her back, hoping to comfort her in some way. He'd spent the past year as a bodyguard honing his protective instincts, and they now came to life, alarm bells ringing through his skull. Something was very, very wrong.

When she finally spoke, she surprised him with her question. "Who's the party for? Sierra was cagey about it on the phone earlier."

Zack glanced back at the house. "Oh. Uh, for Taylor and Colt. They got married in Vegas last weekend."

Alexa's head whipped around. "What? But didn't they *just* get together?"

"Yeah."

"They're crazy." She shook her head, but he could hear the smile in her voice.

"That's what I said."

Gently, she laid a hand on his arm, the tips of her fingers warm against his skin. "Are you okay?"

Fuck, she was so sweet. He was supposed to be comforting her and finding out why she'd suddenly burst into tears, and she was worried about him because his ex-girlfriend had eloped.

He laid a hand over hers, allowing himself the luxury of tracing his thumb over her delicate knuckles. "I'm fine.

Just surprised, like everyone, I think. You gonna tell me what's wrong?"

She sighed heavily. "I don't even know where to start."

"Beginning's usually a good place."

She scoffed out a laugh. "*That* would take too long."

He turned to face her. "Did someone hurt you? What happened, Alexa?"

A tremble coursed through her, and he wished he were wearing more than a T-shirt and jeans so that he had a jacket or a sweater to offer her. But he didn't, so instead he pulled her close and tucked her against him. "Please tell me. I want to help."

She swallowed thickly and looked up at him, meeting his gaze. "I…I think my dad's a murderer and that I might be in a lot of trouble."

CHAPTER 3

Alexa stared at Zack, wishing she could call back the words that had just fallen from her mouth. But he'd been so nice to her that she'd wanted to open up. His deep-brown eyes held hers, his brows drawn together. After a second he rubbed a hand over his thick dark-brown hair. The muscles in his arm bunched and flexed as he moved, and, despite the night she was having, butterflies floated through her stomach at the movement.

But then again, Zack had always had that effect on her, from the moment she'd first laid eyes on him and he'd flashed her that smile, with the perfect white teeth and the dimples and the stubble.

He was the sexiest man. Ever. Period. And that was *not* what she was supposed to be thinking. For so many reasons, the first being that he was her friend's ex-boyfriend, and that was a line that probably shouldn't be crossed. Heck, it was a line she probably shouldn't even get close to.

The other reasons were more…personal. Painful. Stemming from a past she wanted to forget, and yet she knew she couldn't. Not after what she'd overheard her father say earlier.

"Tell me everything." His voice was low and intense, and it made her want to curl into him again, to seek out the shelter of his body.

She pulled back from him and wrapped her arms around herself. She decided to start with the simplest facts and work up to the more complicated ones.

"I had dinner at my parents' house tonight. My dad had a party, and even though I don't live there anymore, I was expected to put in an appearance."

Zack nodded, studying her intently, his body angled toward her. "And what happened?" She sighed heavily, twisting her hands together in her lap, the words she needed not coming easily.

He laced her fingers with his and gave her hand a gentle squeeze. That small bit of gentleness almost undid her, because she'd been to his fights. She knew the violence those hands were capable of. The power and strength and destruction in them. And he was showing her gentle, and soft, and sweet.

His touch soothed her, and she swallowed around the lump in her throat. "My mom was getting on my nerves, as usual, and I needed a minute alone, so I excused myself and went upstairs. There's a small room off the library I used to hide out in as a kid, and I went there."

His face softened, the hard lines giving way to something gentler. "You used to go hide out as a kid?"

She shrugged. "Yeah. Sometimes. Believe it or not, that was *not* an easy house to grow up in."

"I'm sorry." He squeezed her hand again, and that small gesture, coupled with the two simple words he'd offered, made her want to keep talking.

"Thanks. There was a lot of pressure, growing up. A lot of expectations, which I never seemed to meet. I'm pretty sure I was a constant disappointment to my parents. Nothing was ever good enough, you know? I wasn't booking enough jobs. I wasn't pretty enough. I wasn't thin enough. I wasn't interesting enough. I wasn't…" She swallowed as blood rushed to her cheeks and she stared at her knees, her eyes tracing the contours as she fought down the sickening shame that always rose up when she thought about it. She took a breath before continuing. "It wore me down, and sometimes I just needed to get away. Hide out and be left alone."

"Assholes." Zack muttered the word and then shook his head. "Sorry. I know they're your family, but that's horseshit, that they made you feel that way." He paused and rubbed his free hand over his mouth. "None of it's true. I hope you know that."

She sent him a small smile, warmth spreading over her skin and unknotting her shoulders slightly. "Thanks. I do, thanks to some very expensive therapy. I'm in a better place now than I was a few years ago, but…it's hard to shake that stuff completely, you know?" She shrugged one shoulder. "I still struggle with it sometimes, and I probably always will. I'm just a little bit better at dealing with it now, I guess."

The sounds of the party drifted out the open windows, but she liked it better out here, in the peaceful dark with Zack, his long, thick fingers woven with hers. His skin was warm and slightly rough against hers, and she traced her thumb over a scrape on one of his knuckles.

"So what happened tonight?" he asked, steering them back on track.

She cleared her throat, some of her tension returning. "I

was in that room, the one off the library, when I heard my dad talking to one of his business associates, a producer named Gordon Kramer." She paused, her pulse pounding in her temples as she replayed the conversation in her mind, her brain whirling as she tried to make sense of what she'd heard. "They…they talked about killing Jeff Astor."

"The producer who disappeared last week?" Zack asked, his eyes wide, his brows drawn. "You heard your *father* talking about killing Jeff Astor?"

She nodded and pushed herself to continue. "I know it sounds crazy, but it's what I heard. It sounded like Kramer did it, but my father…" She trailed off, trying to sort through everything as she spoke. "It sounded like he'd…like he'd ordered it. Like he'd *made* Kramer do it. It was almost like Kramer was reporting back to him."

Zack's grip tightened on her hand, his dark eyes intense, shining like deep pools in the faint light. "Alexa, did anyone see you? Know you were there?"

She bit her lip and shook her head, trying to keep her breathing steady as the scene replayed itself over and over again. "No. No one saw me go into the library, or the room off of it. They couldn't have known I was in there."

"And did anyone see you leave?"

She frowned, thinking. "I don't think so. I waited until they were long gone before going back downstairs. I said quick good-byes to everyone and left. I said I wasn't feeling well, that I was going home."

"But you came here."

She glanced down at her lap and shrugged. "I didn't want to be alone."

He nodded and squeezed her hand again, warmth flowing over her skin. God, just that small touch was doing ridiculous things to her. It was wrong for her to enjoy the feel of his hands on her the way she was. *Wrong*, she reminded herself. But something hot and wanton crested through her at the word, the single syllable taunting her.

"And that's everything you heard?"

His question chased away the warmth, because they were headed into the part of the conversation she was dreading having to repeat because of the questions it would raise. And yet…she wanted to tell him. She needed to tell someone who could maybe help her figure out what the hell she was supposed to do.

She squared her shoulders and tipped her chin up slightly. "No. There's more. They talked about other people, a cop named Morales and someone named Crosby."

"Do you know who they are?"

"No. I don't know any cops. And whoever Crosby is, my father wants him dead too, and he promised Kramer that…" She sucked in a deep breath, as if about to dive underwater, and then forced the words out. "He promised him that if he does it, if he kills Crosby, that Kramer…he could have *me*." The last few words tasted like sawdust in her mouth, and she swallowed, fighting down a wave of nausea.

Zack frowned and leaned toward her, his voice quiet but full of intensity. "What do you mean, have you?"

With a shaky hand, she gestured to her body. "Have me."

Zack's eyes followed her hand and then trailed down her body. His brows drew together and then slowly inched up his forehead as understanding dawned. "He can't do that." His voice was low and fierce, and she had the sudden urge to rub her thighs together.

Instead she let out a mirthless laugh and shrugged one

shoulder. "He's a powerful man, Zack. There are very few things he can't do. What chance do you think I'd have if Kramer felt entitled?"

Zack studied her for a second, his jaw tight, a strange light in his eyes. "Has he ever done anything like this before? Promised another man he could"—he paused, his nostrils flaring as he practically spat out the next word—"*have* you?"

She opened her mouth, her heart pressing up into her throat, and for a split second, she thought she might tell him everything. But with his fingers laced through hers, and a hot, protective glower on his face, the words wouldn't come. He probably wouldn't look at her that way, touch her that way, if he knew the truth.

"No," she lied.

"I just can't believe…He's your father. It's so fucked up, Alexa."

"I know." She took a shuddering breath, her chest constricting as tears stung her eyes. "I know. I've always known that he isn't a saint, but this…" She tried to take another breath, but it came out as a sob, and as she blinked she felt hot tears cut paths down her cheeks.

"Shit. Come here." Zack's voice was slightly rough as he pulled her against his chest, his big hand stroking her hair. "I'm not going to let that happen, Alexa. I promise." Her tense muscles relaxed, as though her entire body wanted to melt into him, into his warmth, his strength, his protectiveness.

"I don't know what to do," she whispered, tucking her face into his neck. Zack's scent filled her, and he didn't smell like cologne or laundry or anything other than warm skin and the faintest hint of masculine spice. God, he smelled good. His heart beat steadily in his chest, and she closed her eyes, letting the rhythm soothe her, synchronizing her breaths with it.

Two beats in.

Two beats out.

He rubbed a hand over her bare shoulders, her skin tingling at his touch. His hand was warm and strong against her, and her nerve endings felt like flowers, blooming and stretching toward the sun. Gently, he eased her away from him and slipped a hand under her chin, tipping her face up and forcing her to meet his eyes.

"We'll figure it out."

"*We?*" she asked, a slight tremor in her voice.

"Hell yes, *we*." He cursed softly. "No way am I letting you deal with this alone." The corner of his mouth tipped up in a half smile. "I'm glad you came here instead of going home. I'm glad I saw you in the hallway. And I'm glad you talked to me."

She nodded, his callused fingertips rasping against the underside of her chin and sending an electric chill through her. God, she was coming apart because of the crazy night she'd had. It was the only way to explain the insanity roiling through her body every time he touched her.

"Thanks," she said, easing out of his arms, needing to think, to get herself together so she could figure shit out.

"For now I think we should go inside and talk to Sean. He'll know what to do."

She bit her lip, considering. "I don't want to interrupt the party with my drama, but you're right. We should tell Sean." She toyed with the hem of her skirt, running her fingers along the seam. "Let's go inside, enjoy the party, and talk to Sean after. I would hate to do something to take the shine off of Taylor and Colt's night."

A breeze ruffled the leaves of the trees and the palm

fronds around them, and a soft, rustling hush enveloped them for a second. A strand of her baby-fine hair blew across her face, and Zack reached up and tucked it behind her ear. For the briefest second, she thought his hand might linger on her face, but he took it back almost immediately. He leaned forward, his muscular forearms braced on his thighs, his hands clasped.

He looked up at her over his shoulder. "You're too fucking sweet, you know that?"

"What do you mean?"

He shook his head and then rubbed a hand over the back of his neck, the muscles in his arms and shoulders straining against his T-shirt. "You heard your father—*your father*—talking about murdering someone tonight and offering you up as bait in exchange for more murder, and you're worried about upsetting Taylor and Colt."

She shrugged. "Well, it's their party. They did get married."

"Yeah. They did." He nodded slowly.

"You're sure you're okay?" she asked, and she slipped her hands under her thighs, sitting on them to prevent herself from touching him.

He huffed out a quiet laugh. "Like I said, you're too fucking sweet."

She didn't know how to process his compliment, so she tucked it away to examine later. "Let's go inside. I could use a distraction and a drink."

* * *

Zack watched Alexa from across the room as she hugged Colt and Taylor, laughing with them and congratulating them. She'd washed the tear-smeared mascara from her cheeks before heading into the party, and, to most people in the room, she probably looked like she always did: sweet and pretty and happy. She was doing a good job of hiding her fear, her sadness, and the ugliness she'd overheard earlier. She didn't look like a woman who'd been crying in his arms less than fifteen minutes ago. He wasn't sure if it was her need for a distraction or the fact that she always seemed to put her friends' happiness above her own that had her laughing and smiling as though nothing were wrong.

Which was fucking bullshit, because everything was wrong. He couldn't stop everything Alexa had told him from echoing through his mind, her words pinging restlessly around his brain. Jesus, her father. He couldn't even wrap his mind around it. So fucking wrong.

And then there was the way she'd felt in his arms. How soft and warm her skin had been. How good she'd smelled. How badly he'd wanted to take on the world for her.

How badly he'd wanted all kinds of things he couldn't have. He didn't have room in his life for any kind of relationship right now, and especially not with someone like Alexa. He'd fucked up so badly with Taylor. He'd hurt her. He hadn't meant to, but he had, and he couldn't risk getting himself into the same situation again. He spent too many hours training in the gym and was too focused on his fighting career, and he knew he'd make a lousy boyfriend. And if his career took off, there was a chance he'd move away to train—the best gyms were in places like Albuquerque and Coconut Creek, Florida, and Montreal and Brazil. If the opportunity came, he'd leave. Just the idea of hurting Alexa the way he'd hurt Taylor had his stomach clenching.

No. He couldn't let that happen. Instead he needed to focus on what he could do to keep her safe. He'd made her a promise that he wouldn't let her father hurt her, and he damn well meant to keep it.

Zack slipped his hands into his pockets and clenched them into fists, his eyes glued to Alexa. She was listening to Taylor, her head cocked, a wide smile on her face. She was a better actress than her family apparently gave her credit for.

He believed everything Alexa had told him, but fuck, it was shocking. He knew who Jonathan Fairfax was—millions of people around the world had seen his movies, but apparently nothing was as it seemed. All he knew for sure was that he didn't want to let her out of his sight, safe as she might be at the party. The idea that her own father would…Jesus, he couldn't even think the words without his skin crawling. Her father couldn't just offer her up like that.

The idea of another man's hands on Alexa made Zack want to punch things, but it wasn't only that. The fact that her father, a man who should've been protecting her, would throw her to the wolves like that…No. He couldn't let that happen. As soon as the party was over, he'd find Sean, and they'd figure out what to do to keep Alexa safe.

He had to keep her safe.

Because it was his job.

Great. Now he was lying to himself. Perfect.

"You stare at that lass any harder, you're likely to burn a hole in her dress. But maybe that's what you're aiming for." Ian MacAllister, another Virtus bodyguard, tipped his beer at Zack and shot him a thin-lipped smile. It was rare to get any kind of smile out of the Scot, so Zack returned it.

"Didn't mean to stare. I'm just tired." It was a half truth that saved him from wading into the murky waters of Mac's comment.

Mac nodded, a lock of his curly reddish-blond hair falling across his forehead. He brushed it away with a scarred hand. "Training going well?" he asked, his brogue twisting the words as they came out.

Zack tipped his head, his eyes still on Alexa, his mind still spinning with what she'd told him. "Yeah, pretty well."

"When's your big fight?"

"In less than a week."

"Zack-man! I was looking for you!" A slightly drunk Jamie Anderson clapped him on the shoulder, leaning back when his hand made contact. "Holy fuck. This thing's like a rock. You been juicing?" Jamie winked and laughed at his own joke, his eyes bright.

Zack smiled down at the floor, shaking his head. "Are you driving his ass home?" he asked, pointing at Jamie and making eye contact with Carter Davis, the hulking ex-NFLer following on Jamie's heels.

Carter rubbed a hand over his short black hair and chuckled, his deep baritone infectious. "Someone's gotta be the responsible one." He shrugged his massive shoulders, smiling and shaking his head.

"So I guess you're not making it to training tomorrow morning," Zack said, watching as Jamie picked at the label on his beer bottle. Although he didn't compete at the same level as Zack, Jamie trained at the same mixed martial arts gym and liked to take the occasional fight.

"Nah." Jamie rolled the piece of damp paper between his fingers, his eyes slightly glassy. Taylor's friend Chloe smiled at him from across the room, and Jamie narrowed his eyes and took a long pull on his beer. Then he smiled and wiggled his eyebrows. "Excuse me." Without a backward glance, he headed in Chloe's direction.

"What the hell's got into him?" asked Mac, scratching

his stubbled cheek. Normally Jamie wasn't much of a drinker, but he'd clearly been hitting it tonight.

Zack watched as Jamie flirted with Chloe with dogged determination, and realization dawned. "Shit. It's June eleventh."

Carter and Mac shot him puzzled looks, but Zack shook his head. "It's not my story to tell, but it's a tough day for him. Let him do what he needs to do."

Colt's best friend Roman made his way over, a beer clutched in one hand, his shoulder-length hair twisted up into a knot. Roman was another bodyguard, but he worked freelance, not for Virtus. In the few instances Zack had worked with him, he'd found Roman to be tough as fucking nails and smart. The guy had great instincts and was easy to work with, normally cracking jokes and entertaining everyone with his cocky bravado. But right now he was glowering at Jamie and Chloe, his nostrils flaring as he watched them flirt.

Not long ago Roman had had a thing for Chloe, but for whatever reason it hadn't gone anywhere. Zack didn't know why, and Roman wasn't exactly the caring-and-sharing type.

"What are you guys talking about?" Sierra asked, sidling up to them. She took a sip of her wine, her cheeks slightly flushed.

"Beyoncé," said Zack, grinning at her.

She snorted out a laugh. "*Sure* you were. There's like a metric ton of testosterone in this corner."

"So what do you think we were talking about?" challenged Carter, his arms crossed over his chest.

She shrugged, frowning slightly. "I don't know. Sports. Work. Cars. Sex. How great I am at throwing parties."

Colt came up and pulled her in for a hug, kissing her quickly on the cheek. "Yes, you are. Thank you."

"You're welcome." Then Sierra fisted the collar of Colt's T-shirt and tugged his face down to her level. "If you hurt her, I'll castrate you." She smiled prettily at him, and Colt returned her smile.

"If I hurt her, I'll do it myself."

Something in Sierra's expression softened, and she let go of his shirt, rubbing his arm. "You would, wouldn't you?"

"Hey, back off. You've already got your own hot bodyguard," said Taylor, a bright smile on her face.

Sierra laughed and then glanced at her engagement ring. "Damn right I do."

Taylor turned to Colt and smacked him on the ass. "Take me home, *Husband*," she said, then leaned toward him and whispered something in his ear. Colt slipped his arms around her and pulled her against him, apparently not caring that they were surrounded by people. He closed his mouth over hers in a hot, slow kiss, and Zack looked away, feeling a bit like a voyeur. His eyes landed on Alexa, who stood only a few feet away, her eyes glued to Taylor and Colt, her lips parted slightly, a delicate pink flush creeping across her cheeks. She took a deep breath, her breasts rising and falling. Watching Taylor and Colt make out like teenagers, she looked…Fuck, what was the word?

Wistful. Sad, and longing, and at least a little turned on.

She pulled her eyes away from Taylor and Colt, and those gorgeous blues slammed right into him, and he felt his cock swell, just a little. Her eyes widened slightly, and he wondered if she could tell that he was thinking about how fucking good it would feel to kiss *her* like that.

Needing to regain control, he headed back into the kitchen and fished a bottle of water out of one of the coolers. He twisted the cap off the bottle and drained half the water, trying to ignore the heat crackling over his skin.

The entire night had become a goddamn confusing mess. Taylor was married, and he felt slightly awkward joining in the celebration, given the way things had gone down between them. And then there was Alexa. Keeping her safe. The complicated mix of lust and protectiveness he felt toward her.

The party was starting to dwindle, and Alexa came into the kitchen, a stack of dirty paper plates in her hands, and just setting eyes on her sent warmth flaring up his spine. She sent him a small smile and shoved the plates into the garbage, then wiped her hands on the kitchen towel. He hadn't even realized his legs had started to move until he was right in front of her.

"How you holding up?" he asked, fighting the urge to cage her against the counter. He crossed his arms over his chest, and he didn't miss the way her eyes dipped down and trailed over his arms.

She sighed heavily, and her shoulders slumped as she leaned against the counter. "I'm confused and exhausted."

"Why, what's going on?" Sean came into the kitchen behind them, a garbage bag in his hands. He paused as he studied them, one eyebrow raised.

Zack met Alexa's eyes, and she just stared at him, uncertainty warring with fear across her pretty features. After a second she bit her lip and then nodded rapidly.

Zack turned to face his boss. "We need to talk to you. Alexa's in trouble, and she needs our help."

CHAPTER 4

Jonathan Fairfax eased back into the leather chair behind the massive mahogany desk in his office and rolled his cigar between his fingers. The tip of it glowed softly, the rich, loamy smell of the Cohiba filling the air. It wasn't often he broke out the Cohibas, but the fact that Astor was now out of the picture called for a celebration.

A tendril of smoke curled lazily up from the tip of the cigar, and he smiled as he brought it to his mouth. Crosby was the last pin to knock down. The last thorn in his side. And then it would be blue skies, and everything he'd worked for, everything he'd fought to maintain, would be his.

Power.

Influence.

Wealth.

They were his drugs, and he was proud to be an addict.

And now, when all the dust settled, he'd be a king in everything but name. He cocked his head, staring at the black-and-white framed photograph of his father and grandfather that he kept on his desk. It served as a reminder. Motivation. But as much as they'd done for the family, he had a feeling that even they'd be impressed with how things were coming together.

It had all started with his grandfather in the 1920s. George Fairfax had moved to Hollywood, bitten by the acting bug. He'd come from a wealthy family in Colorado, the Fairfaxes having made their money in mining. Lacking any acting experience, he'd bought his way into his first roles, using his wealth, good looks, and charm to talk directors into giving him parts.

When his first movies had flopped and his studio had dropped him, he'd taken matters into his own hands, using family money to pay cinema chains to show and promote his films. It was fairly small stuff, really. Bribery. Coercion. A little extortion here and there. Higher-ups in RKO and United Artists found out what George had been doing and saw the simple elegance in his solution to slumping ticket sales. They banded together, and the Golden Brotherhood was born. They invested in other film studios, in film lots, in bars, and in other properties around Los Angeles. Money, power, and influence followed, and George won his first Academy Award for Best Actor in 1929.

In the early thirties, shortly after Jonathan's father, Robert, was born, the Golden Brotherhood got wind of corruption among the local heads of the biggest cinema workers' union in America. Projectionists were being bribed into disrupting showings, threatening work stoppages, showing films upside down, and dropping stink bombs into the aisles. Big payoffs were extracted from cinema chains in order to prevent further disruptions.

George and the Brotherhood flipped. They'd thought they'd had the cinema racket cornered and were livid that the union was dipping into their pool. George and a few other members of the Golden Brotherhood met with the union leaders and struck a deal. The Brotherhood would allow them to continue their scam—for a 50 percent cut. The union knew the Brotherhood had the power to crush it and accepted the deal. The deal also meant an even greater influence over the film industry for the Brotherhood. Back then, some of the biggest cinema chains were owned and operated by the film studios. Control over the projectionists meant control over the cinemas, which meant control over the studios. By the midthirties the studios realized the control the Golden Brotherhood had and set up a system of regular payments to keep everything running smoothly.

In the late thirties, a rival organization, the Rizzolis, had tried to penetrate the movie industry. Tried and failed, because the Brotherhood's enforcers had taken them out, solidifying their power. George then realized he needed to step back from the Brotherhood, but only publicly. He wanted the Fairfaxes to thrive in Hollywood, and he needed to keep his business dealings separate from his professional persona. George couldn't be connected with murder.

But that didn't mean the family legacy wouldn't continue. George had groomed Robert, and, while pursuing an acting career of his own, Robert had expanded their operations. In the early 1950s, he'd invested in Las Vegas, opening five casinos. Loan-sharking and money laundering had followed, and by the time Jonathan was born in 1957, the Fairfax family had amassed almost $300 million, thanks to the activities of the Golden Brotherhood.

George had died from a heart attack when Jonathan was a baby, and shortly before he died, Robert had promised him that he'd groom his son the same way George had groomed him, to carry on the family business—both the public and the private one. The extortion of film companies continued, raking in millions of dollars a year, and, finally, in the 1960s, Robert had started Fairfax Films, which almost overnight became the biggest, most powerful film studio in Hollywood. It had crippled the other studios and had the wealth and power to do whatever it wanted. It had given the Golden Brotherhood a legitimate front, further hiding the business from law enforcement.

Jonathan remembered distinctly his eighteenth birthday, when his father had given him a gun and a man to kill, a former Brotherhood member who'd turned informant.

"I will never ask you to kill someone who doesn't deserve killing. Killing isn't about violence. It's not personal. It's business. There are no bad guys, and there are no good guys. Everyone wants money. Everyone wants power. Some are just better at getting it and keeping it." He'd patted him on the shoulder. "You're a man now, and this business is in your blood. Pull the trigger."

And he had. So easily. He hadn't even hesitated. He'd claimed what was rightfully his, and he hadn't looked back.

When his father had died five years ago—another heart attack, which had spurred Jonathan to start watching his cholesterol—the family's net worth hovered somewhere around $2.5 billion, but it wasn't enough for Jonathan. He still felt the need to prove himself, to go above and beyond what his father and grandfather had done. He'd made moves to increase their circle of influence, wanting more. Wanting to make his father proud. He'd started buying politicians for the tax breaks and blind eyes needed for the Brotherhood's illegal activities to continue undetected. He'd recruited biker gangs to move drugs for them. And while things hadn't always gone to plan, with Jeff Astor's death and the impending studio acquisition, things were looking up.

As long as he could get that damn journalist Crosby out of the way, and maybe Morales if it came to that, the next part of his plan would come to fruition and mark a new chapter in the Golden Brotherhood's power and wealth.

He puffed on the cigar, blowing out smoke rings and sitting back, propping his feet up on the desk, basking in all that he'd accomplished. Him, and the men who'd come before him. Moonlight sparkled over the pool, light dancing over the water, and a peaceful contentedness settled over him.

A soft knock sounded, and the library's door swung open. Elijah Todd, Jonathan's second in command, stepped in. With his bald head, hip Warby Parker frames, and elegantly tailored suit, he looked much more studio head and much less mobster. It was his ability to do both jobs flawlessly that set him head and shoulders above most others in the Brotherhood.

Elijah stopped a few feet in front of Jonathan's desk and slipped his hands into his pockets, rocking back slightly on his heels. "I think it went well tonight, no?" he asked in his deep, melodically cultured voice.

Jonathan nodded. "I do. I spoke to Kramer. Let's see what he can do with Crosby."

"And if he fails?"

"Then it'll fall to you."

"Understood." Elijah nodded and looked down at the floor. He paused and frowned, stooping down to pick something up. "An earring," he said, approaching the desk with his hand extended. Gently, he set down a diamond stud on the leather blotter in front of Jonathan. The earring was platinum, with a princess-cut diamond surrounded by round brilliant diamonds all totaling almost two carats. He knew, because he'd given the earrings to his daughter, Alexa, just a few months ago for her twenty-fifth birthday.

"It's Alexa's," he murmured, picking it up and twirling it idly in his fingers, watching as the moonlight caught the diamond's facets, glinting coldly.

"And does that mean we have a problem?"

Jonathan sighed and replayed the evening in his mind. Alexa had been at dinner, had been her usual quiet self, and had left early, saying she didn't feel well or something. Really, he hadn't been paying much attention, preoccupied as he was with Kramer.

He sat up a bit straighter and once again went over the evening's timeline. Drinks. Dinner. The discussion in the library with Kramer. In almost every instance, he could place Alexa, but he couldn't be certain she'd still been sitting at the table when he and Kramer had retired to the library. Obviously, given the earring, she'd been in here at some point, but she couldn't have been in here at the same time as he and Kramer. There was nowhere to hide.

And yet his instincts were telling him that something was off. Alexa had been pulling away lately, moving out of the house and becoming increasingly stubborn and distant. She was a far cry from the pliant girl she'd been in her teens and early twenties, and it frustrated him. Her usefulness was in her ability to publicly uphold the Fairfax name and do what he needed her to do.

"Jon?" prompted Elijah, frowning slightly.

Jonathan dropped his feet from the desk and leaned forward, examining the earring in his hand. An eerie trickle worked its way down his spine. What if the reason Alexa had been distancing herself was that she suspected there was more at play than winning Oscars and running studios? He'd always kept her out of the Golden Brotherhood's business, knowing she didn't have the personality or the stomach for any of it. He'd always hoped for a son, but Alexa was his only child. So he'd made the best of it.

Had she been in here because she was spying? Had she heard something? Or was he being paranoid?

"I don't think so. This is Alexa we're talking about." He wasn't sure if he was trying to convince himself or Elijah.

"Is that really a stone you want to leave unturned?"

He sighed heavily because Elijah was right. He needed to find out if she knew anything, if she'd somehow started to piece things together. And if she had, he'd need to figure out what to do about it. "No. You're right."

"What do you want to do?"

He tipped his head, thinking. "Search her place. See if there's evidence she knows anything. And leave it a mess. Scare her a little, just in case she's been snooping. Take a few things, make it look like maybe it was a break and enter, in case she doesn't know anything." A few ruffled feathers, and if she *had* been snooping, she'd settle back into place. And if she hadn't, it would look like a simple robbery, no harm done.

"You want us to bring her in?"

"I don't think that'll be necessary. Alexa's easy to manipulate. This should take care of the situation."

And if it didn't, he might have a big, messy problem on his hands.

* * *

Sean raked a hand through his hair as he settled himself behind the desk in his study, gesturing for Alexa and Zack to take the two chairs facing it. A few guests still lingered downstairs, but Taylor and Colt had left, easing Alexa's guilt a little. At least she wasn't stealing attention away from them. Her cheeks heated as she remembered the way they hadn't been able to keep their hands off each other in the hallway, Taylor's fingers toying with Colt's belt as they whispered in each other's ears.

It didn't matter if Alexa wanted that—or something like that—for herself. Chances were that, even if she had it, she wouldn't know what to do with it. And maybe she liked only the idea of it. In all likelihood she wouldn't like the reality. She hadn't in the past, anyway. She shook her head as she sank into the low-backed leather chair; she had bigger worries than her mess of a sex life right now.

Sean's home office was comfortable and masculine, with gray walls, hardwood floors, and floor-to-ceiling windows behind the desk. A framed antique-looking map of the world hung over the fireplace, and the mantel held several framed photographs. A much younger Sean in a baseball uniform with who she assumed were his parents; Sierra's college graduation photo; a recent photo of Sean and Sierra together on a beach. Bookshelves lined the walls on both sides of the desk, which was really more of a table on which a laptop and a lamp sat.

Alexa smoothed her hands over her skirt, knowing she was cataloguing the office's decor in an effort to center herself. It was one of the techniques the therapist had given her to deal with the panic attacks she'd started having shortly after her sixteenth birthday. It was a relaxation method that worked for her. Taking slow breaths in and out, she'd focus on her surroundings, and her heart would slow and the dizziness would subside. Paying attention to the reality around her somehow diminished the anxiety expanding through her chest and replaced the repetitive, panicked thoughts with something more mundane.

Sean leaned back in his chair and folded his impressive arms over his equally impressive chest, the fabric of his T-shirt stretching over his biceps. "So what's going on, Alexa? What did Zack mean when he said you're in trouble?" He furrowed his brow in concern, lines creasing his forehead.

She opened her mouth, and her skin prickled uncomfortably as her anxiety surged back up. The more time she put between herself and what she'd heard, the more uncertain she became about everything. She smoothed her hands over her skirt again and then fiddled with the hem, trying to make her brain stop spinning long enough to form a few words. A sentence even. She could feel the weight of Sean's and Zack's eyes, and she knew she needed to say something. Her anxiety spiked, her heart thudding in her chest as sweat formed along her hairline. She sucked in a breath and then another, but somehow she wasn't getting enough oxygen.

Zack's hand, big and strong and warm, landed on her bare knee. He gave her leg a squeeze and rubbed his thumb in gentle circles over her kneecap, and she felt as if she could breathe again. That touch, so easy, so simple, anchored her, and she nodded, finding her voice.

She met Sean's calm, curious gaze. "I know my father's not a saint. Maybe better than most," she added, giving her head a slow shake. "Earlier tonight, I heard him talking with another man. Talking about murder."

Sean sat up straighter in his chair, dropping his hands to the desk. "Murder?" He glanced at Zack before returning his attention to her. "You're sure?"

She nodded and told Sean the entire story.

He frowned and drummed his fingers on the table. After a second he nodded. "Alexa, I'm gonna ask you some questions, and I want you to know that I'm not trying to be an insensitive asshole. Okay?"

Zack's hand tightened a tiny bit more. She nodded. "Okay."

"Have you heard any of the rumors about your father?"

She nodded again. "Yeah. That he bought his Oscars. That he's a bully within the industry. That he manipulates people and uses them. Anything to succeed. That he's not someone you piss off. I don't think those are rumors."

"No?" he asked mildly.

She bit her lip and shook her head, surprised at how freeing it felt to admit out loud what she'd known for a long time. "No. I know firsthand that he…Well, like I said. He's not a saint."

"Some of the rumors say that he's in the mob."

She opened her mouth to deny it, but as she turned that single syllable over in her mind, the longer she sat with it, the harder it became to reject outright. Finally she shrugged her shoulders, some of the heaviness returning. "I don't know. It's…not impossible," she conceded.

Sean sat back in his chair again, scrubbing a hand over his close-cropped beard as he thought. "And you're sure he doesn't know that you overheard that conversation?"

"No. He doesn't know."

Sean tapped his fingers against his mouth. "Good. But we still need to be careful with how we proceed."

"What do you mean, be careful?" Zack cut in, a low intensity in his voice. "He offered her up as a prize for murder. She needs our protection. We can't let that happen." He looked at her, his deep-brown eyes full of emotion. "*I won't.*"

Sean held out his hands. "Whoa. Easy. I agree that Alexa needs our protection, if she wants it." He glanced at her, and she nodded, knowing she didn't want to face whatever the hell this was alone. "But we need to think this through. If she's suddenly got security when she didn't before, that might set off alarm bells with her father." He shoved a hand through his hair again. "He's provided you with security in the past, right?"

"Yeah. Always his own guys. I'm not living at home anymore, though, so I have a bit more freedom. I haven't been doing a lot of public appearances lately, so I haven't been using any security, and the few times I've needed a bodyguard in public, Ian's worked for me."

"He has?" Zack asked, frowning.

Sean nodded. "Yeah, a few times recently." He tapped his mouth again. "Do you want to go to the police?"

The question caught her off guard, and she inhaled sharply. "I…" She forced air into her lungs, and a hint of dizziness teased her. She closed her eyes, exhaustion pulling at her. For the past several hours, she'd felt as though she'd been scrambling to keep up with what was happening around her, to make sense of it. "I don't know." She bit her lip and then admitted the ugly truth swirling through her. "He's still my father. I can't make any decisions tonight. I just can't." Her voice cracked on the last syllable, and she felt hot tears slip free and track down her cheeks.

"Shit, Alexa. I'm sorry. I know it's been a long night. I'm just trying to figure out how best to help you."

She sniffled and nodded heavily. "I know. I'm not—" She hiccupped inelegantly before continuing. "I'm not mad at you. I'm overwhelmed. And tired. And scared." Everything was crashing in, and she didn't have enough energy to process it.

Zack moved his hand from her knee to her back, rubbing soothing circles between her shoulder blades. "Deep breaths. We've got you. We'll figure it out."

She nodded and wiped at her eyes, trying to ignore the hot lurch in her stomach at Zack's touch. "I don't want to go home," she said, her voice creaking and rusty. The idea of going home alone to her empty house only heightened her anxiety.

Zack started to speak, but Sean beat him to it. "Stay here tonight. You shouldn't be alone right now. I need to think about what our best course of action is, and you need to figure out if you want to talk to the cops." He pushed out of his chair and leaned forward against his desk. "For what it's worth, I think you should, but you need to do what you're comfortable with. Given who your father is, it wouldn't be a stretch to say that you're under duress, fearing for your safety, which would protect you from any legal repercussions from not coming forward. Criminal or not, he's your father, and I get how complicated that is. If you decide you do want to talk to the police, I have contacts at the LAPD. And whatever you decide, we're not going to let anything happen to you."

Zack's hand slid up from her back to the nape of her neck, and with subtle pressure he turned her head to face him. A thrill shivered down her spine at the ease with which he could work her body, moving it the way he wanted with gentle control. But as much as that touch threatened to undo her, it was his expression—dark, determined, and fiercely hot—that had her heart unraveling and tangling.

He ground the words out, his voice low and dangerous. "Damn fucking straight."

CHAPTER 5

Zack slammed first one fist, then another, into the heavy bag in front of him, sending it swaying on its metal chain. He flexed his hands, stretched his neck from side to side, and bounced on his feet a few times, warming up, fighting through the exhaustion clouding his focus. He'd barely slept last night, tossing and turning in his bed, the sheets tangled around him as he'd replayed everything Alexa had told him over and over again.

Replayed her words. How she'd felt in his arms. The fear in her eyes. The way she'd trembled slightly when he'd promised her he wouldn't let anything happen to her. And he might not be a knight, but he kept his promises. He hadn't wanted to leave last night, but he'd known she was safe at Sean and Sierra's. And besides, what the hell could he have said or done? He didn't even fully understand *why* her safety felt like his responsibility. It just was, and that wasn't going to change. That much he knew.

Hands on his hips, he glanced around the gym, early-morning sunlight streaming in through the windows lining the far wall. Other fighters worked nearby bags, the slap of skin on leather blending with the hip-hop pumping through the gym's speakers. Fluorescent lights gleamed against the polished hardwood floors, and a few more fighters walked by, crossing the room to the weights on the other side. A couple of others took up space in the center, jumping rope and chatting.

He adjusted his stance and started working the bag, alternating low and high kicks with jabs, hooks, elbows, and knee strikes. Slipping into the familiar rhythm, he focused on his form, picking up speed as blood flowed into his muscles. He kept working, moving around the bag, a single drop of sweat streaking down from his hairline and over his temple. Sufficiently warm, he dropped down to the ground and stretched out his legs in a side split, working his hips as close to the ground as possible.

"You ready to hit the cage?" Zack's trainer, Oliver Jenkins, asked, a set of punching mitts already on his hands. The gym's lights shone against his weathered dark skin, and he twitched his thick mustache, black with streaks of gray.

Zack eased up out of the stretch. "Let's do it." He followed Jenks into the cage and skipped around the perimeter, swinging his arms as he moved, a familiar anticipation buzzing through his blood. He met his trainer in the center of the octagon and circled around him, landing a series of quick jabs against the mitts before ducking under Jenks's swing.

"Good. Again. Diaz is fast. You wanna win this weekend, you gotta be faster. Don't give him time to get out of the way. Make sure you're not hitching your shoulder before you throw. Don't telegraph those jabs."

Zack nodded as he absorbed the instruction and threw

another series of punches, visualizing how Diaz would try to duck and weave out of the way and how he'd connect when Diaz least expected it.

How he'd win that championship belt. How he'd prove to everyone he was worth something. How he'd show the world he was more than a dumb, dyslexic jock. For Zack fighting was more than just an outlet or a distraction. It wasn't about violence or being tough, or athletic, or whatever. No, it was about proving to himself that he could succeed at something. Sure, he was relatively successful at his job, but it wasn't the same thing. Being a bodyguard wasn't his passion. It didn't fuel him the way fighting did. Fighting was about discipline, and hard work, and dedication. About being the best at something that made him proud, that made him feel alive. Plain and simple, mixed martial arts was the best thing that had ever happened to him, and he was damn well going to pour everything he had into it.

He landed a kick against the pad covering Jenks's torso, and as his shin made contact, he wondered how Alexa had fared last night. If she'd been able to sleep at all. If Sean had assigned someone to her and had figured out what their next step should be. He landed another kick, sending Jenks back a few steps, as he thought about how Mac had apparently been helping her out in the recent past. He wondered if Alexa had decided whether to go to the cops with what she'd heard. He was anxious to get eyes on her again, tension sparking through him.

Alexa. God. Even her name sent heat that had nothing to do with his training session flashing through his body. Heat, and protectiveness, and something more. A need to keep her safe, no matter what, but even *need* didn't feel like a big enough word to describe what was churning through him.

Jenks's punching mitt caught him upside the head, hard, and Zack took a step back, shaking off the hit.

"Hey! What the hell's the matter with you?" Jenks tapped his mitts together, shooting Zack a look, and pointing at him. "Focus, De Luca."

He pushed Alexa from his mind, and *this*, he reminded himself, was why he didn't date. Why he couldn't. Everything he'd worked for was right in front of him, and he was taking head shots because he was thinking about Alexa.

"Yeah, sorry," he said, adjusting his stance and circling around Jenks again. Refocused, he landed another series of elbows and knees against the pads.

Jenks held up his mitts, bringing their training to a pause. "Whatever her name is, you've got bigger things than pussy to worry about."

Anger flashed through Zack at his coach's harsh, coarse words, and he ground his teeth together, his jaw tight. He didn't like Jenks talking about Alexa that way. He forced a breath out through his nostrils. "It's not like that. It's work stuff."

"Right. You and your damn day job."

Zack shot him a smirk, his arms out at his sides. "Hey, if you're offering to train me for free…"

Jenks laughed and shook his head. "Don't get crazy now. You're lucky you've got some good sponsorships starting to come in."

Before he could respond, a pair of shin guards came flying up over the side of the cage, landing at Zack's feet. "Don't leave your shit everywhere, De Luca," said Jamie, looking disgustingly fresh and chipper given how many beers he'd had last night. Zack crossed the octagon and leaned his forearms against the padded rail along the top of the cage.

"Didn't think you'd be dragging your sorry ass in this morning."

Jamie shrugged and dropped down onto a nearby bench, retrieving a pair of hand wraps from his gym bag. "What can I say? Hitting stuff cheers me up." Both martial arts enthusiasts, Zack and Jamie had met when Zack started training at Take Down, more as a hobby than anything. But even when he'd been a relatively inexperienced twenty-two-year-old, Jenks had seen Zack's potential and had encouraged him to get serious about his training. He had, and he'd spent three years dominating the Southern California amateur MMA circuit. He'd taken his first pro fight two years ago and had stepped up his training even more. Now, at the age of twenty-eight, he had a pro record of fourteen wins and two losses. Jamie had been the one to suggest he try to get hired as a bodyguard at Virtus Security—he had the skills and the experience despite not having gone to college, and it paid a hell of a lot better than bartending.

Zack opened his mouth, wanting to ask if Jamie had heard anything about Alexa, but shut it, not wanting to get into it in front of Jenks.

Jenks cleared his throat and stared him down. "If you ladies are done with your chat, we've got work to do." When Zack returned to the center of the octagon, Jenks once again pointed his punching mitt at him. "Whatever it is, it's messing with your focus. I can't have that, not days out from the fight. Get your head in the game." He tapped his temple. "Compartmentalize."

Zack nodded, his anger ebbing. He knew Jenks was right. He'd trained too long and too hard for this opportunity to let it slip through his fingers because he was distracted. He should step back and leave Alexa's protection to someone else on the team. He needed to stay focused on his training.

Easier said than done, considering he was already planning to head over to Sean's as soon as his training session was over.

* * *

Alexa tugged on the T-shirt and jeans she'd borrowed from Sierra, then ran her fingers through the messy waves of her hair. The plain heather-gray T-shirt mostly fit, even if it was a little tight across her boobs. The jeans, however, were a different story. Given that Sierra was smaller than Alexa, they'd been a bit of a struggle. They fit, but barely, squeezing Alexa's hips and butt. But at least she had clean clothes to wear, thanks to her friend. And really, she had much bigger problems than having to wear jeans that were slightly too small for her for an hour or two until she could get back to her place.

She glanced over at the unmade bed behind her, the sheets a rumpled, twisted mess. She'd had one of those nights when it felt as though she hadn't slept at all, even though the night had passed too quickly for that to be true. Any sleep she'd caught had come in restless, fitful spurts, her mind whirling and spinning with what she'd heard the day before.

She pushed open the curtains, letting the morning sun into the room, and sank down onto the bed, the jeans digging into her skin. Closing her eyes, she took a deep breath, trying to sort and organize everything in her mind.

Fact: her father had been involved in a murder, and had ordered another.

Fact: he didn't know that she'd heard his admission.

Fact: if she didn't go to the police, someone else might end up dead.

Fact: if she went to the police, she'd likely destroy her relationship with her family and put herself at risk.

Fact: she needed protection, and she very badly wanted that protection from Zack.

Over and over again last night, those thoughts had swirled through her mind, weaving a web of fear, confusion, anxiety, and guilt. She'd spent time crawling down each thread, poking and prodding at it. Her father. Her family. Going to the police, or not. And eventually—inevitably—Zack.

He was Taylor's ex. He'd dated her friend, and according to the rules—of friendship, sisterhood, decency, whatever—he was off-limits. Not to mention that she was crazy for thinking he'd be interested in her. He'd chosen Taylor, not her. And if Taylor, with her brash humor, confident sexuality, and rock-star lifestyle, was the type of woman he was drawn to, it was clear Alexa wasn't Zack's type. She didn't have a hope of competing with Taylor when it came to sex, considering she didn't even *like* it. She needed to let this stupid crush go. It couldn't happen—it *wouldn't* happen, she corrected herself—for so many reasons.

Standing, she scooped her only remaining earring off the nightstand and dropped it into her purse. She'd lost the other one at some point last night, and in the turmoil of everything that had happened, she hadn't noticed until she'd gone to take them off to go to bed. She also gathered her dress, tossing it over one arm, and began to descend the stairs, pausing when she saw the front door open. Zack and Sean stepped inside together, Sean in a suit and Zack in a T-shirt and sweatpants. She backed up a couple of steps, retreating out of sight. It was either that or run down the stairs and come to a skidding halt in front of Zack like a lovelorn puppy. She'd clung to him enough yesterday. Today she would be stronger.

"Alexa still here?" asked Zack, his voice echoing in the spacious foyer and vibrating through her. Her toes curled slightly at the sound of her name on his lips.

"Yeah. Upstairs, I think."

"You talked to her yet this morning?"

"No, not yet. I went to check in at the office first thing. I was just coming back to see how she's doing."

"You left her alone?"

"No. Mac's been here the whole time."

Zack muttered something she couldn't quite make out. Something that sounded a lot like "of fucking course." There was a slight pause before Zack continued. "So listen. I'm glad I caught you, because I wanted to talk to you. About Alexa."

"Yeah? What about her?"

Alexa's heart skipped and fluttered in her chest, and she wasn't sure if she should brace herself for what might be coming.

"I'm going to be up front with you. I'm torn, because I've got this big fight coming up, but...fuck, I can't stop thinking about it. I want to help."

"You have."

"No, I mean...I know she's worked with Mac. But I'm the one she confided in yesterday." There was a possessive pride in his voice that sent happiness swirling through her. She hadn't confided in him just because he'd happened to be the first person she'd seen at the party last night. No, she trusted him, pretty much unquestioningly. Trusted him and believed in his ability to protect her.

There was a slight pause before Zack continued. "I want to be lead on this." Alexa suddenly found it a bit harder to breathe, and she pressed her fingers to her lips.

"You want to be Alexa's bodyguard?"

Zack's voice was steady and confident. "Yeah. I do."

Something warmed inside her, hot and sweet and sticky, like honey and chocolate, relaxing the tension that had crept into her shoulders. She slumped back against the wall, and her heart felt too big for her chest, thumping away happily. She felt like a teenager who'd just overheard that the homecoming king had a thing for her. Or at least what she imagined that would feel like. She'd never actually set foot in a real high school, having earned her diploma through tutors hired by her family and the studios she'd worked for as a teen.

"Good. Because I have an idea, and I think it'll work best with you," said Sean.

"What?"

"I need to mull it over a bit more, but I'll keep you posted. You want some coffee?" Footsteps echoing through the foyer, they retreated to the kitchen. Feeling foolish even as she did it, Alexa dashed back into the guest room, fluffed her hair, and slicked on a coat of lip gloss. It was the only makeup she had in her purse, so it'd have to do. The wand still in midair, she stilled, shaking her head and laughing at herself.

Zack wanted to help her. But it didn't mean anything. He was only doing his job, maybe even feeling obligated because of the way she'd confided in him yesterday. She bounded down the stairs, unsure if she should admit she'd overheard their conversation or not.

"Morning," she said as she stepped into the kitchen, and four sets of eyes turned toward her. Sean, Zack, Ian, and Sierra were in deep conversation. The scent of coffee and toast filled the air, and her stomach lurched slightly as her mouth went dry. Despite the fact that there were several other people in the kitchen, her eyes went immediately to Zack. He was so tall, nearly a foot taller than her, which likely put him at at least six foot three. His hair was wet, the thin cotton of his worn T-shirt stretched across his shoulders. Long, strong fingers curled around his coffee cup, and the corner of his mouth twitched up. She took a step forward, and his lips parted slightly, his eyes roaming slowly down her body, lingering on her breasts and then her hips. When his eyes returned to hold hers, his gaze had darkened slightly, and her entire body heated, warmth flooding her veins. She wondered if anyone saw her hands trembling slightly as she tugged the hem of the shirt down.

"Did you sleep much?" asked Sierra, passing her a cup of coffee and offering her a muffin from a nearby plate.

Alexa took the food with a smile and settled onto one of the stools lined up against the island in the center of the kitchen. "A little." She took a sip of the coffee and peeled the wrapper off the muffin, picking at a raisin and popping it in her mouth. "Not really."

Sierra rubbed a hand in a soothing circle over Alexa's shoulders. "I'm so sorry, honey. I can't even imagine..." She trailed off, shaking her head.

"Have you thought any more about going to the cops?" asked Sean, looking every inch the professional bodyguard in his simple black suit, his shoulder holster peeking out from under his jacket.

"I've thought about it a lot." She sighed and broke off a piece of the muffin, then chewed it thoughtfully. "If I do, I'm putting myself at greater risk, but it might prevent another murder from happening. It might also destroy my relationship with my family. And bad guy or not, he's still my father." She took a sip of her coffee. "I don't know." Once again her eyes met Zack's, who was watching her intently, tension coiled in his muscles. "What do you think I should do?" she asked him, the question popping out before she could stop herself.

Zack crossed his arms over his chest, the muscles in his arms rippling as he moved, and he tilted his head, thinking. "My main concern is that your father's offering you up as bait. Not only is that fucked up, but it's dangerous. I'm confident that I—we—can keep you safe. I think you need to wait until you're sure before you involve the police."

She nodded slowly, picking at her muffin, crumbs falling from her fingers and speckling the granite surface of the island. "I need more time. I'm not ready to decide. For now I just want to go home."

"I'm not sure that home is a safe spot for you," said Sean, pushing a hand through his hair. "Until we figure out how to play this, I'd feel better with you here."

"And what about me?" asked Zack, his brow furrowed.

Sean turned to Alexa. "I'm assigning Zack as the lead on this case. Obviously he'll have the support of the team, but he'll be your main guy. Is that okay with you?"

She nodded and shot Zack a small smile, feeling suddenly shy. "Sure."

"Good," said Sean. "So that means he'll be staying here too, for now."

"Are we at all concerned about how that might look?" asked Ian. "Won't it seem suspicious that you're staying here?"

"My father probably won't even notice," she said, shrugging. "And if he does, I'll tell him my place is being fumigated, or a pipe burst, or something. I think we're okay." But then she frowned as she turned to Zack. "What about your training? Your fight?"

He smiled, the half smile that made her heart flutter. "The fight's still on, and don't worry about me."

She swallowed, and just when she thought she was regaining control over her haywire body, Zack winked and mouthed, "Too sweet."

Her mouth fell open, and she exhaled slowly before shoving a piece of muffin in her mouth. She stared at the granite as she chewed, blood heating her cheeks, her fingertips tingling. She crossed her legs and felt the urge to squeeze her thighs together.

"We've got you covered, lass," said Ian, nodding at her, probably mistaking her silence for fear. And shit, fear might've been better, because at least she knew what to do with that. But right now, in this moment, she wasn't afraid.

She was aroused.

"We do," said Sean, nodding. "I'm sorry you're going through this, but we're not going to let anything happen to you, regardless of what you decide."

"No matter what," added Zack, his hands braced on the island, the corded muscles of his forearms moving beneath tanned skin.

She looked around at these three men, all so strong, so confident, so capable, and a completely welcome sense of security enveloped her, gratitude and relief filtering over her like sunshine.

Now she just had to figure out what the hell to do.

About everything.

CHAPTER 6

Zack pulled open the passenger side door of his Jeep and took Alexa's hand to help her up into the vehicle. Her hand was so small, so delicate in his, and he glanced down, not letting himself savor the sight of her fingers against his palm. But looking down was a mistake, because now he was staring at her denim-clad hips, the jeans barely containing her curves.

Fine. He was staring at her ass. For a sliver of a second, the image flashed through his mind before he could stop it, his hands around those hips, her ass pressed against his thighs as he buried himself inside her.

Shit.

With a brief smile, he made sure she was tucked inside before closing the door and walking briskly around the front of the Jeep to hop up into the driver's seat. Without a word he jammed the key in the ignition, cringing as Jay-Z blared through the Jeep's interior at full volume. Quickly, he reached out and twisted the knob, turning it down.

"Sorry. Postworkout adrenaline," he said as he put the Jeep in drive and maneuvered to the bottom of Sierra and Sean's circular driveway.

She shrugged one shoulder and shot him a sweet smile. "Hey, it's cool. Ain't no one fresher than Hova."

Fuck, she was cute. Cute, and off-limits. She'd already been off-limits for a number of reasons, but now he was officially her bodyguard, which added another layer of what might as well have been yellow caution tape around her. Fraternization with clients was against Virtus's policy. Not because Sean was trying to control the love lives of his employees, but because he knew firsthand how distracting it was to date a client while trying to keep her safe.

Part of the reason that Zack had offered himself up for the job was that he didn't want to leave her safety up to anyone else. And her safety had to come first.

Fuck, her safety was the only thing that should be coming anywhere at all.

Easing the Jeep into traffic, he tightened his grip on the steering wheel as he struggled to refocus his thoughts, refusing to poke into the deeper reasons why he'd been so reluctant to leave her security up to someone else on the team. Refusing to let his mind linger on all his Alexa-fueled fantasies, and not just because he didn't want to get hard while wearing sweatpants.

"Thank you," said Alexa, her hand landing on his thigh and completely eviscerating his tenuous control over his dirty thoughts. Immediately, he imagined her hand sliding higher, her fingers brushing against his package...

Jesus, maybe taking this job had been a mistake. And yet it didn't feel like a mistake. Having eyes on Alexa, knowing he could keep her safe...Fuck, it felt right. Really goddamn right.

She gave his thigh a squeeze and quickly took her hand back, and he adjusted his grip on the steering wheel, forcing images of different choke holds into his brain, pushing out anything remotely sexy. If he wanted to keep her safe, he needed to get a grip on his nearly out-of-control crush on Alexa.

Alexa, who was too sweet for him. Too good. Too distracting. Too out-of-bounds.

"For what?" he asked, focusing on the traffic around them.

"I overheard you and Sean earlier. Thanks for volunteering."

He cleared his throat before speaking, slightly embarrassed. "You're welcome." He rolled to a stop at a red light and turned to look at her, truth bursting free. "I like you, Alexa, and I care about your safety. It's important to me. I want to help you."

She inhaled sharply, her breasts straining against her T-shirt, and she nodded, pressing her fingers against her mouth. "Thanks. I...appreciate the help, Zack."

He almost groaned at the sound of his name because it sounded so damn good coming from her. God, she'd probably be so sweet in bed. Hot and yielding and giving and incredible.

This assignment was going to be either a disaster, or the best thing he'd ever done.

And he couldn't let it be a disaster. So he pushed away everything—how attracted he was to her, how much he liked her, how good she smelled, how amazing she'd felt in his arms yesterday—and started mentally going through a security plan. He navigated the morning traffic on Fountain

Avenue, descending from Sean and Sierra's house in the
Hollywood Hills and heading west toward Alexa's neigh-
borhood, which was between West Hollywood and Beverly
Hills.

"You're going to be okay. We'll figure it out, and until
then I've got you. Okay?" The Jeep crawled toward Mel-
rose, and he met her eyes, feeling a kick in his gut when
he did.

It was ridiculous. Morning haze above him, cars surrounding him, a hundred other things to be focused on, but
he was absorbed in the silvery blue of her eyes, and in that
moment he swore a silent oath that he'd do whatever it took
to keep her out of harm's way.

"So you had training this morning?" she asked, a slight
flush on her cheeks.

He nodded, resisting the urge to honk when a Porsche
cut him off. "Yeah. I train at six a.m. most mornings."

"Wow. That's really early. I'm completely useless at six
in the morning."

Immediately, the image of Alexa in bed, sleepy and
warm, sheets wrapped around her naked body, seared
through his brain, and Zack cursed his vivid imagination
as it conjured up several uses for Alexa at the crack of
dawn.

"When I'm prepping for a fight, I train twice a day, once
in the morning and once again in the afternoon or evening,
depending on my work schedule."

She peered at him thoughtfully. "That must be tough."

"It takes up most of my time. It's partly why things
didn't work out with Taylor." Well, shit. He hadn't meant
to take the conversation down that road.

She nodded slowly, her lip caught between her teeth. "I
get that. You're already committed to your fighting career.

That takes a lot of dedication." She sighed softly, her fingers twisting together in her lap. "It must mean a lot to you."

"It does."

"Can I ask why? I mean…Crap, that sounds rude. I don't mean it to be. I'm just curious. I've seen you fight before, but I've never really…I guess, wondered why you do it."

He eased back against the seat, the conversation relaxing some of the tension in his muscles. "First of all, I want to lay down a few ground rules if we're going to be working together."

"Ground rules?" Her brow furrowed. "Like what?"

"Well, like that we need to be able to communicate. So don't feel uncomfortable asking me questions." He turned to look at her as they stopped at yet another red light. "I need you to be honest with me, to tell me what you need, and I'll do the same for you. So you ask me whatever you want. We need to be clear with each other."

She smiled and licked her lips. "Okay. What else?"

"Along with communication, we need to listen to each other. If I ask you or tell you to do something, it's not for shits and giggles. And it's my job to listen to you and make sure you're getting the protection you need."

"Agreed. I'll try not to be too difficult." Her lips twitched, and his dick mirrored the movement.

"And that feeds into trust. I need you to trust me to do what's best for you, even if it doesn't seem like it at the time. Your safety is my top priority."

"I believe you, and I do trust you, Zack. I wouldn't be here with you right now if I didn't." She huffed out a soft laugh. "Hell, I wouldn't have told you everything if I didn't."

Something in his chest melted and softened, and he sent her a smile. "I'm glad you did."

Her hand returned to his thigh, and this time it stayed, her fingers pressing into him. "Me too." After a second she continued the conversation. "Okay. Communication, listening, honesty, trust. What else?"

"That's pretty much it. Those are the biggies."

"What are the smallies?"

He chuckled, relaxing even further. She made everything feel so good, so right, infusing everything with her warmth—even a simple conversation like this one. "If and when problems come up, we'll tackle them together. We're a team now."

"A team." She echoed his words back to him and gave his thigh a squeeze that she probably intended as friendly, but that his mind took to filthy places.

So much for honest communication.

His mind drifted back to the dream he'd had about her last night. In it they'd been in a limo, driving God knew where. Sitting on the bench across from him, Alexa, wearing the same strapless dress she'd had on the night before, had merely watched him, one finger pressed against her pink bottom lip. She'd smiled, something both sweet and bold, never taking her eyes off him.

"Yes?" she'd asked him. And in that weird way where you just *know* stuff in a dream, he'd known exactly what she meant.

"Hell yes." He'd spread his arms over the back of the limo's bench as they watched each other. And then, without another word, she'd tugged her dress down, freeing her full breasts. She'd tilted her head, one eyebrow cocked as all those silvery blond waves tumbled around her pretty face.

"Come here," he'd said, his voice feeling far away. Small and foggy.

With a smile that was all sweetness, she'd pushed slowly off the bench and settled herself on his lap, straddling his hips, her breasts inches from his face and begging for his mouth, her sweet pink nipples hard and peaked. He'd slid his hands to her gorgeously curved ass, giving her cheeks a firm squeeze.

"Is this what you want?" he'd asked, starting to inch his fingers under the hem of her dress, her skin smooth and soft and warm beneath his touch.

"Is this what you want?" She'd echoed his question back to him, her tongue skimming along her bottom lip. He'd opened his mouth to speak, to assure her that fuck yes, he was game, but then he'd woken up with a jolt, sweaty and tangled in his sheets.

He glanced at Alexa and shifted in his seat. His dick twitched in his pants, and he forced his brain to switch gears. Mentally, he rehashed this morning's workout, the various combos and holds he'd practiced.

Alexa ran her hands through her hair, her breasts straining against her T-shirt, and he knew he needed to up his distraction game, because his dick was already halfway to punching a hole through his sweatpants.

Baseball. Cars. Motorcycles. Will Ferrell.

She yawned and let out the tiniest, sweetest sigh, and he wondered what kinds of sounds she made during sex.

Shit. He was at erection DEFCON 1.

You fucked her friend, and she's out of your league. On top of that, she's never given any indication that she's into you. And she's your client now, so it can't happen. Get your fucking shit together, De Luca. Put your dick away and keep her safe.

He held on to all the reasons he couldn't have her, repeating them on a loop, the mental equivalent of a cold shower.

It was working. Sort of.

He changed lanes as he turned onto North Robertson, glancing over his shoulder as he maneuvered the Jeep through traffic and Alexa gave his thigh another squeeze. He ground his teeth together and tried to ignore the way his skin seemed to tighten when she did that. He stared at the landscape around him, at the tall, shaggy Mexican fan palms that stood out in the distance against the hazy light-blue sky. Scrubby mountains rose in his rearview mirror, their bumpy outline barely visible against the smog. He focused on the trees and mountains and not the heat thrumming through his body, still fighting against the erection doing its damnedest to make an appearance.

"You never answered my question," she said, pulling his attention back to her.

"You're right. I didn't." He drummed his fingers on the wheel, trying to figure out how much to tell her and at what point in the story to start.

"So what are you fighting for? What draws you to it?"

"A lot of things, really. I like the physical challenge of it. It's a good outlet. It focuses me."

She studied him. "But there's more to it than that. I've seen a couple of your fights. It's about more than just beating another guy up." She smiled, her nose wrinkling slightly. "Which you're very good at, by the way." Her gaze trailed over his hands and up his arms.

"Yeah, there's more to it than that. It's the discipline, you know? Working hard to be the best at something, to push my body to new limits. There's something primal about it that makes me feel alive, and to know that I could potentially be the best at something like that…"

"To succeed," she added, nodding slowly. "But why MMA specifically?"

He shrugged as he turned onto her street. "I never went to college. I was working as a bartender when I started training at Take Down. Honestly, I was looking for a hobby. The bar I worked at showed the fights on TV sometimes, and I wanted to try it. Turned out I was really good at it. It gave me a sense of purpose, a goal to work toward. And it was a hell of a lot more fulfilling than pouring shots for frat boys, I can tell you that."

"How come you didn't go to college?"

"Which one's yours?" he asked, peering at the house numbers.

"Eight-eight-two-five."

"College wasn't for me. I'm dyslexic, and school was…Fuck, I hated school."

"Oh. I didn't know that."

"It's not a huge deal. Really."

She nodded, staring at him, and he could almost hear the wheels turning as she put all the pieces of his story together. He liked when she looked at him like that, as if she wanted to figure him out. As if knowing more about him was worthy of her time.

"I never went to college either."

He glanced at her. "No?" he asked, unable to keep the note of surprise from creeping into his voice.

She shook her head. "I guess I could've, if I'd really pushed it, but it was never something talked about in my family. From as early as I can remember, everything was about being a Fairfax and living up to the family name."

"What did you want to be when you grew up? A ballerina? Doctor? Or did you always want to be an actress?"

A silence stretched between them, and when he stole a glance at her, her bottom lip was caught between her teeth again.

After several seconds she answered. "You know, I don't think I ever thought about it the way other kids do. I was just always going to be an actress."

"Because that's what you wanted to do?"

"Because it's what was always going to happen." He could almost hear her unspoken "whether I liked it or not." She gave her head a small shake and smiled. "Maybe someday I'll go to college. I'd like to. You've found your thing with fighting. I'm still looking for mine, you know?" She sent him another smile. "One thing at a time, I guess."

Sadness tugged at his chest as he thought of how alone she must've been growing up, with only cold, manipulative adults around her. So much wealth and fame that she'd been trapped by it.

When he'd first started talking, he'd felt the tiniest bit of worry that she'd look at him differently once she knew he hadn't gone to college and that he was dyslexic. But it had been worry for nothing because she was still looking at him with that sweetness and light he found so damn appealing.

He pulled into the driveway of the small 1920s bungalow, with ivy crawling up one side of the house, obscuring the off-white stucco.

"Cute place," he said, putting the Jeep in park. "It suits you."

Pink spots jumped up on her cheeks, and she smiled, glancing from him to the house. "Thanks. I like it here.

It's the first time I've lived away from my parents, and I'm really loving it."

"Must be freeing," he said, cutting the ignition and snapping off his seat belt, then taking in the details of the property as he pushed open his door. The driveway ran along one side of the house, and a walkway paved with patio stones led to the front door. A low shrub hedge separated her yard from the neighbors', and a couple of palms lined the far side of the driveway. A large cedar took up most of the front yard, shading the front of the house, and a pair of shaggy cypresses flanked what he assumed was the living room window.

He helped Alexa down from the Jeep, frowning as he followed her up to the house. No outward signs of a security system. No decal announcing the presence of one, no visible motion-detecting lights, no cameras. The windows looked newer and secure, but there was no front porch. Only a set of three concrete steps leading up to the front door, which, he was glad to see, was solid wood with a deadbolt. She wouldn't stay at Sierra and Sean's forever, and they'd need to look at upgrading her security for when she moved back into her house.

Alexa fished her keys out of her purse and moved to unlock the front door. But just as she brought the key to the lock, the slight pressure of her touch sent the door swinging open. It hadn't been locked, hadn't even been fully latched. She glanced at him over her shoulder, her eyes wide. "I *know* I locked it before leaving yesterday."

A surge of protectiveness pushed up through Zack's chest, sending his blood pumping through his veins. He grabbed Alexa's hand and pulled her back toward the Jeep, not wanting her out of his sight for even a second. He considered having her wait in the car while he checked out the house, but doing that could play into a trap. Separating was never a good idea, and leaving her alone was an even worse one.

He pulled open the passenger side door and unlocked the glove box, then yanked out the loaded Smith & Wesson M&P9 he kept there. Slamming the door—there was no point being quiet, because anyone in the house would've already heard the Jeep's engine and their doors' opening and closing when they'd arrived—he turned to face Alexa, whose face was pale, her sweet blue eyes wide as she stared at the house. Those blues swiveled from the house and dropped to the gun in his hand, and she wrapped her arms around herself, rubbing her hands over her arms.

"Don't leave me out here alone," she said, her tone soft and pleading.

"No. I wouldn't do that. I'm going to update Sean, and then we're going to go check it out."

After a quick call to Sean, letting him know they'd found Alexa's place unlocked and the door slightly ajar, he nodded at Alexa. "Stay behind me and keep your hand on my back so I know you're there. I want you close."

"I'll stay close. I promise."

He turned and made his way back to the house, Alexa tucked behind him. Gun raised in front of him, he nudged open the front door, sweeping both the weapon and his eyes back and forth across the small entryway and what he could see of the living room. The house was completely silent.

Silent, and trashed.

CHAPTER 7

From behind Zack, Alexa gasped as she took in her ransacked house, fear cascading over her like icy water. She curled her fingers into Zack's T-shirt, a slight tremble coursing through her. Gun raised in front of him, Zack took a slow step forward, and she followed, her heart racing, the sound of her pulse in her ears almost deafening.

The mirror above her fireplace was smashed, shards scattered across the hardwood floor and glinting in the sunlight coming in through the window. The flat-screen TV was gone, her decorative knickknacks—candleholders, a porcelain horse, a small silver tray—strewn on the floor, most of them broken. A framed picture, an antique print of a horse, lay against the wall, the glass cracked. The baskets in which she kept magazines and books had been upended, their contents littering the floor, torn pages sticking out at odd angles.

"No security system?" Zack asked over his shoulder as they made their way through the living room. A sickening sensation crawled over her skin. Someone had been in here, in her house, going through her things. Some of her fear gave way to anger, and she clenched her shaking hands into fists.

"No. I'd asked the landlord to put one in, but it hadn't happened yet."

"Son of a bitch." The lines of the muscles in his forearms were taut, and she kept herself firmly behind him, watching the way he led them toward the kitchen with graceful, easy confidence. He was so strong, so sure, so capable that she didn't even have words for what she felt, sheltered as she was behind him. Grateful and relieved, yes, but there was more to it than that. She felt safe, despite the sense of violation that made her want to scream and break things.

They made their way past the table and chairs at the front of the kitchen. A painting that had hung on the wall where the living room and kitchen met was missing, but it was no great loss, since she'd painted it herself and it wasn't worth anything.

"Stuff's missing?" he asked softly, his gun trained in front of him.

"Yeah. The TV from the living room and a painting, so far," she said, relaxing a little as she realized the unlikeliness of the thieves' still being in the house.

They stepped over a toppled potted plant, the dirt crunching softly beneath their feet. The kitchen was relatively undisturbed. Drawers were half-open, cupboard doors were ajar, but there wasn't anything worth stealing in here.

If it had been, in fact, a robbery.

As though he could pick up on her thoughts, Zack murmured, "Pretty goddamn fishy that this would happen the same day you…heard what you heard."

"I know."

"We'll check out the rest of the house, you can grab your stuff, and we'll get out of here."

She nodded, tucking herself close behind him. Heat from his body brushed her skin, and she wanted to press her face into the muscles of his back, to breathe him in and bask in his protection.

They moved into the sunroom behind the kitchen. The chest she used as a coffee table had been wrenched open, splinters lying on the floor. Books and DVDs lay strewn over the sectional sofa, the cushions all pulled out and opened, stuffing spilling out of the zippers.

"What was in the chest?"

"Nothing valuable. Books. DVDs. A few photo albums. Old scripts."

"Anything missing from in here?"

She shook her head. "No. Still only the TV and painting."

"How many bedrooms?"

"Just two."

"What's this door?" he asked, pointing with his gun at a door off the kitchen.

"Bathroom."

Nodding, he nudged the door open. It creaked as it swung wide, and she jumped slightly, brushing against him. A quick scan of the bathroom revealed nothing out of place. The thieves likely hadn't even come in here.

"Where's your bedroom?"

Despite everything, a warmth flushed over her skin at his words. "The other door off the kitchen."

He pushed the door open.

She'd been lulled by the minimal damage and property missing, and hadn't braced herself for what awaited her in her bedroom. She pressed a shaky hand to her mouth, her heart in her throat.

The mattress lay half-on, half-off the padded king-size bed frame, the sheets pulled away and ripped. Pillows had been torn open, and the mirrored stand beside the bed had been smashed completely, drawers lying askew on the floor, empty of their contents.

"Shit," Zack whispered. He pointed at the gaping hole in the wall facing the bed. "TV?"

"Used to be." Gingerly, she made her way across the floor, stepping over broken glass, pieces of drywall, drawers, and feathers, her chest aching. "I think all my jewelry's gone. A lot of it was in these drawers."

"Anything expensive?"

"A few things, but mostly sentimental stuff. Anything really valuable is either at my parents' in the safe or in a safe-deposit box."

Quickly they checked her en suite bathroom and the second bedroom, from which her laptop had been stolen. The thieves had also knocked over a set of shelves, leaving more damage behind. Zack pulled his phone from his pocket and paced up and down the hallway as he made a call, his gun still clutched in one big, strong hand.

Shaking slightly, Alexa moved into the center of the room, standing in a patch of sunlight and closing her eyes, not wanting to look at the damage around her. The new start she'd been so excited about was completely tarnished now. The new home she'd been thrilled to call her own had been violated and no longer felt safe. Maybe she'd been foolish to move out on her own. But then the thought of moving back home…A clamminess rose up on her skin, the sunshine doing nothing to chase it away.

She couldn't go home. She didn't want to stay here.

A sense of loneliness swamped her, and she swallowed against the thickness gathering in her throat. She blinked, and hot tears dropped down her cheeks as she stared at the blurry patch of sunlight on the floor, tracing her toe around its edges, just trying to breathe.

It was all too much, and everything she'd been through over the past day pressed down on her, a crushing weight on her shoulders.

Everything stopped—her heart, her ability to breathe, the entire world, it seemed—as she wondered if her father knew what she'd overheard yesterday. Her legs went weak as more tears fell, and she was about to sink to the floor when a strong arm circled her waist. Zack held her up, pulling her back against his firm chest.

"I've got you," he whispered, and she relaxed into his strength. Into his warmth. Into him. She took a deep shuddering breath and turned, burying her face against him. Her shoulders shook as sobs racked her, and his arms came up around her, cradling her against him. "Shhh." His warm breath fanned against her temple, and she closed her eyes, timing her own breaths with the rise and fall of his chest against her cheek.

"What if this is related to what happened yesterday?" she asked, her voice cracking slightly.

"It might be," said Zack, tightening his arms around her, his lips brushing her temple as he spoke. A shiver worked its way through her. God, the feeling of his lips on her skin…it was incredible. Just that tiny touch made her want to weave her fingers into his hair and pull his mouth down to hers.

If only that were actually an option.

"We need to go to the police. What if my father knows what I heard? That puts not only me but you and the entire team in danger. I can't have that."

"If you want, we could just report the break-in. You don't have to tell them about your father if you don't want to." He slipped a hand under her chin and tipped her face up. "Whatever you want to do, I'll keep you safe."

Her stomach fluttered, and heat pulsed between her legs. "I have to go to the police. It's selfish if I don't."

Zack's hand slid from her chin to her cheek, and his thumb grazed her cheekbone, brushing away her tears. He pulled her a little tighter against him, his chest rising and falling steadily against hers as his eyes dropped to her mouth. His head dipped slightly, just the tiniest bit, and her breath caught in her chest. She held completely still, terrified of shattering the moment. Terrified of what would happen if he kissed her. She both wanted it and didn't want it, for completely different reasons.

"So sweet," he whispered, and he closed his eyes, his jaw clenched tight. He pressed his forehead to hers for several breaths, his thumb still tracing over her cheekbone, and she had the feeling that as much as she was waging an internal war, so was he.

Which was completely perplexing. Because he couldn't possibly be feeling what she was. He couldn't want her the way she wanted him.

He wouldn't. And even if he did, it'd be wasted on her. It'd be like giving someone who didn't know how to drive a Ferrari. A lovely gift that she wouldn't have the first clue how to handle.

He brushed his nose against her cheek, and she shook slightly, that internal battle ripping her to shreds as she fought to hold still and not do something stupid.

They couldn't. It would be wrong. A mistake. Maybe even dangerous.

With a soft growl that had her belly and thighs

clenching, he pulled away, his brown eyes dark and hot. "Gather up what you need, and let's go talk to the cops."

* * *

Zack raised a hand in greeting when he spotted Sean sitting in one of the chairs in the glass and chrome lobby of the Robbery-Homicide Division, housed in the towering administration building of the Los Angeles Police Department. Sean pushed to his feet, buttoning his suit jacket as he stood, and Zack glanced down, realizing he was still in his post-workout sweats. Not very professional, but, given the circumstances, it couldn't be helped. Their footsteps echoed off of the tiled floor, cops and civilians alike moving around them. Voices swirled together into a low hum, mixing with the click of shoes on tile and the occasional buzz of a cell phone.

After he'd made sure the house was empty and had known that Alexa was safe, Zack had called Sean and filled him in on the break-in. Then he'd almost kissed Alexa, and then he'd called Sean again to let him know that they were going to the police.

Calling the boss to fill him in? Yeah. Good thinking.

Almost kissing Alexa, who was not only a client but not the type of woman he should even *think* about starting something with? Colossally stupid.

"Alexa, honey, I'm so sorry," said Sean, giving her shoulder a squeeze.

She nodded and sent him a small smile, but she was pale, her eyes sad. "Thanks."

They started walking through the bright, airy lobby toward a bank of elevators. "So the break-in made you change your mind?"

She sighed heavily and fiddled with the strap on her purse. She'd changed out of her borrowed clothes before they'd left her house, from the too-tight jeans and T-shirt and into a flowing white top, black leggings, and a pair of black-and-white sneakers. Although Zack missed the sight of all those curves, he had to admit that she looked a hell of a lot more comfortable now.

She leveled a look at Sean. "Be straight with me. In your professional opinion, what are the odds that this is a coincidence? That I heard what I heard yesterday and suddenly my house gets broken into?"

Sean frowned and shrugged as he jabbed a thumb against the elevator's call button. "I don't know about the odds, but from a security standpoint, it'd be foolish to treat it as an unrelated coincidence."

She nodded, chewing on her bottom lip. "That's what I thought. As scary as it is and although he's my father…I can't stay quiet. That wouldn't be right." She shuddered slightly, as though a chill had just run through her, and Zack laid a hand on the small of her back, rubbing in small circles. She leaned into his touch, and it only made him want to pull her into his arms.

Goddammit.

"So why did you want to meet here, instead of just going to a precinct?" she asked as they stepped into the elevator.

"I have some LAPD connections. My friend Antonio's a detective with major crimes, and he gave me the name of someone in Robbery-Homicide we should talk to. Cut through the rigmarole of going to a precinct, filing a report, having to answer the same questions, tell the same story over and over again." Sean glanced down at Alexa. "He also promised that Detective Morales is very discreet. You're in good hands."

Alexa froze, all the blood draining from her face. "Did you say Morales?"

Sean nodded slowly. "Antonio did a directory search, and there are eleven officers with the last name Morales on the force. We have no way of knowing which one your father was talking about."

Alexa nodded, her lips pressed together in a thin line. An ache took root in the center of Zack's chest, because fuck, did he wish he could carry some of this for her. Her world had been turned upside down, and while he was impressed with how she was handling it, he wished she didn't have to handle it at all.

"I guess we'll find out, won't we?" She leaned back into Zack's hand a little more. God, what he wouldn't give to be able to really comfort her. To pull her against him, to stroke her hair, to kiss her and promise her that nothing would ever hurt her.

But that couldn't happen, so instead he stared at the electronic screen embedded in the elevator, watching the numbers go up as the elevator rose. When they reached the seventh floor, the doors opened with a soft chime, and Sean led them out and down a hallway. Turning a corner, they almost ran smack into Mac, who leaned against a wall, one foot propped casually against it, holding a paper cup of coffee.

"I finished up that paperwork early, so I thought I'd come meet you," he said, the syllables running together in his Scottish accent.

"How'd you know where to find us?" asked Zack, and Mac tipped his cup at him.

"I know lots of things. Wasn't hard to figure out where you'd be and when."

Although Zack had worked with Mac for over a year

now, he still wasn't sure how he felt about the Scot. He didn't talk much, and when he did, he seemed to be spouting off riddles and half-complete thoughts, leaving Zack to fill in the blanks. And that was when he could understand him at all. Mac was almost impossible to read sometimes, and mostly kept to himself. Despite the number of jobs they'd worked together, Zack knew almost nothing about him. Didn't know how long he'd been in America or why he'd come. Didn't know the first thing about his personal life. He knew Mac was a former Special Air Service medic and paratrooper, but the only time he'd asked him about it, he'd been met with a glare, stony silence, and, finally, "It's not something I talk about." Zack had never asked again.

Alexa laid a hand on Mac's arm as they walked down the hallway. "Thanks for coming."

He simply nodded at her and patted her hand. A flicker of jealousy burned through Zack's stomach, and his jaw was clenched so tight that his molars were jammed together almost painfully. Rubbing a hand over his mouth, he forced himself to relax. Fuck, he needed to get it together. Focus on protecting her. Nothing else.

They stopped in front of a glass door, and Sean knocked. A woman rose from behind the desk and pulled the door open, waving them in.

"Come in, take a seat. Well, some of you. Two chairs, four people, you do the math." She stuck her hand out in front of her. "Detective Natalie Morales." They all shook hands and introduced themselves before Alexa and Sean settled in the two chairs facing Detective Morales's desk. Zack and Ian stood just behind them, and Zack struggled against the urge to put his hands on Alexa's chair. Or her shoulders. So he crossed his arms in front of him instead.

The detective looked to be in her midthirties and was

tall with a fit, athletic build visible even underneath her gray pantsuit and blue blouse. Her thick dark-brown hair came to her chin, framing her pretty face. She moved around the office with confidence and authority, and Zack was pretty damn sure that Detective Natalie Morales wasn't someone you messed around with. She sat back down in her chair and opened her laptop.

"Detective Rodriguez filled me in, but only very basic details." She turned her attention to Alexa. "I assume you're the woman he mentioned. He didn't give me any names."

Alexa nodded. "Yeah."

"Why don't you tell me the whole story, in your own words, from the beginning? I don't want to start off an investigation with thirdhand information."

Alexa nodded again and, with a shaky breath, began telling Detective Morales the whole story. What she'd overheard her father say during the conversation with Gordon Kramer, essentially confessing to the murder of Jeff Astor. The way he'd offered her up as bait in exchange for the murder of someone named Crosby. The subsequent break-in at her place.

"How long were you out of your home? I'm just trying to pinpoint a time frame during which the robbery occurred," said Morales.

"I guess from about five p.m. yesterday afternoon until about ten this morning."

"Where did you stay last night?"

"At Sean's house. I didn't want to go home."

Morales nodded, typing on her computer as she spoke. "And there's no security at your current residence?"

Alexa shook her head. "No. I'd asked the landlord about installing a security system, but it hasn't happened."

Morales sat back in her chair and tucked her hair behind her ears. She pressed a hand to her mouth, deep in thought. "Hang on a sec," she said, pushing out of her chair and stepping out of the office. She returned almost as quickly with two thick file folders in her hands. She dropped them down onto the desk and flipped one of them open, once again tucking her hair behind her ears.

She glanced up, her eyes darting from Alexa to Sean and then back again. Finally, she nodded, as though having made up her mind about something.

"Alexa, have you ever heard of the Golden Brotherhood?"

Zack's mouth fell open, and his skin tingled. He'd dealt with the Brotherhood only a couple of months ago, when they'd come after Taylor.

Alexa shook her head slowly. "Um, no. I don't think so. Why?"

"Because I'm the organized crime liaison between the LAPD and the FBI, and we've been investigating your father for a long time."

"You have?" Alexa's voice was small, quiet. Zack could barely hear her over his racing heartbeat.

Morales leaned forward on her desk, her hands clasped on top of the open file. "Yes. And what you heard last night, it's just the tip of the iceberg."

Alexa's hands were clasped together in her lap, her knuckles white. "It has to be you," she whispered.

"Excuse me?" Morales arched an eyebrow.

"My father, when he was discussing Astor and Crosby, mentioned a cop named Morales who knew too much. If you're the organized crime liaison, it has to be you. He knows, Detective. He knows you've been investigating him."

Morales squared her shoulders and folded her hands together calmly in front of her. "Well, shit. You're sure you heard my name? Morales?"

"I'm positive, yes."

"There are other Moraleses on the force," said Sean, although he didn't sound convinced.

"Other Moraleses investigating the organized crime ring her father happens to be the head of?" challenged Morales. "It's me. He was talking about me." She turned her attention to Alexa. "Thank you for telling me."

"Organized crime? What exactly are you saying?" she asked, her voice shaky.

"I'm saying that I think your father is the kingpin of one of the most elusive organized crime operations in California. And you, Alexa, can help us bring it down."

CHAPTER 8

"Did you find anything at Alexa's?" asked Jonathan as he skimmed through the news headlines on his tablet. He picked up a piece of toast from the plate in front of him and crunched down. He brushed away a few crumbs that had landed on his pants. A soft breeze swirled around him, rustling the fronds of the palm trees surrounding the pool. Glancing up, he shielded his eyes as Elijah's silhouette moved into the shaded alcove where Jonathan ate his breakfast every morning.

Elijah sat down across from him and helped himself to a freshly baked croissant from the basket in the center of the table. He broke it in half, a little puff of steam rising up and evaporating almost instantly. "No, nothing. But one of the tech guys is still going through her laptop. So far nothing suspicious to indicate she knows anything."

"And you made it look like a robbery so as not to arouse suspicion?"

Elijah nodded and popped a piece of croissant into his mouth. "Just like you asked. We took the two televisions, some art, her jewelry, and her computer. Made a mess."

Jonathan sat back in his chair, his fingers tented. "I'm surprised she hasn't called to tell me about it. You know how needy she can be."

"Maybe she's spoken to Melanie?"

"Maybe who's spoken to me about what?" Melanie sauntered toward them, dressed for the pool and the sun in a black one-piece bathing suit, a floppy straw hat, enormous sunglasses, and a diaphanous black robe. She held a script in one hand and a champagne flute filled with orange juice—and probably a lot of champagne—in the other.

"Have you heard from Alexa this morning?" he asked.

Melanie gave her head a little shake. "No. Why? What's she done now?"

"Probably nothing. But…" He reached into his pocket and placed the earring on the table. "I found this in the library last night after the party."

She arched an eyebrow at him. "And? Spit it the fuck out, Jonathan."

Even when she was annoyed with him, he loved her strength. He wished Alexa had inherited at least some of it, but she was all soft and weak where Melanie was angles and resilience. "I had my conversation with Kramer vis-à-vis Astor and Crosby in the library last night during dinner."

Melanie scoffed out a laugh. "What, you think she was hiding in there? Spying on you? Please. You're getting paranoid."

He picked up the earring and twirled it slowly between his fingers, watching the facets catch the light. "It's not paranoia. It's caution. I had her place searched last night."

She tapped her foot impatiently. "And did you find anything?"

"No."

"So that's it, then. She doesn't know anything."

Jonathan twirled the earring again, the diamonds glinting at him. Winking at him, as though they had tricked him, somehow.

"I still think we should keep her close. Just to be sure."

Melanie sighed and took a sip of her orange juice. "Fine. Whatever floats your boat." She paused and took a few steps closer, then set her glass down on the table. Slowly, she pulled her sunglasses from her face. "And if she *does* know?"

"Then we'll have to deal with it."

* * *

Alexa dug her fingers into her thighs, trying to anchor herself against the onslaught of emotions crashing through her, twisting her into knots. She felt as though she were drowning, choking on confusion, disbelief, and fear.

"What…what did you say?" she asked, her voice sounding far away, muted by the blood rushing through her ears. She took a shaky, shuddering breath, and for a brief moment she wanted to scream. Her entire world was unraveling around her, spinning out of control, and she didn't know what to do with herself or how to process any of it. Breathing and blinking were all she was capable of, and she could feel herself getting swept away by the nauseating chaos of the situation.

Zack's hand—strong, but gentle—landed on her shoulder, and she dropped her head forward, some of the tension going out of her neck. Two wet splotches appeared on her leggings, and she realized she'd started silently crying.

"I know it's a lot to take in. I'm sorry," said Detective Morales, her tone sympathetic. Zack's thumb traced slow, soothing circles at the base of her neck. The room spun for a second but then settled back into place. Alexa looked up, past Detective Morales and out the window.

The sun still shone. The windows of the *Los Angeles Times* building across the street winked metallically in the light. The sky was still blue. Horns still honked occasionally from below. Phones rang in the offices adjacent to Morales's. A photocopier hummed, people laughed.

Everything was still so *normal*, despite the fact that Alexa's world had just tilted on its axis, upending everything. Upending her life, and everything she thought she'd known.

Despite the shock of the detective's words, Alexa realized that she believed her. "How do you know?" she asked, her throat thick.

Without a word Morales slid one of the file folders across to her. With shaking hands Alexa accepted it, and the rest of the room dropped away. On one side were full-color mug shots, held in place with a paper clip. She sorted through them, recognizing face after face. Men and women she'd seen in her house growing up, who she'd assumed were friends of her parents and nothing more. Not loan sharks, and blackmailers, and drug dealers, and arms traffickers. Pimps and fraudsters and corrupt businessmen.

Murderers.

Alexa gasped when she landed on a very familiar face. "It's Jack," she whispered, pulling the photo free from the pile and handing it to Sean. He stared down at the picture of Sierra's ex-boyfriend, a former state senator now serving twenty years for kidnapping, forcible confinement, assault, election fraud, and stalking, plus other fraud and weapons charges. Jack, who'd tried to kill both Sierra and Sean, two people Alexa loved dearly. Heat flushed through Alexa's body as a flicker of anger rose up, sharpening her focus. "Jack's involved with this Golden Brotherhood?"

Morales tipped her head. "It's complicated, but yes, I think so. There was never enough evidence to prove it, and he wouldn't talk. Probably because he knew he'd have a date with a shiv the second he found himself in gen pop."

"Fucker," Sean ground out before tossing the photo back on Morales's desk.

Alexa continued flipping, her heart pounding faster and harder with each face she recognized. Faces of criminals she knew to be associated with her father in some way.

"Wait, go back," said Sean, twirling a finger in the air. She did, and he snatched a pair of photos up off the desk. "*Son of a bitch.*"

She knew she'd seen the men in the photos before but couldn't seem to get her brain to work fast enough to place them. "Who are they?"

Sean jabbed a finger at the first mug shot, the one of a bald biker-looking guy. "Frank Ross. Taylor's father." His expression grim, he flipped to the other picture. "Ronald Baker."

"Taylor's stalker…Holy shit," Alexa said, tracing her fingers over the face in the picture as recognition snapped through her. "They were involved with the Golden Brotherhood too?"

Morales nodded. "Yes. Again, no one will talk, but there's a lot of uncorroborated evidence pointing in that direction. The FBI is still investigating."

"My father was involved in almost killing my friends.

In almost killing the people I love." Her voice came out flat, almost monotone as she tested out the words, weighing them as she spoke. She pulled the folder closer, flipping through page after page of evidence. Interviews, investigations, words blurring together. A litany of awful things her father was allegedly responsible for.

Given what she knew from her own experience with her father, the only word in that sentence that felt out of place was *allegedly*.

"How do you know I'm not involved?" asked Alexa, frowning up at Morales.

"Because we've been investigating you too. I don't think you're involved. And I don't think you would've given me the heads-up about your father's threat against me either. If you were here simply for information, to try and find out just how much I know, I don't think you would've tipped me off." Morales clasped her hands in front of her on the desk and leaned toward Alexa. "I'll ask you once, and then we'll be done with it. Alexa, are you involved with the Golden Brotherhood?"

Alexa met the other woman's gaze and shook her head slowly. "No." For several seconds Morales held her eyes as though searching for something, and then she nodded once.

"Has he ever hurt you?" asked Morales.

Alexa's fingers tightened around the folder, the manila bending slightly under her grip. Shame crackled over her, hot and prickly, and she swallowed, her mouth dry. "Not…not intentionally." She forced the words out, struggling with what to say. Zack's hand tightened the slightest bit on her shoulder.

"What do you mean?" asked Morales, her eyes narrowing slightly.

"I don't…It's far in the past, and it wasn't criminal.

It doesn't matter." She already felt as though she'd been hit by a truck after everything that had happened over the past day, and she could barely make sense of everything as it was. Now wasn't the time to layer on another complication. And especially such a personal one.

Especially in front of Zack.

Morales stared at her for several seconds before letting it go. Alexa had a feeling she wasn't off the hook indefinitely, but she could handle only so much right now. Opening up that old wound wasn't happening. Not today.

She reached for the second folder and began paging through it, not really taking in any of the information in front of her as her mind reeled and spun with what she'd already found out. Her eyes skimmed over the terms *money laundering* and *larceny*, and her mouth opened before she even realized she was going to speak. "My father is a mobster who played a role in hurting my friends. He's hurt a lot of people. He's dangerous. And I can help you? That's what you're telling me?" She pushed the folder away. She'd seen enough, and she swallowed thickly, fighting a wave of nausea. "He's a criminal, who's hurt people I care about," she murmured, letting the words sink in. Wishing that they weren't so easy to believe. Wishing she had even the tiniest bit of doubt that Morales was telling the truth.

But everything in front of her, coupled with what she'd learned yesterday and over the past ten years of her life…it made sense. A damn boatload of it. A shard of guilt pierced her, but she shoved it away. If all this was true—if he'd tried to kill her friends, if he'd hurt other people to feed his own selfish need for power—he wasn't worthy of her guilt. That much she knew for certain.

Morales nodded, flipping the first folder closed. "You

present an opportunity this investigation has never had before. The biggest problem is that no one will talk, and the Brotherhood is pretty much impossible to infiltrate. Believe me, we've tried." She pressed her index fingers to her lips before pointing at Alexa. "But you...You're in a unique position, because you have inside access and aren't involved. He has no idea you're here?"

"No, I don't think so."

"Okay, let's just back the fuck up for a second here." Zack's voice came from behind her, sending a ripple down her spine. How was it possible that she was so aware of him, so responsive to him when she shouldn't have room for anything except the chaos of the past day?

Alexa swiveled around to look up at him. A muscle in Zack's jaw ticced, and his gaze swung down to meet hers. His deep-brown eyes were hot, an angry glower knitting his eyebrows together and sending a pulse of heat straight through her. "You're *not* doing this," he said, his voice almost a growl. "It's way too fucking dangerous." He turned that glower on Morales. "I can't believe you'd suggest something like this."

"You don't even know what I'm suggesting," said Morales, a hint of irritation adding an edge to her voice.

"It doesn't matter. She's not doing it."

Alexa pushed to her feet and spun to face Zack. "*She* can make her own decisions, thanks." God, she'd had enough of other people dictating her life, and she'd be damned if she was going to let Zack start.

"And I'm telling you, this is a bad one." He leaned forward slightly, taking up some of her space, and a part of her wanted to shove him back, while another wanted to wrap herself around him.

"It's *my* choice, Zack, if I want to do this or not. Not

yours." She jabbed a finger into his chest, everything—the fear, the anger, the shock, the confusing tangle of her attraction to Zack—melting together and bursting out of her. "Just because you're my bodyguard doesn't mean you get to boss me around and make decisions for me."

His jaw tightened and his nostrils flared. He glanced down for a brief second to where her finger was still pressed firmly against his chest. His very hard chest. "Actually, it does. It's my job to protect you, and that means keeping you out of harm's way. Not letting you walk right the fuck into it. God." Nostrils flaring again, he rubbed a hand over the back of his neck, tension practically radiating off him.

"What about your rules? Communication and honesty and trust? Was that all bullshit?" When she swore, his eyes narrowed slightly, and he pressed forward the tiniest bit, her finger still jabbed into his chest, her nail bed white from the pressure. "Because what it sounds like to me is that you want to be in control. That I should just do what you want, when you want." Heat flared in his eyes. Tension, thick and hot, gathered around them, but she wasn't backing down. She couldn't, not when her father had done these awful things. Not when she had a chance to try to make it right.

When Zack spoke, it was through clenched teeth. "I'm *communicating* to you that I *honestly* believe this is a terrible idea, and I need you to *trust* me to do my goddamn job."

She took her finger away and stepped around the chair, getting right in his face. "I thought we were a *team*."

"We are."

"Right, but you're the captain and I'm a benchwarmer."

"I need to keep you safe." His hand came up and curled

around her arm, his grip firm but gentle. Something in his eyes shifted, the anger giving way to something softer. Something almost…imploring.

"Zack," she said, some of the fire going out of her. She found it incredibly hard to think with his hand on her. All she could focus on was the warm, reassuring strength in his touch.

His gaze dropped to her mouth for a second, and then, with a sharp exhale, he took a step back. He dropped his head forward, shaking it as he stared at the floor. Finally, when he looked up, it was at Sean, not her. "And you're going to let his happen?" he asked Sean, his hands out at his sides.

Instead of answering Zack, Sean looked up at Alexa, his hands clasped between his legs, a thoughtful expression on his face. "Do you want to do it?"

"Are you fucking kidding me?" Zack scoffed out a frustrated sigh.

"What do you want Alexa to do?" Sean asked the detective, his voice cool and calm in comparison to Zack's.

Morales shot Zack a pointed look first. "You done?"

Zack took another step back and crossed his arms over his chest. The muscles in his forearms bunched and flexed, and some of Alexa's anger dissolved into something hotter, sinking through her and settling between her thighs.

"I haven't heard your plan yet, so probably not," he said, his voice a little rough.

Morales gestured to the empty chair in front of her desk, silently asking Alexa to sit back down. She did, and even though the chair was solid beneath her, she felt as though she were a boat on a storm-tossed sea, unanchored and rocking violently as she fought against capsizing.

"The way you can help is simple, Alexa. Do you have access to your parents' house?"

She nodded. "Yes. I see them regularly."

"Good. What we need you to do is to plant bugs—listening devices—so that we can build a stronger case against your father."

"With the idea that he goes to prison?" she asked, her stomach swirling sickly. Criminal or not, the betrayal would cost her.

Morales nodded. "Yes. Are you in?"

"Yes. I'm in. I'll help you."

She heard a muttered string of curses from Zack.

Morales nodded. "Good. And I think it's best if you stick with Virtus for your security. Putting a police detail on you would only raise questions, and…" Her voice trailed off, and she shrugged. "Given that your father already had my name, clearly there are people around here who can't be trusted. I hate to say it, but the fewer cops involved, the safer you are right now." Her mouth and nose twitched as though she'd just smelled something offensive.

Obviously struggling for control, Zack cleared his throat before speaking. "So how do we play this?" he asked Sean. "You mentioned that if Alexa suddenly hires security, it might tip her father off that she knows something, or at least suspects something, and I agree. It wouldn't make sense for her to have security around her family if she's got nothing to be afraid of. When she goes to plant those listening devices, how am I supposed to keep her safe if I don't even have a valid reason for being there?"

Sean smiled confidently. "This is where the idea I mentioned earlier comes in. You're right, it doesn't make sense for you to walk into the Fairfax mansion as Alexa's bodyguard. No way that wouldn't set off immediate alarm bells." Sean paused, glancing from Zack to Alexa. "It's a bit unorthodox, but given the situation, I think it's our best option for keeping Alexa safe, and allowing her to help the police with their investigation."

"What's your idea?" she asked, sitting forward in her seat.

"Until all of this is resolved, Zack's not just going to be your bodyguard. He's going to pretend to be your boyfriend."

CHAPTER 9

It was a stunningly simple solution to a complicated problem, Zack had to admit. Pretending that they were a couple gave him a completely reasonable excuse for being around Alexa and for going with her the next time she visited her parents. It allowed him to stay close to her without tipping their hand.

It also gave him the chance to pretend Alexa was his. It gave him an excuse to touch her, to flirt with her, to make her laugh and blush. His entire body hummed just thinking about it. How the fuck he was going to survive that part of the plan...Well, he hadn't figured that out yet. He'd just have to keep reminding himself that it wasn't real. It was pretend. To keep her safe. To protect her.

To torment him with a taste of something he couldn't have. Something that could never be real.

After discussing it with Morales, they'd decided that he'd use a fake last name when he met Alexa's parents so that it'd be harder to tie him to Virtus and his job as a bodyguard. The less the Golden Brotherhood knew about his real identity, the safer it was for all involved. So, instead of Zack De Luca, bodyguard, he'd be Zack Caruso, bartender.

Hey, at least he wouldn't struggle with that part.

They'd spent at least an hour in Detective Morales's office, hashing out the plan—Zack's new identity, how the listening devices worked and where to place them, and various safety protocols. Alexa would help Morales, and by extension the LAPD and the FBI, with their investigation into the Golden Brotherhood by planting the bugs and keeping Morales apprised of any pertinent information. Meanwhile Virtus would work behind the scenes to keep her safe. Zack would pretend to be her boyfriend in public while acting as her primary bodyguard, and another member of the team would spot them when necessary.

Alexa's shoulders had looked stiff and tense the entire time, and she'd barely glanced at him, but she hadn't said anything to indicate she wasn't okay with pretending to date Zack while she helped with the investigation. Granted, she'd probably been quiet because the map of her whole damn world had just been completely redrawn. He knew he owed her an apology and an explanation for the semi-caveman act he'd pulled. He kept turning words over in his mind, trying to find the right ones.

Now, back at Sean and Sierra's after a late lunch and running home to grab several days' worth of essentials, it was time for another part of the plan.

Believable chemistry. Somehow Zack didn't think that was going to be a challenge.

"Hi, Dad, it's me," she said into her cell phone, and Zack followed her into the house. "So…listen. My house was broken into last night." She paused as she listened, nodding slightly as she followed Morales's instructions to behave as naturally as possible, which included calling her father to tell him about the break-in. "No, I'm fine, and they really didn't take much. It was probably stupid kids...Right, I know. I talked to the landlord about a security system, but...I know. I'm okay, really...No, I don't want to come home. I'm going to stay with friends for a little while. And..." At this pause she turned and glanced at Zack over her shoulder, biting her lip. "My boyfriend's here with me too, so I'm fine...Yes, boyfriend. No, you don't know him...It's new. The point is, I'm not on my own, okay?...His name's Zack...No, like I said, not long. I have to go...What? Yes, I filed a police report about the break-in. I really have to go, Dad. I just wanted to let you know what's going on and that I'm fine...Okay. Yeah. Bye." She swiped her finger across the screen and ended the call.

He followed Alexa into the living room, dropping both his duffel bag and her suitcase on the floor by the stairs. At the twin dull thuds, she turned, a carefully schooled neutral expression on her face. For several seconds she stared at him. Not angry, not sad, not anything, all emotion hidden. Just waiting and giving him the chance to say something.

Fuck the right words. "Yeah, I know. I was an asshole. I'm sorry."

She leaned against the wall, arms crossed as she studied him, her lips curving in a tiny smile. "Mmm. I don't know if I'd say *asshole*, but..."

"The idea of you putting yourself in a dangerous situation...I get it, Alexa, but I don't like it. I snapped back there, and I shouldn't have. You're right. I don't get to tell you what to do. I meant what I said earlier, about being a team." He shoved his hands into the back pockets of his jeans. If he had a hope in hell of getting through this charade unscathed, he'd have to learn to keep his hands to himself as much as possible.

She took a step toward him, her delicate brow furrowed. "So you snapped because I'm putting myself in danger?"

"Yeah." He sighed heavily and rubbed a hand over the back of his neck, his skin suddenly hot and itchy.

"Oh."

"You thought it was for another reason?"

She nodded, biting her lip as she glanced down. "Because I wasn't doing what you wanted me to do."

Unable to help himself, he closed the distance between them and slipped a hand under her chin. Gently, he tilted her face up until her eyes met his. "The idea of you putting yourself in danger…Yeah, I don't like it, and I didn't handle it well back there. But I support your choice, okay? So if this is what you want to do, this is what we'll do. And I will do whatever it takes to keep you safe. I promise."

Her expression softened. "I thought you might be mad at me for pushing back. I was worried you were upset with me."

"No. Communication and honesty, remember? Even though I'm pretty much always right," he said, winking at her, "you're allowed to disagree with me." God, she really was too damn sweet.

She shot him a rueful smile. "I guess that's our first fight as a couple out of the way."

"Guess so." Too bad there'd be no makeup sex to follow. There was no makeup sex in pretend relationships.

Pretend. The word ricocheted around his skull, and he tried to hold on to it, but it kept bouncing away.

Stepping away from him, Alexa headed farther into the living room, then plopped down on the couch with her legs out in front of her, toes pointing toward the opposite end. "So…how did we start dating?" she asked, her pretty face drawn with exhaustion. "He's going to want to meet you, and probably sooner rather than later, which I guess is good for us."

Zack sat down next to her and pulled her legs into his lap. She let out the tiniest, sweetest gasp when he did, and it was a good thing he'd changed out of his sweatpants and into jeans and a gray hoodie, because just that tiny inhale had blood flowing to his dick.

"Good question," he said, rubbing a hand lazily over her shin before he remembered that he was supposed to be trying to keep his hands to himself. "Probably not through work, right?"

She thought, scrunching her nose and mouth to one side.

So fucking cute it almost hurt to look at her.

"I don't go to a lot of bars, and if you're a bartender, I doubt you spend much time on film sets. Not that I'm acting much anymore."

"Why is that?"

She shrugged. "It doesn't make me happy. It doesn't fulfill me. For the longest time, I did it because it was what was expected of me. I was never allowed to choose my own path."

"So what makes you happy?"

She smiled, and her entire face lit up, like the sun coming out from behind thick clouds. "Helping people. About a year and a half ago, I volunteered with UNICEF and spent three months in a village in Laos building a school and putting in a water and sanitation system. It was amazing, and I'd love to do something like that again." She let out a sad little chuckle, shaking her head. "I passed on a movie to do it, and my parents were so mad. Totally worth it, though. Instead of spending three months making a movie, I spent three months building a school." She reached out and squeezed his arm. "A school, Zack."

He smiled and laid his hand over hers, his thumb tracing over her knuckles. "That sounds amazing."

"Helping those kids…God, I just felt like I'd made such a positive difference, you know? It was almost like a high. I do a lot of volunteer work at the Children's Hospital here in LA now."

"Hey, maybe that's where we met," he said, trying to focus on the story they were concocting and not how soft and small her hand was beneath his.

"Volunteering at the Children's Hospital?" She paused for a second, considering, laying her head against the back of the couch, snuggling in. And then she smiled. "Yeah. I like that."

"What do you do there?"

"Mainly just hang out with the kids. Visit with them, read to them, cheer them up and distract them. Play games. Whatever makes them smile. I'm also on the fund-raising committee for the hospital."

He nodded slowly, and his heart felt too big and too warm for his chest. "I think I'd like to come with you, next time you go. I like kids."

"Yeah?" Her fingers curled around his bicep, the touch casual and easy. It was ridiculous how natural sitting with her like this felt. How right and not as if they were pretending at all.

At least that's how he felt. Alexa, on the other hand, was just being her usual sweet self. And he was taking that sweetness and turning it into something it wasn't.

"Yeah. The gym I train at runs free clinics for local kids who want to come and learn martial arts. I help out sometimes."

"That's really sweet," she said, her thumb tracing circles on his bicep.

Fuck. Now he was blushing. If his blood wasn't rushing to his dick, it was rushing to his face. Stupid blood.

"It's fun, and it's good for the kids. It's exercise, and it teaches them a little bit about discipline, respect, and hard work. And it's pretty amazing when they accomplish something they hadn't been able to do before, knowing that you helped them get there."

"That sounds really rewarding."

"It is. I used to volunteer at the SPCA, before I got serious about fighting. Once I started training more, I just didn't have the time."

"What did you do there?"

"Whatever they needed, really. Clean cages, walk the dogs, answer the phone. I miss it sometimes. I love animals, especially dogs. Part of the reason I started volunteering there was because I knew I wasn't home enough to get a dog of my own, so it was a way for me to get my dog fix in. Sometimes it was hard when the dogs got adopted. I was happy for them, but man, I'd miss them after they were gone."

She smiled at him, warmth shining in her silvery blue eyes. "Zack De Luca, lover of small children and puppies. I never would've guessed."

"If you tell anyone, I'll deny every word," he said, winking at her.

She laughed, and he wanted to close his eyes and bask in that sound. Her laugh wasn't a high-pitched giggle, but a lower, almost raspy, feminine chuckle, hot and sweet and perfect.

He swallowed thickly, reminding himself that this was just pretend.

Pretend. Pretend. Pretend.

"I hope you don't mind that I suggested bartender when we were coming up with your undercover ID," she said, running a finger along her bottom lip in an absentminded move his own fingers itched to repeat. "I thought it might be easier if it was something you knew."

"I don't mind. And you're right, it is easier that way. At least if someone asks me for a Bloody Mary, I know what to do."

She let out a soft little groan. "God, I could really go for one of those right now."

"Want me to make you one?"

She thought about it for half a second before shaking her head, her cheeks going pink. "I kinda just want to keep sitting here with you. If that's okay," she added hurriedly. "Plus, it's like two in the afternoon. A bit early for alcohol, don't you think?"

He shook his head, sending her a smile. "Nah. Bloody Mary's a lunchtime drink. You're covered."

"Man, I bet you got killer tips working the bar." Her face flushed redder. "I mean…That sounded like…And I didn't…I just mean that you're nice to talk to. Sorry. Came out weird. Sorry."

He couldn't decide if he should turn up the dial on the flirting or if he should back off because she was clearly embarrassed. But was she embarrassed because it seemed as if she were flirting with him when she wasn't, or because she *had* been flirting and was getting just as snarled up in pretending as he was?

This pretending shit was going to get really old really fast, he suspected. He wasn't used to second-guessing his instincts around women like this. He didn't like it.

She cleared her throat softly. "What's your favorite movie?"

He hesitated for a second, not because he was surprised by her question but because he was still caught up in admiring the way she'd blushed. "Probably *Rocky*. You?"

"*Dirty Dancing*. Or possibly *Romancing the Stone*. Or *Bridesmaids*."

"I've only seen *Bridesmaids*."

She gasped, an adorable expression of mock horror on her face. "I don't think this relationship's going to work out."

He laughed. "Sorry, sweetheart. For the time being, you're stuck with me."

She smiled softly and let out a long sigh. "Thank you."

"Of course. I'm glad I'm able to help."

She met his eyes and bit her lip, her fingers digging into his bicep with a bit more pressure. Her head still propped against the couch, she smiled up at him, something warm and soft passing between them. Something that didn't need words, an easy, quiet comfort.

In that sweet, peaceful moment, the realization slammed into him that he'd never felt quite like this with a woman before. Like he didn't have to try so hard. Like he could be himself, and give what he had to offer, and that would be enough. Like he'd do just about anything to take care of her, make her laugh, smile, whatever she needed. Like just sitting here quietly with her was the best part of his day.

The front door opened, and as Sierra's and Taylor's voices echoed through the hallway, Alexa jerked her legs away from him as though she'd been electrocuted, tucking them up under herself. A flicker of hurt stole up through his chest.

"Dude," said Taylor as she came into the living room, her attention focused on Alexa. "Are you okay? What the hell's going on? I tried to get it out of Sierra, but she was all, 'That's not my story to tell.'"

"Because it isn't!" called Sierra from the hallway.

Alexa's eyes darted back and forth between Zack and Taylor, and she nodded. "Yeah, I'm okay. Or at least I will be. I think. Everything's kind of a mess right now." She shook her head slowly, as though she still couldn't believe it. "My dad…He's not who he seems. He's…" She swallowed thickly. "He's a criminal. And I need to talk to you and Sierra and apologize for so much, and…" Alexa took a shuddering breath and hugged her arms around her middle, obviously struggling to hold it together. More than anything, Zack wanted to wrap his arms around her, pull her tight against him, and hold her until she felt okay. Until she knew that he'd never let anything happen to her.

"Aw, honey," Taylor said, plopping down between him and Alexa and throwing an arm around her shoulders. "Welcome to the shitty father club. The initiation package includes confusion, guilt, fear, and drinking, the latter of which helps with all of the other shit." Taylor turned to look at Zack, and once again Alexa's eyes ping-ponged between them. "Sierra said that you're assigned to her."

He nodded. "Yeah."

"We're pretending to date." Alexa blurted out the words as though they'd been eating at her, desperate to break free.

Taylor frowned slightly and glanced from Zack to Alexa. "Uh…okay. Why?"

"I'll explain everything. You're not mad, are you?" asked Alexa.

God. She was in danger, her life turned upside down, and she was worried about hurting Taylor's feelings.

"Of course I'm not mad. Really fucking curious, but no. Not mad."

Sierra came into the living room and sank down onto the floor in front of Alexa, laying a hand on Alexa's knee. "Sean said that you guys found out some stuff at the police station?"

Alexa nodded, and then her face crumpled. "I'm so sorry, guys. I'm so sorry." She reached out a hand and touched Sierra's shoulder while leaning harder into Taylor. "You almost died and…and it was all his fault."

"Whose fault?" asked Sierra gently.

"M-my father's. The police think he's involved with something called the Golden Brotherhood." At that, Sierra and Taylor slowly turned to look at each other, solemn expressions on their faces. "But I'm going to fix it. I'm going to make it right." She sniffled, wiping at her eyes with the backs of her hands. "That's why Zack and I are pretending to date. So he can be my bodyguard without my father knowing that I *have* a bodyguard."

Zack's phone buzzed from the front pocket of his hoodie, and he slipped it out, feeling as if he was intruding on this moment between Alexa and her friends. "Shit. I have to go. I'm late for my afternoon training session," he said, pushing up off the couch. "Do you want to come with me?" he asked Alexa, reluctant to leave without her.

She sent him a wavering smile. "Another time, yes. But right now I think I need a hot shower and a nap."

"She'll be okay here, Zack," said Sierra.

"Colt's off today. I can ask him to come by if that'd make you feel better," said Taylor, her eyes lighting up at the prospect of seeing her new husband.

Zack nodded. "That's a good idea. I don't want to take

any chances." He gave Alexa's shoulder a soft squeeze. "I'll be back later."

She wiped at her eyes again, yawning. "Have a good practice."

Taylor rose from the couch and followed him to the door. When she spoke, her voice was barely above a whisper. "I can't believe her dad's involved with the Golden Brotherhood. Insane."

"I know. I couldn't believe it when the detective said it. But she had folders full of info, including mug shots of your dad and Baker."

Taylor shuddered slightly, wrapping her arms around herself. "If anyone can handle these guys, it's you. Thanks for looking after my friend." He nodded and had turned to go when Taylor laid a hand on his arm. "Keep her safe, Zack. Sierra and I, we love her. We need her safe."

He simply nodded again, because he damn well needed the same thing.

CHAPTER 10

Alexa stood in the upstairs hallway of her parents' mansion, the house dark and silent. Every single door was closed, and she shivered, wrapping her arms around herself. She took a step forward, almost tripping when her legs became tangled in the pure-white gown she wore.

Her father's laughter echoed from behind one of the doors, followed by the sharp bang of a gunshot. Gasping, she gathered up her heavy skirt and started to run for the stairs. But as though the house had yawned, the hallway stretched ahead of her, longer than it had been a second ago. Struggling against her skirt, she redoubled her efforts, but the staircase stayed exactly where it was, twenty feet in front of her.

Her feet tangled in her dress, and she tripped and fell, landing on the floor with a hard thud that echoed in the silent hall. Finally, practically swimming through the yards of white silk around her, she reached a door and shoved it open.

Bright lights blinded her, and she raised a hand to

shield her eyes. An octagon stood before her, surrounded by padding and a chain-link fence.

Zack stood in the center of the octagon, wearing a T-shirt and shorts, punching a bag that hung from a heavy metal chain. Hope and relief filled her at the sight of him, and, gathering her skirts up, she started to run toward the cage.

"How could you?" Taylor's voice came from behind her. She stood a few feet away, a guitar in her hands and a wounded expression on her face. "I thought you were my friend. I thought you were good."

"I didn't…I would never…We…It's pretend…," she rasped out. Her dress had turned from white to a dirty, sullen gray.

Another gunshot sounded, and Alexa shut her eyes tightly. Silence surrounded her, and when she opened them, she was in her father's library.

He sat behind his desk, wiping blood from his hands with a handkerchief. Her eyes darted to the corner, and she caught a glimpse of herself, age seven, her tiny face barely visible through the slit in the door that led to her hiding spot. An unconscious man sat roped to a chair in front of the desk, his face beaten and bloody.

She'd watched her father slam his fists into the man's face as her father's friend Elijah stood by. They'd taken turns asking him questions that she hadn't understood. They hadn't liked his answers, though. That much had been clear.

"What happened to your dress?" Her father looked up at her from his desk. She glanced around, making sure he was speaking to her, the adult Alexa, and then down at her dress. The gray had deepened, dull and smeary.

"I'm sorry," she said, smoothing her hands over the fabric.

"*You should be. Mr. Hendricks wasn't impressed with you at dinner.*"

At the name, her stomach revolted, and she swallowed hard, fighting against the wave of nausea roiling through her. "*I'm sorry,*" she said again, hating that she'd disappointed him and hating herself for hating it.

"*I think you might still have a chance at the role, though,*" he said casually, dropping the bloody handkerchief onto his desk. "*He's staying over. He'll be in the main guest room. If you go see him in his room, I'm sure he can be persuaded.*"

Hot tears rolled down her face as shame and humiliation washed over her. "*No. Not that. I won't do that again.*"

Calmly, he rose from his desk and closed the distance between them. "*You'll do what I tell you to do. If that means playing the whore, that's what you'll do. Seems to be the only thing you're actually good at.*"

His words were like a knife, piercing her heart and twisting. Tugging and sawing until it wasn't recognizable as a heart anymore.

"*I won't. I don't want to do that anymore.*"

He slapped her with the back of his hand, and pain crashed across her face in a hot, dizzying wave. "*You'll do what I tell you to do.*"

"*I wouldn't do that if I were you,*" said Detective Morales from the doorway, her gun pointed at Alexa's father.

All the blood drained from her father's face, his fists shaking with rage. "*How could you?*"

"*I'm...I'm not sorry,*" she whispered, and watched as her dress changed from gray to black, inky patches blooming on the silk like dye in water.

"Then you'd better run, little girl," her father snarled at her, and she gathered up her skirt and pushed out of the library, running and running and running, feeling as though she were underwater, moving slower with each step. Finally, she reached the stairs, but as soon as she moved to place her foot on the top step, they vanished, and she fell, her dress disintegrating into ash.

Alexa jerked in bed, her skin slick with sweat and the sheets bunched around her. The duvet had fallen completely to the floor, and as she moved to untangle herself from the sheets, cool air greeted her overheated skin. Lying back down, she pressed a hand to her chest, her heart pounding fiercely against her palm. She closed her eyes, trying to focus on her breathing, but when she did, all the images of the dream came rushing back at her, jumbling together until her head throbbed and she thought she might throw up. With a frustrated sigh, she reached over and turned on the lamp. Pulling her legs up to her chest, she rested her chin on her knees and let the tears come, knowing there was no use fighting them.

God, she was probably dehydrated, she'd cried so much over the past day.

And right now they were selfish tears. She wasn't crying for her father's victims, or even because she felt bad about what was happening. Right now, alone in the middle of the night, she was crying for herself. For the scared little girl she'd been. For the abuse she'd suffered as a teenager. For the life, the identity she'd lost, everything she'd known turning to ash around her, just like her dress in the dream. For the way she ached for Zack, a man she had no business wanting.

She was a horrible person. A disloyal daughter and a greedy, uncaring friend. A naive fool. A whore. Damaged and broken. A liar who hid her true face from everyone she loved, lest they see her for who she really was.

"Ugh, *stop*," she chided herself, wiping her tears away and shoving her hands through her slightly tangled hair as she tried to stop the downward spiral. She had friends who cared about her. A safe place to stay. A plan to help prevent her father from hurting more people in the future. Zack to keep her safe. So many things to be grateful for.

She picked up her phone from its spot on the bedside table to check the time. 12:42 a.m. She'd taken a nap earlier when Zack had gone to his training session, and after a dinner that she'd barely been able to eat, Alexa had crawled into bed, completely worn out. She'd slept soundly until that damn nightmare. And now she was wide awake and, truth be told, a little hungry.

With a resigned sigh, she padded barefoot across the room to the door. Opening it, she paused for a second, listening. The house was dark and quiet. Peaceful. She knew there was leftover pizza in the fridge from the party, and her stomach rumbled encouragingly at the thought.

Stepping gently down the stairs, she emerged into the living room and was surprised to find that the main level wasn't completely dark. A dim light glowed from the direction of the kitchen, and she took a few steps forward, wondering if Sierra or Sean was still up. Standing on the threshold between the living room and the kitchen, she froze at the sight of a wonderfully broad, deliciously muscled bare male back. Even in the dim light, she knew just from the outline of his shoulders and his hair that it was Zack. A tattooed series of Asian characters formed a line between his shoulder blades, and she wanted to trace those swooping lines with her fingers.

With her mouth.

Her lips and fingertips tingled at the thought, which she pushed gently away. She couldn't let herself go there. A hint of the shame she'd felt during the dream came back, a shadowy whisper of guilt.

Sweatpants hung low on his hips, his abs flexing as he moved around the kitchen. Cut lines along his hips disappeared into his sweatpants, along with the trail of dark hair that started under his belly button and arrowed downward. His chest was strong and smooth, the muscles cut and defined, and once again her lips and fingertips tingled as warmth swirled over her skin. He apparently hadn't seen her, and she watched as he tossed his phone down on the island and then opened the fridge, sticking his head inside. She noticed another tattoo, this one on the underside of his left bicep. About the size of her fist, it looked like a crescent moon emerging from behind clouds, but she couldn't tell for sure. A tribal dragon, faded and more crudely drawn than the others, decorated his right shoulder.

He emerged with an orange in his hand, and as the door fell shut, he began peeling it, his strong, thick fingers working the peel free. The sharp scent of citrus cut the air. She inhaled, pulling the scent into her lungs, and he turned to look at her, his white teeth flashing as he started to smile.

"Alexa? Are you okay?" His voice was a little bit rusty. As she took a step toward him, his eyes dipped down her body, lingering on her breasts. She glanced down to find that her nipples had pebbled into hard nubs under her thin T-shirt.

From watching him. From staring at all that skin, all that muscle. The tattoos. His hands. The way he moved.

Every little thing about him.

She shook her head slightly, stepping farther into the kitchen. "I had a dream and couldn't get back to sleep."

She tipped her head at the fridge, trying to ignore how suddenly hyperaware she was of the scrape of the fabric of her shirt against her hardened nipples. "Did you see any pizza in there?"

He set his orange down on the counter. "I sure did. You want a slice? You must be hungry. Didn't eat much at dinner."

She nodded, both surprised and touched he'd noticed that she'd barely touched her food earlier. "Please."

He pulled the fridge open again. "You want to talk about it?" He pulled a container out. "The dream, not the pizza. You want it heated up?"

"No, cold is good." She stepped up next to him and pried the lid off of the container, then pulled a slice free, taking a hearty bite. Zack slid the container back in the fridge and stood across the island from her, his hands braced on the granite. She couldn't stop her eyes from doing a slow walk down his body, over each chiseled muscle, and something hot pulsed low in her stomach.

As she chewed she mulled over his question. Did she want to talk about the dream? Just thinking back to it had her on edge, a restless uncertainty crawling through her. Telling him about it would mean opening up about her past, not to mention revealing the quagmire of her feelings for and attraction to him. She could leave that stuff out, but then she'd be lying about the dream, and that wasn't really the point of talking about it, was it?

She almost jumped when Zack's knuckle brushed her temple. She'd been so deep in thought that she hadn't seen him move.

"I can hear you thinking from all the way over here." Her eyes darted up, and he smiled crookedly. "You don't have to talk about it if you don't want to."

"No, I do. I'm just trying to figure out how to explain it. I'm still processing," she hedged, because she found that, despite her reservations, she did want to talk about it. She didn't want to carry it alone. Taking another bite of her pizza, she found she wasn't nearly as hungry as she'd been a moment ago as she rolled the details of the dream—still fresh, still vivid—through her mind. She swallowed, and the food lodged uncomfortably in her chest. A surge of anxiety tore through her, and she grasped for something else to talk about. She pointed at his shoulder before she could stop herself. "Is there a story behind the dragon?"

He frowned and glanced down at his shoulder. "You mean the ugliest tattoo you've ever seen?"

Her eyes widened, and she shook her head. "No! That's not what I meant."

He laughed quietly, his brown eyes gleaming in the soft light. "I got it when I was eighteen. I thought it was badass, but I was too cheap to go to a good studio to get it done, so now I'm stuck with it."

"You could get it covered up with something else, couldn't you?"

He shrugged, muscles moving beneath his skin, and then shot her a smile. "So you admit it's ugly."

She bit her lip, a smile struggling to break free. "I…It's not *not* ugly," she teased, amazed that, given the nightmare she'd just had, she was smiling.

Zack's mouth fell open in mock surprise, his eyes sparkling. "Hey, don't make fun of Cliff. He's sensitive about his looks."

She started to laugh, but as the images from the dream flashed through her mind again, it died on her lips. She grabbed a paper towel from the counter and laid the piece of pizza down on the island, not sure if she was going to finish it. Gently, she pushed it away, and she noticed that her hand was trembling. Distantly, as though she were seeing herself through a fog, she knew she was on the verge of falling apart. Everything was just too much.

Zack must've noticed too, because he cursed quietly and came around the island. "Let's sit down. Come on." He laid a hand on the small of her back, and she relaxed into his touch, his warmth soaking through her thin shirt as he led her into the dark living room, the only light coming from the kitchen and the moon shining through the windows. The moonlight only heightened his chiseled features, deepening the shadows in the muscled grooves of his chest. It was the kind of chest women drooled over and men were jealous of. It was the kind of chest she wanted to touch and explore and claim in ways she had no right to want.

God, Zack. As they walked into the living room, an ache bloomed in her chest. A tangled snarl of longing and guilt and shame and lust and regret.

She shivered as he eased her down onto the same couch they'd sat on earlier that day, and he grabbed a throw from the nearby armchair, then wrapped the plush blanket around her shoulders before sitting down beside her. Tucking her legs up under her, she turned to face him, snuggling into the back of the couch.

"I'm not even sure where to start," she said, her eyes meeting his in the semidarkness. She pulled the blanket tighter around herself, and her eyes dropped to his gorgeously strong arms, wanting them around her instead of the blanket.

He reached out a hand and tucked a strand of hair behind her ear, letting his thumb linger on her jaw for a second. His fingers still smelled like orange, and she wasn't sure she'd ever be able to smell that scent again without thinking of this moment. She closed her eyes for a second and pressed her cheek into his palm.

"You're overwhelmed. Anyone would be. What was your dream about?"

Really, she should tell him everything so that he'd know exactly who she was and why he should stay away from her. Why she wasn't worthy of his kindness. Why her own attraction to him was wrong.

She grabbed fistfuls of the blanket and stared at her hands, knowing she'd be unable to concentrate if she kept looking at him. "I was standing in the upstairs hallway at my parents' house, and I was wearing a white gown. I heard laughter and gunshots, and I tried to run for the stairs, but it didn't matter how hard I tried, they never got closer. Like the carpet was a treadmill or something. I found a room with—with my father. I think…maybe it was a memory I'd repressed."

He traced the shell of her ear with his fingers, massaging her earlobe gently for a second. Something tight and sharp soared through her and settled between her legs. She pressed her thighs together, trying to stifle the growing ache there, but wanting more of his touch.

His fingers skimmed down her neck before he dropped his hand. "What happened?"

She swallowed and forced herself to continue. "He'd beaten a man, and his hands were all bloody. I saw myself as a kid, hiding in the corner. My dress changed from white to gray." She swallowed again and kept going, glossing over another part of the dream, because, as much as she wanted to unburden herself, she couldn't bring herself to say the words out loud. "Morales was there, and my father said, 'How could you?' and my dress changed from gray to black. I ran, and the stairs disappeared, and I fell. As I was falling, my dress disintegrated around me."

"And this is something you remember?"

She nodded. "I think so. It's fuzzy, but I remember being in that room that I used to hide out in and watching…" She shook her head slowly. "Growing up in that house was really hard. It was lonely and scary. I felt so isolated, like there was no one I could talk to. No one who would keep me safe." She glanced up and met his eyes, dark pools that she wanted to dive into and never surface from. "I think I've known for a long time that my father is a criminal. I just didn't want to believe it."

"I'm sorry," he whispered, and raised a hand as though he was going to touch her again, but then dropped it just as quickly. "I'm sorry," he said again.

She nodded, and, as if a puzzle piece had clicked into place, the significance of the dress dawned on her. "I don't know who I am anymore. I've always tried so hard to be the good daughter, to do whatever he wanted me to do, to please him, but I can't be both a good person and the dutiful daughter he wants. I know that now."

She took a shuddering breath as the truth washed over her and then another as panic started to mount, clawing at her insides and struggling to break free. Everything that had informed her sense of place in the world was gone, replaced with a nightmare. She closed her eyes, trying to center herself, and she felt the warm rasp of Zack's palm on her cheek.

"I know this is a lot to try and figure out, but you're still Alexa." Something hot glowed in his eyes, and he moved a bit closer.

"And who is she?" she whispered, feeling hollow.

He pulled her into his arms, and she went willingly,

wanting the comfort but unprepared for the perfection of his bare skin under her cheek as she laid her head on his chest. She wanted to melt into him, to lose herself in him, in his body, his warmth, his touch.

He adjusted the blanket, wrapping it around both of them. One arm held her tightly against him while the other stroked over her hair as she curled into him. A tremble coursed through her when he gently kissed the top of her head.

"The Alexa I know is sweet, and funny, and probably one of the kindest people I've ever met."

The pain of wanting, and not being able to have, tightened her throat as he spoke.

"She's smart, and she gives so much to the people around her. She's brave."

She snorted softly at that. "I don't feel very brave right now."

"You are. You were given a choice earlier today in the detective's office, and you chose to do the right thing. The hard, scary, brave thing. *You* made that choice, and, although it cost you, you did what you felt was right. To me that's bravery. That's strength. That's courage."

"I feel like I'm betraying my family." She slid her arms around his waist, snuggling in closer, wanting more of his comfort.

"I know it's complicated, ba—" He cut himself off sharply before continuing. "Alexa. I know. But you don't get to pick your family, and your father threatened to…" He trailed off and cleared his throat softly. "You're doing the right thing." He eased back slightly and tipped her face up. "The Alexa I know is beautiful, inside and out." His lips brushed over her temple, and she closed her eyes as another tremble shivered through her. Words failed her as he brushed his lips over her temple again. All she managed was a soft, raspy moan.

"I know," he whispered, tipping her chin up a bit higher so his mouth was close. Close enough that she could smell the citrus on his breath. His eyes found hers. She couldn't read whatever was flickering through his mind, dark as it was in the room, but his entire body practically vibrated with tension.

"Zack." She whispered his name, and she knew she didn't want him to stop. Just those tiny touches felt so good, so right.

"I'm here." He cupped her face with both hands and brushed her nose with his. "I'm here, and I'll keep you safe, princess." He dipped his head and brushed his lips over hers, the tiniest bit of contact. A warm, heavy throb settled between her legs, beating in time with her frantic heart. He brushed his lips over hers again, and then he froze. She held completely still, waiting, her heart sinking when he placed a chaste kiss on her forehead and eased her away. "This isn't a good idea."

"Oh," she whispered, disappointment curdling through her. She wanted to ask him why but also knew that maybe she didn't want to know the answer.

"Sorry," he said, pushing to his feet and heading for the stairs without a backward glance. She watched him go, knowing she had to. Knowing that as much as she wanted it, it was for the best. Knowing he'd likely gotten caught up in the moment and would regret almost kissing her in the morning.

It was what she deserved, and she tried with everything she had to cling to that idea as she climbed back into her bed and turned the light off. But alone, in the dark, she let herself imagine what it would be like to curl into his warmth, to feel the strength of his body around her as he sheltered her from everything. She'd never fall asleep in Zack's arms, and it didn't matter how close he'd just come to kissing her. The dream had frightened her, but it had also reminded her of who she was, and the pain she'd suffered at her father's hands. Zack had dated her friend, and she shouldn't cross that line. And what would he say if he knew the truth about who she was? If he knew that she was damaged?

A flicker of anger pushed up through her, not at her father and not at herself, but at the idea that because she wasn't "pure," she was damaged. It was so deeply ingrained in her, in society, that for the longest time she hadn't even questioned it. She'd swallowed the garbage society had fed her, subconsciously buying into the fucked-up idea that women could be only whores or virgins. As though her worth were tied to her sexual experience somehow.

She didn't want to see herself as damaged. She didn't want to define herself by her past. All she wanted was to find a way out of this murky situation.

And Zack. She wanted Zack. Despite the myriad reasons she shouldn't—he was Taylor's ex, she was his client, and she had a lot of personal shit to work through—she did.

She let herself go back to imagining his arms around her and fell into a deep sleep.

CHAPTER 11

Jonathan snatched his phone and laptop off a nearby table and sank down onto the chocolate-brown leather sofa in his trailer. The distorted reflection he caught of himself in the dark screen of the massive TV on the opposite wall made him look even more tired than he felt. He'd been on the set of *Deepest Sympathies*, an ensemble drama about a family-run funeral home, since five that morning. He glanced at his phone, grimacing at the number of texts, e-mails, and missed calls that had accumulated during the six hours he'd been working.

He tipped his head back, letting his eyes fall closed for a second as a bone-weary exhaustion weighed him down. He sucked in a deep breath through his nose and forced his eyes open. Even though he was on a break from filming, he still had work to do. He sat up straighter, and as he dialed into his voice mail, he flipped his laptop open with his free hand. After listening to his messages, he called Elijah back. Although the Alexa issue wasn't the most pressing, it was the one weighing most heavily on him.

Elijah answered on the first ring. "Yes?"

"It's Jonathan. Bring me up to speed."

"We've finished going through her laptop, and there was nothing suspicious, but just to be safe, I put a tail on her this morning."

"And?"

"She stayed at a friend's house last night, as did her boyfriend. He also went with her to volunteer at the hospital this morning. He went out alone beforehand too, to a mixed martial arts gym. Worked out for a while, went back to the friend's house."

Jonathan drummed his fingers on the table as he stared unseeing at the computer screen in front of him.

"What do we know about the boyfriend? The friends?"

"Not much about the boyfriend, but I'll see what we can dig up. The friend is Sierra Blake, and her fiancé, Sean Owens."

Jonathan's scalp prickled because this was all hitting a little too close to home for comfort. Over a year ago, he'd made the ultimately foolish decision to help Jack Nikolaidis win a seat in the state senate. The senator—Sierra Blake's ex-boyfriend—hadn't been able to pay the Brotherhood back for its services, and he'd come off the rails trying to get the money. Jack had gone so far as to shoot Owens, making an even bigger mess of the whole thing.

Alexa—sweet, dumb Alexa—didn't know the truth about who he was, and so neither did her friends. But still, there was that prickle working its way across his scalp again. "Keep watching her and let me know if anything suspicious comes up. I think it's time for me to meet this boyfriend of hers."

"Sounds good. I'll be in touch."

Jonathan ended the call and pulled up Alexa's number,

a feeling he couldn't quite name working its way through his chest as he listened to it ring. A mixture of anxiety, fear, anger, and suspicion churned through him as his gaze swept across the lavish trailer.

"Hello?"

"Alexa, honey, it's me. How are you?" he asked in his most soothing tone.

"I'm okay. Just finished volunteering at the hospital."

"You're still staying with your friends?"

A slight pause. "Yeah. After that break-in, I don't want to be alone."

"You should come home. You don't want to be a burden on your friends." It would be so much easier to keep tabs on her if she were still under his roof.

"I'm not." She snipped the words out, her tone sharper than he was used to, but he let it go. It wouldn't do to push her away even more, especially because that snippiness had him on edge.

"In any case, come for dinner tomorrow night. Bring your new boyfriend. Your mom and I would love to meet him." Meet him, get his fingerprints, run a background check.

She hesitated before answering. "Um, yeah. Okay. I'll see if Zack's free."

"Wonderful. Tomorrow at seven."

"All right. I gotta go, Dad. See you tomorrow."

"Bye, darling." He ended the call and tossed his phone down on the table. He opened his e-mail and sorted through several messages, including the copy of the police report Alexa had filed. He'd had it forwarded to him by one of his men on the LAPD. Quickly, his eyes skimmed down the document, but nothing was out of place. Just a typical B&E report, filed by a Detective Antonio Rodriguez. He saved the e-mail and opened another, pleased to find preliminary acquisition information for Innkeeper Films. With Astor gone, Innkeeper was in chaos, and it was ripe for the picking. With its addition, Fairfax Films would grow and become even more powerful and influential. Increased market share. Increased revenues. Increased control.

But now he needed to focus on the larger task at hand, which was getting his hands on Crosby, that damn journalist from the *Times* who knew way too much. He'd been snooping around for years and had uncovered the Brotherhood's latest business venture: weapons production. After all, why buy someone else's guns when you could make your own? They'd managed to acquire a factory through one of the Brotherhood's shell corporations and were set to start up production soon. Producing their own untraceable guns and ammunition would give them control over the arms market, and Jonathan was a little mad at himself that he hadn't thought of it sooner.

But he'd gotten wind of an exposé that Chris Crosby, who'd started investigating the real estate transaction for the factory, was planning to write for the *Times*. Thankfully, their source at the paper had tipped them off before the piece had run. They'd tried the usual intimidation tactics, but Crosby hadn't backed off and had gone to ground. He knew too much, and he posed the threat of discovery. It was the worst thing that could happen to the Brotherhood, as far as Jonathan was concerned, and he'd do whatever it took to make sure it didn't happen.

* * *

"Don't freak out, but we're being followed." Zack tightened his grip on the SUV's steering wheel, cutting his eyes back and forth between the road ahead and his rearview mirror. To protect Alexa, he'd switched out his Jeep—which was registered to Zack De Luca—to one of Virtus's vehicles. If anyone ran a trace on it, it'd come up as registered to Zack Caruso, with a different address, phone number, and driver's license number on file. Clay, Virtus's private investigator and tech whiz, had set everything up for him.

"Shit. We are?" To her credit Alexa didn't turn in her seat to look out the back window but stayed completely still, staring straight ahead through the windshield. "How do you know?"

Keeping his foot steady on the gas pedal, Zack signaled and changed lanes, squinting through his sunglasses as the setting sun emerged from beneath a cloud, piercing the sky with low rays. Glancing once again in the rearview mirror, he watched as the nondescript black sedan did the same.

"The same car has stayed exactly four car-lengths back almost the entire time we've been driving. We picked him up shortly after we left Sierra and Sean's. I've taken a few weird turns, and he's still four cars back. It's not a coincidence. He's definitely following us."

"What do we do?" He heard her swallow even over the hip-hop playing quietly through the SUV's speakers.

He shook his head. "Nothing. We let him follow."

She shifted in her seat, her fingers now wrapped around the shoulder strap of her seat belt. "You're not going to try to lose him or something?"

"No. It would tip him off that I've noticed we're being followed, which in turn would reveal a lot more than we want to. We have to act like everything's normal. I'm a fighter heading to the gym to train, and you're coming with me to watch. We can't give anything away."

She sighed, nodding slightly. "Right. Of course. God, I am *so* out of my depth here. My first instinct would've been to hit the gas and get the hell away from him."

"That's why I'm here, princess. To keep you safe." He eased his foot off the gas slightly, keeping his speed consistent with the traffic around him.

Alexa pried her fingers away from the seat belt and hugged herself, turning toward him and biting her lower lip in a way that had blood flowing south of his waist, despite the tense situation they were in. "I like it when you call me that."

He shrugged. "Well, I figured that, if we're dating, I'd probably have a nickname for you." Now wasn't the time to tell her that he'd spent the past year thinking of her as a princess. Not in a spoiled, untouchable way, but as someone who deserved the best of everyone around her. Kindness and protection and everything good in life.

"Oh, right. Good call." Her face fell slightly for a second, and then she managed a small smile that didn't quite reach her eyes. He didn't have time to dig into what her reaction meant, and he adjusted his grip on the steering wheel, needing to focus completely on their surroundings. He glanced in the rearview mirror again, keeping tabs on the black sedan, which had gained a car-length on them, still following.

He scanned the traffic around them, on the lookout for anything suspicious, wondering if they had more company than just the one vehicle. The traffic on West Olympic wasn't heavy, despite the fact that they were hitting the tail end of rush hour. Low-lying stucco buildings faced the street, the cracked sidewalks devoid of pedestrians. Scruffy palms and overgrown cedars lined the road, dotting the gated yards of the few residences on the street. Now that he knew they were dealing with the Golden Brother-hood, he needed every protective instinct on constant high alert. Using the SUV's Bluetooth system, he called Sean.

"Owens."

"I'm with Alexa, headed to the gym. We've picked up a tail. Black Toyota Camry, newish. Blacked-out windows, so no idea how many inside. Plate is six-Foxtrot-Romeo-November-one-six-four."

"Got it. I'll send Priestley out after you to keep tabs, and I'll call it in to Morales, let her know what's up. What's your POA?"

"Plan of action is to proceed as normal, like I haven't noticed the tail. Still heading to the gym. ETA is under ten minutes, give or take five for traffic."

"Check in when you get there. Morales will run the plate. Maybe that'll tell us more about who's following you."

"Right," Zack said, nodding. There wasn't a doubt in his mind that it was the Brotherhood who was following them. The real question was *why*. Did they know what Alexa knew? That she'd hired security?

"Stick to your plan, keep eyes on Alexa, and Colt's backing you up. He'll loop back to the gym and keep an eye on things once the tail's taken care of."

Zack disconnected the call, his knuckles protesting at the iron grip he kept wrapped around the steering wheel. "Does your father ever have you followed? Keep tabs on you?" he asked.

Alexa frowned. "Not that I've noticed, but I haven't exactly been looking for that kind of thing."

Zack's jaw tightened, tension shooting down his neck and straining his muscles. "Can you think of anyone else who might follow you? A fan? A stalker? Paparazzi?"

She looked lost as she shook her head again, her blond waves fluttering against her face. "No. I don't think so. But my father's not happy that I moved out, and he knows about the break-in. He's...*protective* isn't the right word at all, but he's...he's territorial. It's not impossible that he'd have me followed just to keep an eye on me. It doesn't necessarily mean that he knows anything."

Zack glanced at her. "It also doesn't mean that he doesn't know. We have to treat this as a threat. For me to keep you safe, I need to prepare for the worst case scenario."

"Yeah, well, Dad figuring out that I know the truth and that I'm helping the LAPD investigate him is pretty much as worst case scenario as it gets."

Zack nodded, her words hanging between them. She was risking a lot. Not just her relationship with her family, but potentially her own safety. He couldn't even imagine the complicated shit she was struggling with. He pursed his lips, mulling over the question he wanted to ask. He licked his lips and then opened his mouth, unable to contain his curiosity. "You mentioned in Morales's office that your father had hurt you. What happened?"

She took a deep breath, and as she released it, it looked as though she were deflating, collapsing in on herself like a balloon he'd just pierced with a needle. "Is that your gym?" She pointed at the big black-and-yellow Take Down sign as he turned onto West Pico. Changing the subject. Interesting. And doing nothing to satisfy his curiosity.

He debated for a second whether to press her on it, but as he swung the SUV into the Take Down parking lot, he decided to let it go. For now. But he wanted to know—badly—just what she'd meant by that comment. Mainly because he needed to know just how badly to hurt

Jonathan Fairfax when he got his hands on him. No way was he going to let someone get away with hurting his girl.

Only she wasn't really his girl. A detail—a fact—he was having a hard time holding on to.

He pulled the SUV into a space and threw it into park, then cut the ignition and came around to Alexa's door. He pulled it open and helped her down, his eyes skimming the parking lot and the street beyond as Alexa's body slid against his.

"Oh," she said, the tiniest sound, as her breasts flattened against his chest. The black Camry turned the corner and headed toward them, not pulling into the parking lot, but slowing as it neared. Zack's blood surged through his veins, and something hot and protective gripped him. He caged Alexa against the SUV, his palms flat against the vehicle, blocking her from view and shielding her from anything that might be coming their way.

He dipped his head and grazed his nose against her cheek, tracking the Camry in the side-view mirror of the SUV. "They're driving by right now. Colt's going to follow them, and we're going to go inside. He'll circle back and keep an eye on the gym. How you doing?"

She inhaled deeply, pressing her breasts against his chest again, and it took every ounce of control he had not to press his hips into her. But he couldn't let himself get caught up in their charade. It was far too risky. Far too dangerous.

"I'm okay," she said, her voice barely above a whisper. He closed his eyes for a second and, with his nose pressed to her temple, inhaled the coconut scent of her shampoo, but he held himself in check. God, a dangerously large part of him wanted to say, "Fuck pretending" and find out just how good it would feel to kiss her.

When she spoke again, her voice was firmer. "I'm okay." Her eyes flashed up to his. "Thanks."

He swallowed and nodded, glancing back at the side-view mirror. The Camry had passed, and he knew he should step back. But damn, it felt good being so close to her. "They're gone. For now."

She patted his chest, letting her hand linger against his pec. "That was a good move. I think…" She swallowed before continuing, her fingers circling over his pec and driving him insane. His fucking traitor of a brain imagined those fingers wrapped around his cock, which swelled in response. "I think Sean's plan was a good idea."

"The plan to pretend." He held her eyes as he spoke, and her pupils dilated as she stared up at him, the black eating up nearly all of that stormy silvery blue.

"Yeah. Pretend."

For several seconds they stood completely still, and he couldn't tear his eyes away from her. Her eyes moved to his mouth, down his body, back to his mouth, and, finally, back to his eyes. He didn't move, letting her gaze wander over him. Last night, when he'd nearly kissed her, he'd been surprised that she'd wanted it as much as he had. Maybe this wasn't entirely pretend for her either. The thought sent need and something hot and possessive rippling through him.

But even if she wanted him, she was holding back. He'd seen it in her eyes last night and again just now when he'd asked her about how her father had hurt her. He had fighting and a less-than-stellar dating track record as his reasons for holding back, not to mention that she was a client. What were hers? Did it matter? She wasn't his, and he needed to keep reminding himself of that.

"I feel safe with you," she said, still circling her fingers over his chest.

He pried one of his hands away from the SUV and laid it over hers, holding her fingers over his heart, which thumped against her touch. "You should. I'll do whatever it takes to keep you safe, Alexa."

She smiled, but it didn't quite reach her eyes. "Including pretend to be my boyfriend, which has got to be above and beyond the call of duty."

He eased back slightly, the intensity between them fading out, just a little. "Yeah. It's such a hardship pretending to date a beautiful, sweet, smart woman like you." He winked and turned to grab his gear bag to stop himself from hauling her against him and showing her what a *hardship* it was.

CHAPTER 12

For the past forty-five minutes, Alexa had stood rooted to the spot, unable to tear her gaze from Zack's gorgeously muscular and shirtless body. Although she'd seen him fight before, she was now riveted by the mass of tattooed skin and athletic muscle moving in a violent clash less than ten feet away from her. Zack and his sparring partner moved fluidly around each other, their feet never stopping, gloved fists darting out with impressive speed. Several other spectators circled around the octagonal cage to watch, murmured conversation blending with the music throbbing through the gym's speakers. Zack kicked at his opponent, sending him stumbling back into the chain-link fencing lining the octagon. The cage rattled as the man pushed off it and launched himself at Zack, sweeping his feet out from under him with a low kick. On his way down, Zack managed to get his legs around his opponent's torso, and he tumbled him to the ground. Lightning fast, Zack climbed on top of his sparring partner, practically mounting him, and Alexa's stomach quivered. His muscles, slick with sweat, strained and flexed as he struggled against his opponent, and she traced all those gorgeous lines on his arms, on his back, on his thighs, with her eyes. The tips of her fingers tingled, and she licked her lips, heat flushing through her. What would it feel like to be underneath all that muscle, to be surrounded and pinned down by all that strength?

The fighters were back on their feet, and she drank in the sight of Zack, his hair damp with sweat, his chest heaving. Something pushed up right into the center of her chest, lodging there, a hot, heavy, frustrated weight that made her want to pace and fidget and scream. Back in the parking lot, she'd wanted so badly to kiss him. To pull him against her and chase away the fear and the worry and the guilt, to obliterate them with the feel of his mouth on hers. She'd never wanted to kiss a man like that. Wanted his mouth for purely selfish, greedy reasons. Wanted it for her own pleasure, and not necessarily his. Wanted him for herself, not because someone had told her to. Not because it would help her career somehow.

Reciting it like a prayer, she went through the litany of reasons she couldn't allow herself to go there with Zack. The fact that he'd dated her friend, whom he'd chosen first. Her past, which was complicated, to say the least. The upheaval she'd gone through over the past couple of days. The dangerous investigation she'd signed up for.

What if, somehow, her father knew she was helping the police? She shivered as a chill worked its way down her spine at the sobering thought. Tomorrow they'd have dinner with her family, and she'd find a way to plant those bugs throughout the house. She'd studied them, memorizing the weight and feel of them, reciting over and over again Morales's instructions about where to place them and how to activate them. Hopefully, once the bugs were in place, she could step back and let Morales, the LAPD, and the FBI take over.

She didn't know what would happen once the bugs were in place. She didn't want to think about it, because when she did she almost drowned under the confusing eddy of guilt and anger and sadness that pulled at her. Guilt over what she was doing, anger at everything her father had done, sadness that so much of her life, of what she knew, had been a lie. She'd broken herself for him, to make him happy and keep the peace, to live up to the expectations he'd held. She wasn't sure if helping the authorities take him down would help her feel whole again, or just break her even further.

She wrapped her arms around herself, holding it together, somehow. She glanced around the gym, and for a second she felt as though she were floating. Everything took on a surreal yet harsh quality. The fluorescent lights were too bright, the music and conversation around her too loud, the scent of sweat and rubber and leather too strong. Closing her eyes, she forced herself to take a deep breath, fighting back the panic threatening to take hold. Another breath. Another. Her skittering heart slowed, and she opened her eyes.

Zack had locked his sparring partner's arm between his legs at what looked like an excruciating angle, and the other man tapped his free hand rapidly against the mat. Zack released him immediately and hopped to his feet, catching her gaze and sending her a smile and a wink. Something settled over her, a peaceful sense of security, and the lingering panic subsided.

She didn't have words for how grateful she was to have him on her side. He made her feel safe and protected in a way she never had before. And yet she hoped this situation was over as soon as possible because, although they'd barely begun, she wasn't sure how much more pretending she—her heart, her brain, her long-dormant libido—could take. She was trying to keep it together, but every time he touched her, she felt as if she could come undone. She'd never responded to a man's touch that way before, and it unnerved her.

A trainer yanked open the padded door to the octagon and stepped in. Zack and the other man listened as he gave them feedback. Then they followed him out and toward a long row of punching bags on the other side of the room. She followed, obeying Zack's instruction to stay close. As if she could've done anything else.

Zack worked the bag, connecting with a series of punches and elbows, correcting his form when his coach gave him pointers. She watched, completely fascinated by the way his muscles moved beneath his skin. Fascinated by all that controlled strength, all that deadly accuracy. His fight was fast approaching, and her stomach clenched hotly at the thought of watching him again.

She lost track of time as she watched him, her only marker the fact that it was now completely dark outside. Around her the gym was slowly but steadily emptying, but Zack was still practicing what looked like various grappling holds with his coach. Finally, his coach patted him on the back, dismissing him and ending the training session. But instead of heading toward the locker room, Zack turned and made a beeline for her.

"I talked to Jenks, and he said we can stay for a while," he said, tipping his head in the direction of his coach.

"Why do you want to stay? Are you worried about leaving because of what happened earlier?"

"No. I want to teach you some basic self-defense because of what happened earlier."

"You…Oh. Um…I've never, you know…" She shrugged, feeling self-conscious. "I'm not exactly Ronda Rousey."

He smiled, the corner of his mouth tipping up. "It's okay, princess. I don't expect you to be a ninja." Something in his expression darkened, and he stepped closer. "But I need to do everything to keep you safe, and that includes giving you the skills to defend yourself. Self-defense isn't about beating up someone else. It's about getting away from your attacker as effectively as possible so you can get someplace safe. I'd also like to teach you how to throw a basic punch and kick so that you can do the most damage without hurting yourself should the need arise. Plus it might help relieve a little stress. Might feel good to move." She barely concealed the shiver that raced through her at the idea of relieving stress and feeling good and moving with Zack. Her mind was taking that comment in a completely different way than he'd intended.

She swallowed, her mouth a little dry. "I don't like violence."

He took a step closer, and suddenly his hands, still wrapped in black fabric, were on her shoulders. Even through all the fabric separating them, she could feel the heat, the weight of his touch. "And I don't like the idea of you getting hurt because I failed to teach you how to look after yourself."

The truth of his words settled over her, and she nodded. "Okay. Teach me what to do."

He led her to a quiet corner of the gym with a punching bag and several mats set up on the floor. He faced her with his arms crossed. "The most important thing to remember is hard to soft. That means using the hardest parts of your body," he said, reaching out toward her, "your elbows, your knuckles, your knees, even your head." He gently tapped each part of her body as he named it, and she couldn't decide if she wanted him to put a shirt on or not. It'd be a shame to cover up all that glorious skin and muscle, but it was also immensely distracting. She tore her eyes away from his abs and forced herself to pay attention.

"You want to use these parts against the softest, most vulnerable parts of your attacker," he continued. "You're not Ronda Rousey, but if you jab someone in the eye with your fingers, it'll hurt regardless of how much bigger than you they are. So use the hardest parts to go for the eyes, the nose, the throat, and, of course, the groin."

"Okay. That makes sense."

He smiled, the skin around his deep-brown eyes crinkling. "I'm going to show you a few moves that exploit these weak areas. Now say someone is coming at you like this…"

He spent the next hour showing her how to break various holds and how to exploit those soft areas. What to do if someone grabbed her arm, her leg, her torso, from various angles. She'd been hesitant starting out, but she'd improved as the lesson went on, gaining confidence and speed. His touch had been distracting at first, but as she'd focused on the lesson, she'd gotten used to the feel of his hands on her.

Her panties were soaked, and her entire body was throbbing, that throb only getting hotter and heavier with each touch, making her want more.

A fine sheen of sweat coated her skin, and she had to admit that he'd been right. It felt good to take action, to take back a little bit of control. To let off some steam and feel a little bit less powerless.

Zack lunged forward and grabbed her wrist, but she was ready for him. She circled her shoulder, wrenching away from him, while bringing her other arm up against his shoulder, grabbing him in an arm bar.

"Good, Alexa! And what would you do next?"

Without hesitating she brought her knee up to his stomach, barely touching, not hurting. She then mimed kicking his hip and shoving him away from her as hard as possible. "And then I run like hell."

He nodded. "Last one, and then we'll work on punches and kicks. Ready?"

She nodded. "Bring it."

He circled around behind her and grabbed her in a bear hug. She chucked her weight forward, tipping him off balance. "And now what?" he asked, his breath hot against her ear, his arms still wrapped tightly around her, his body draped over hers.

Her mind went blank; she couldn't think with his body pressed against hers like that.

"Think, Alexa. Hard to soft. What's available to you right now? You want to get out of my grip."

"I…I could stomp on your foot."

He took a breath, his chest pressing against her back. "You could, but that might not make me drop my arms. Where are your hands?"

She glanced down and saw that her left hand was only inches from his groin. Her heart picked up its pace as blood rushed to her cheeks. "Oh."

"I have a cup on, it's okay."

Oh God. She couldn't take this. She was going to spontaneously combust.

His arms tightened around her slightly. "What would you do, Alexa? Show me."

Her hand trembled slightly as she laid it as lightly as possible over the shell of his cup. "I'd squeeze and pull and twist. Hard. Cause pain." She swallowed, heat racing over her skin.

"Good." His voice was slightly husky, and he let her go.

Cold air washed over her as he stepped away, goose bumps rising up on her overheated skin. Instantly, she missed the contact, the reassuring solidity of his body around hers.

"As soon as he lets go, you run. Never stay and fight. The object is always to get away from your attacker." He cleared his throat. "Punches and kicks," he said, his voice still a little rough around the edges as he tipped his head toward the punching bag.

She followed him, grateful for an outlet for the electricity snapping through her veins. If she couldn't jump Zack, she could at least take out her frustrations on the punching bag.

* * *

Zack turned away from Alexa, trying to adjust his cup as subtly as possible to accommodate the monster erection he'd been sporting for the better part of the past hour. Although he knew that teaching her self-defense was the right thing to do, he hadn't taken into account the challenge of having to put his hands all over her to do it. He was so wound up that he was about ready to come, just from touching her and wanting her.

He cleared his throat as he turned to face her. Her hair was tousled, her cheeks flushed, her skin glistening with sweat. Her nipples were hard, pressing eagerly against her T-shirt even through her bra. She met his eyes, and her lips parted slightly.

God. It would be so easy to tug her against him and kiss her until neither of them could breathe. But he knew that he'd be hard-pressed to stop if he did. Kissing her would be like pushing a boulder downhill: good luck stopping it once it was in motion.

No. It couldn't happen, as much as he might want it. He cleared his throat again before he spoke. "We're gonna work on two more things today: a straight punch and a simple front snap kick. You're right-handed, right?" She nodded, eyeing the heavy black punching bag in front of them warily. "Oh. That reminds me. Got you a present."

She smiled, her face lighting up. "You did?"

"Can't have you hurting yourself, princess." He turned and jogged into the locker room to retrieve his bag. After setting it down, he rummaged through it and pulled out a small pair of pink-and-black women's MMA-style gloves.

"Oh," she said softly, and reached out to take the gloves from him. "You got these for me?"

He nodded. "Yeah. I saw them here in the shop this morning, and they made me think of you." He winked at her, and she smiled, the blue of her eyes bright and sparkling as she tugged the gloves onto her small hands.

He moved into a relaxed boxer's stance, calling on every ounce of self-control and discipline he had. "See how my left foot is slightly ahead of my right?" He pointed down and she nodded again. He brought his loose fists up in front of him. "This is called an orthodox stance. You try."

She copied him, except for the fact that her hands were too low. He nudged her elbows upward. "You don't want to leave yourself exposed when you throw your right. Gotta keep those hands up." He turned back to the bag and fell into stance. His right fist shot out, connecting hard with the bag, leaving it swaying on its thick chain. "That's a straight punch. Let me show you slower, and I'll explain what I'm doing. When you punch, not all of the power comes from your hands and arms. See how I'm pushing off with my right foot and twisting my hips and shoulders so that I'm square with the bag? That's where the power comes from. You're creating momentum when you push off and twist slightly." He did it again, slower, this time leaving his arm extended. "Once you're fully extended and you've made contact, you want to snap your fist back to your chin to try to avoid getting punched back. And always keep that left fist up, even when you're throwing the punch. Okay. You try. Go slow. Technique is important."

She caught her bottom lip between her teeth, lust flashing in her eyes as she looked up at him, and he knew she'd picked up on the completely unintentional double entendre in his words. So he crossed his arms over his chest and tipped his head at the bag. He couldn't allow himself the luxury of fantasizing about all the techniques he could show her, and how he'd take his sweet time doing it too.

She got herself into proper stance and, after huffing out a breath, threw her right fist into the bag.

"Hey, not bad," he said, nodding approvingly. "Don't twist your shoulders quite so much, though." He moved around behind her and placed his hands lightly on her upper arms. "Like this." He guided her gently, showing her how to move.

"And what about my hips?" she asked over her shoulder, looking up at him.

He dropped his hands to her hips, and before he realized what he was doing, he'd flexed his fingers into her. "Hit the bag," he said, his voice coming out a little rougher than he'd intended.

She did, and he gripped her hips, showing her the right

degree of pivot to get the most power in her strike. A door shut toward the front of the gym, and as he did a visual scan of the space, the music shut off. As he'd been working with Alexa, everyone else had wrapped up their workouts and cleared out. The only sounds were a soft hum coming from the gym's ventilation system and his blood rushing through his ears, although how there was blood anywhere but his achingly hard dick, he had no idea.

She glanced up at him again over her shoulder, and he gripped her hips harder, pulling her back against him. The need he felt for her was taking over, possessing him like hunger takes over a starving man. He dropped his head a few inches, and her eyes fluttered closed. She arched back against him.

"Fuck, Alexa," he said, unable to stop himself from lowering his mouth toward hers. She trembled slightly against him, and he knew he was about to cross a line. Not just cross it, but fly over it with no thought of hitting the brakes.

He couldn't deny the truth any longer: he'd wanted her from the day he'd met her. Sweet, lovely, kind Alexa. He'd never stopped wanting her. Probably never would.

Metallic music burst from his bag, and Alexa leaped away from him, an almost guilty expression on her face. Fuck. His phone. He scrambled to answer it in time.

"De Luca."

"It's Owens. You guys still at the gym?"

He glanced at Alexa, who'd moved away to retrieve her purse from where she'd set it in the corner. "Yeah. Just finishing up. You got anything?"

"Morales ran the plate. It's a fake, so it was a dead end. But Priestley followed the Camry to a private residence in

Bel Air. Real estate record search shows it's Elijah Todd's property."

Zack frowned and wiped at his sweaty brow. "That name sounds familiar."

"He helps run Fairfax Films. Morales says they think he's the second in command in the Brotherhood."

"Well, shit." His heart sank.

"Yeah, that about sums it up. I'll get Clay in on this too," Sean continued. "See what he can find that could help us. And in the meantime, tread carefully. We don't know what they know. Could be Fairfax is just checking up on his daughter. Regardless, Alexa's safety comes first. Fuck getting the intel if it's too risky."

Hell yeah, her safety came first. "Got it. We've got the dinner with her parents tomorrow, so hopefully we can just lie low after that."

"Sounds like a plan." Sean disconnected the call, and Zack looked up to find Alexa right in front of him.

"Was that Sean? What did he say?"

Zack dropped his phone back into his bag and put his hands on his hips. "Yeah. Colt followed the Camry to a house in Bel Air. Apparently it belongs to Elijah Todd?"

She'd been fidgeting, twisting her fingers together, but she stilled at the name. "He's friends with my father. More than friends. They run Fairfax Films together." She chewed on her lip. "So whoever followed us went to Elijah's house?"

"Looks like, yeah. So it could just be your father checking up on you in the wake of the break-in." He shrugged, and she finished his thought.

"Or the Brotherhood might be watching us."

Zack ground his teeth together, tension radiating through his jaw. "I don't like this. You don't have to plant those bugs. We can go underground, disappear until the FBI finishes their investigation."

"No. We can't just disappear. What about your fight? Won't it seem even more suspicious if we fall completely off the radar and stop living our lives?" She paused before continuing. "And what if the FBI investigation doesn't work out? I can't hide forever."

Zack shoved a hand through his hair. She had a point. "You're right. We'll figure it out. And while we're doing that, I'll protect you. I promise."

Even if protecting her meant keeping his hands to himself.

CHAPTER 13

Alexa stood in front of her parents' house trying to see it through Zack's eyes. The sun was just beginning to set, casting the entire courtyard—with its wrought-iron gates, cobblestone drive, tinkling fountain, and soaring cypress trees—in a purplish-pink glow. The fountain burbled quietly behind them as they stood in the shelter of the portico, massive stone columns on either side of them.

The house spread out before them, wings to the east and west. The property sat nestled against the base of Franklin Canyon, and they were surrounded by rising greenery. None of the neighboring houses were visible. It was opulent and isolated and beautiful and cold. She couldn't imagine what Zack saw. It was like looking in the mirror and not really understanding what others saw because your face was simply yours, something you saw and wore every day. It just was.

She listened to the elegant peal of the doorbell's chimes echo through the house, and she blew out a breath, forcing herself to relax. Zack threaded his fingers through hers and gave her hand a gentle squeeze.

"We've got this," he said quietly, and squeezed again. She bit her lip and nodded, steeling herself for the performance ahead, reminding herself who her father actually was and what he'd done to her two best friends. She wouldn't let him hurt anyone anymore.

Including her.

The heavy wood door opened, and one of the household staff, an older man named Joe, ushered them inside, giving Alexa an affectionate pat on the shoulder. "They're waiting for you in the drawing room," he said, nodding politely as he began leading them down the main hallway. Their footsteps echoed off the polished stone floor, matching the tempo of Alexa's pulse pounding in her ears. Instead of his usual jeans and T-shirt—or those sweatpants she was really starting to love—Zack had opted for a light-blue button-down shirt that brought out the olive tones in his skin and emphasized his broad, fit frame, and a pair of black dress pants. Alexa had chosen a simple sleeveless red cotton maxi-dress, wanting to be comfortable.

Her heart pounded in her chest as Joe led them into the drawing room and both her parents rose to their feet. As per usual, jazz floated through the air from concealed speakers, and her mother held a glass of wine while her father held a tumbler of scotch. The drawing room's ceiling was high, with part of the open second-floor hallway of the east wing looking down onto the room. The stone floor was covered in an expensive Oriental rug, which was bordered by heavy, overstuffed cream-colored furniture. A massive fireplace dominated the far wall, opposite the French doors that led to the backyard's terrace. Despite the golds and creams in the room and the fire crackling quietly in the fireplace, there was no warmth. At least not for Alexa. And once again she knew she was cataloguing her surroundings as a way to keep the anxiety at bay.

She met her father's eyes and smiled, pushing everything else aside and letting herself slip into familiar behaviors. "Mom, Dad, thanks for inviting us. This is my boyfriend Zack."

Zack smiled winningly and held out his hand, which her father shook while eyeing him, a completely unreadable expression on his face. Zack nodded politely at her mother, who was appraising Zack hungrily, her eyes roving up and down his body. Alexa carefully schooled her features to hide her disgust.

"It's a pleasure to meet you both," said Zack, smiling warmly at her parents. He slipped an arm around Alexa's waist and pulled her a bit closer, glancing around the room. "You have a beautiful home." He glanced down at her and winked, the hand at her hip giving her a slight squeeze. "And a beautiful daughter."

"I like beautiful things," said her father, sinking back into his chair and propping his ankle up on his knee. Her mother sat down on the couch, her attention flitting between Zack and her phone. Alexa led Zack to the love seat facing the couch and armchair, sitting much closer to him than she normally would've allowed herself to. Damn, but he smelled good. Like clean laundry and soap and a hint of aftershave. She kicked her sandals off and tucked her feet up under her on the love seat, making herself at home, just as she would've before. Zack laid an arm across her shoulders and nestled her against him, and her entire body heated. God, that felt good. He was so big, so warm, so solid.

"Something to drink?" asked Joe, smiling politely at

them. Alexa didn't want to drink tonight, but she also knew it might raise questions if she didn't.

"I'll have a glass of white wine, please, Joe. Zack?"

"I'd love a beer, if you've got one."

Joe tipped his head and disappeared around the corner.

"Not a very fancy drink for a bartender," said her father, peering down into his drink as though it held the answers to the mysteries of the universe. Alexa wasn't surprised that her father had managed to find the fake information they'd planted about Zack. Clay had created a fake online presence for him, including a Facebook page and an Instagram account.

What would pre-shit-storm Alexa have said? "I don't recall telling you that Zack's a bartender."

"I Googled him," said her mother, not looking up from her phone.

Alexa gave an impatient snort and then smiled sweetly. "I don't recall telling you his last name either." At that her mother looked up from her phone with a slightly guilty expression on her face.

Her father shrugged. "You told me you had a boyfriend; I got curious. So sue me." He tilted his head and gave Zack a scrutinizing look. Joe returned with their drinks, and as Alexa took a sip of her wine, her father wagged his finger at Zack. "You look very familiar to me. I'm wondering if we've crossed paths before."

Zack took a sip of his beer and smiled, meeting her father's gaze, not missing a beat. "I'm positive I'd remember meeting you, Mr. Fairfax."

Her father stared at Zack for a second and then nodded, a small smile on his face. "Mmm. Yes. I'd say you would."

"Alexa, why didn't you mention him the other night?"

She shrugged. "It's still really new, Mom. To be honest,

I was trying to avoid…well, this," she said, raising one palm in front of her. "I knew you'd want to meet him, and you guys are intimidating."

Her mother gave a high-pitched, birdlike laugh. "Oh, we are not."

Zack set his beer on the coffee table beside him and leaned forward slightly, rubbing a hand over the back of his neck. "Respectfully, Mrs. Fairfax, I disagree. I grew up in Thousand Oaks. My mom's a high school science teacher. My dad's a dentist. This," he said, gesturing around them, "is pretty intimidating."

Alexa smiled, glancing down at her wine. He was so charming, this pretend boyfriend of hers.

Her mother laughed, more naturally this time. "Point taken."

"So how did you come to be dating my daughter, Zack…Sorry, what *was* your last name again?" asked her father, his voice low and calm.

Zack eased back against the love seat and once again tucked Alexa against him. "Caruso. We both volunteer at the Children's Hospital."

"Oh. Well, that's nice," said her mother, sounding slightly bored. "So you just met there, and he asked you out?"

"Pretty much," said Alexa, shrugging.

Zack smiled and pulled her a bit tighter against him. "The first time I saw Alexa was almost a year ago. I walked into the room, and she was sitting there, talking to someone else. I felt like everything around me had stopped. All I could see was her."

Something hitched in Alexa's chest, and she had to remind herself that he was making this up. That it wasn't real, no matter how badly she wanted it to be.

"She just had this light about her. I was hooked, almost immediately."

Her mother leaned forward in her seat, suddenly much more interested in the story. "But you said that was a year ago. What happened?"

Zack gave his head a rueful shake. "I chickened out. Alexa and I became friends, and I dated someone else. She dated too."

"But this entire time, you carried a torch for her?" asked her mother.

Zack nodded and glanced over at Alexa, his eyes holding hers. "Yeah. The entire time."

"So then what happened?" asked her mother as her father sighed. It was apparently his turn to be bored with the conversation.

Zack swallowed, hesitating ever so slightly, so Alexa jumped in and began recounting one of the countless situations she'd fantasized about. "I was having a shitty day, and he'd always said that I should stop by his bar for a drink. Didn't matter that it was late, that it was raining, I decided to take him up on his offer. I think a part of me just wanted to see him, you know? I showed up, and we hung out and…just being with him made me feel better. We laughed and talked until like two in the morning, when his shift was over. I even stayed after the bar closed, and there's this really cool old jukebox. He put on some music, and we danced. It was like after knowing each other for a year, we were finally right where we were supposed to be." She looked up at Zack, whose eyes had darkened. "I knew he was for me." His hand dipped a bit lower on her hip. "After that, I knew we had something. It was just so easy being with him."

Her mother's eyes took another walk down Zack's body. "Hmm. I bet. Do you remember the song?"

Zack answered. "It was 'Cry to Me' by Solomon Burke." He glanced at her again, and something passed between them in that moment, but she wasn't entirely sure what. Maybe it was just the closeness that came with being complicit in a series of lies together. Although they *had* danced to that song, at Sierra and Sean's engagement party. It was the first time she'd ever felt his arms around her, and she'd replayed that moment countless times because it had felt so good. So right.

Joe stepped into the room and nodded. "Dinner is served. If you'll follow me." They all rose from their seats, and as Alexa hastily slipped her feet back into her sandals, she shivered slightly, missing the warmth of Zack's body against hers. She sat up, and her eyes fluttered closed as Zack pressed a kiss to her temple. She felt that touch of his lips spread through her, and she smiled. Her parents followed Joe out of the room, and she stood, feeling a little light-headed, despite the fact that she'd had only a few sips of wine.

"That was a good story," she whispered, slipping her hand into his, loving how good his skin felt against hers. How natural her small hand felt tucked into his much larger one.

His jaw tightened, and then he smiled at her, a sadness pulling at his eyes. "Who said it was a story?"

* * *

Zack sipped his beer and hooked his ankle around Alexa's under the table, pulling her leg against his. Not because anyone could see, but because he could and because he wanted to. The lies they'd told pounded through him, and he found himself wishing that they weren't lies. To hold her close as they danced, to tell her the truth of who she was to him…Yes. He couldn't deny that he wanted all of that.

And what he'd said, about the first time he'd seen her…Yeah. That hadn't been a lie at all.

The truth sank into him like an anchor taking hold: he'd been at least halfway in love with Alexa for the better part of a year. It was a truth that made him feel inspiringly alive and despairingly lost at the same time, because fuck if he knew what to do with it. If there was even anything he *could* do with it.

Alexa tossed her napkin onto the table, and he noticed she'd barely eaten half of the salad, steak, grilled shrimp, and sweet potatoes they'd been served. Although he was slightly worried about making weight for his fight—he had to weigh in at 205 pounds—he'd devoured everything on his plate.

"I'd like to give Zack a tour of the house. Is that okay?" she asked, her gaze bouncing between her parents. Her mother had been friendly and chatty during dinner, her father much quieter. More than once Zack had felt the weight of his gaze on him and had ignored it. He had no idea if it was because he had the audacity to (pretend to) date Fairfax's daughter or if there was more to it than that. He wished he knew. What did Fairfax know? Why had they been followed yesterday by someone with ties to the Brotherhood?

Her mother smiled. "Sure. Have a tour, and then we'll have dessert in about fifteen minutes. Helen made crème brûlée."

Given the amount of food still on Melanie Fairfax's plate, Zack had a feeling she wouldn't be eating the crème brûlée. While Alexa resembled her mother in terms of her features—same blue-gray eyes, same nose, same mouth—her body type was completely different. Alexa was petite but curvy, and felt damn good against him. He had the sudden urge to feed her, to cook for her, to watch her enjoy something he'd made. He knew he made a mean lasagna—his nonna's recipe—and for some reason the idea of Alexa eating something he'd made for her turned him on. A lot.

Alexa stood and extended her hand to him. "C'mon, babe. I'll give you the tour." He rose and took her hand, loving how fucking perfect her small hand felt nestled in his.

She led him back toward the hallway and then silently began leading him up the stairs. The staircase was impressive, swooping off into two wings about halfway up. The high ceiling arched gracefully above them. The bugs were stashed safely in Zack's pocket—Alexa had been worried that her purse might be searched at some point if she left it out of sight. And given that it was her parents' home, it would've looked strange if she'd kept her purse clutched to her side all night when normally she just left it in the front hall.

"Library first?" she asked quietly when they were almost at the first landing, and he nodded. She tugged him toward the right. "It's in the east wing, and it's where he spends a lot of his time." They climbed the stairs in sync, her hand still in his. "He takes calls in there, has meetings. We can start there and work our way back toward his office and bedroom."

"Sounds like a plan." He traced his thumb over the back of her hand. "You're doing amazing, by the way. I'm really proud of you."

She flushed, and he smiled, loving that his small bit of

praise had made her blush. "This way." She led him down a hallway and pushed open a door, then pulled him inside and closed it behind them.

The room was quiet and empty but still fairly bright thanks to the light from the setting sun. He quickly scanned the room, taking in the large windows, the floor-to-ceiling bookcases, the heavy, dark furniture. A desk dominated the space in front of the windows, and Alexa crouched down in front of it. She wiped her hands on the skirt of her dress, and he noticed that they were shaking.

Needing to comfort her like he needed to breathe, he crouched down in front of her and took her hands in his. They were cold, and her palms were damp. "You can do this. I know you can. I'm here with you, and I'm not going to let anything happen to you. I promise, princess."

She closed her eyes for a second and then nodded. "Morales said to place the devices in central locations and not too close to anything that would interfere with the sound quality."

He pulled a small sealed plastic bag out of his pocket. It contained several flat black squares, no bigger than postage stamps. They were sound activated, meaning they'd turn on only when someone spoke, giving them a much longer life than the average listening device.

Her hands no longer shaking, Alexa opened the bag and pulled a SIM card and listening device from it. She inserted the SIM card into the listening device and programmed in the appropriate code, just as Morales had showed her. Pride surged through Zack, not only at her bravery and strength in the face of everything going on, but also at her proficiency with everything—their ruse, the self-defense techniques he'd shown her, high-tech surveillance equipment. She was damn capable, and it was extremely attractive.

She pulled out her phone and texted the code she'd used to Morales. Now anytime the device was activated, the audio would feed directly to Morales's phone, thanks to the SIM card. Zack paced the room, eyes snapping back and forth between Alexa and the door as she peeled off the backing on the device and crawled under the desk to affix it.

Zack stood near the door, listening for any signs of activity, and Alexa appeared at his elbow. "One down, two to go." With a quick twist of the knob, she opened the door and led him down the hallway, into her parents' bedroom. Quickly, she set up another listening device, stashing this one on the inside panel of her father's nightstand. The entire hallway was deserted, the wing silent as she led him to their last stop, her father's office.

Morales had wanted to plant more bugs throughout the house, in places like the kitchen and living area, but it was simply too risky. At least these Alexa could plant and activate undetected. Placing the devices in higher-traffic areas would have been much harder. Morales would have to make do with what she was able to gather from these bugs.

Zack followed Alexa into the room, his heart kicking against his ribs. They'd already been gone longer than fifteen minutes, and he was anxious to get this part of the evening over with. He hadn't said anything because he didn't want to rush her—she was tense enough without him getting on her about the time.

Just as she had in the library, she activated the device and crawled under the desk to stick it on. Zack stood near the door, listening intently. An electric current worked its way down his spine when he heard a distinctive creak from somewhere down the hallway. In several long strides, he crossed the room to Alexa, who was just getting to her feet.

"Someone's coming," he said, his voice low.

Her eyes widened, and some of the blood drained from her face. The unmistakable sound of footsteps echoed down the hallway, approaching the office, and Zack did the only thing he could think of to keep Alexa safe.

He pulled her against him and kissed her.

CHAPTER 14

As Zack's mouth closed over hers, Alexa gasped and then melted into him almost instantly. His lips were firm but gentle, warm and sweet as they moved against hers. His hands stroked her back, and as his tongue slipped into her mouth, she slid her hands up his chest, over his broad shoulders, and into his thick, soft hair. His tongue caressed hers, and a sparkling heat exploded over her skin. He groaned softly, and she opened more for him.

Never in her life had a kiss felt like this. It was so much more than a simple touching of mouths, of lips and tongues. It was need, and hunger, and lust. It was waking up after being asleep for far too long. Just this kiss was better than most of the sex she'd had, and the fact that it was *Zack*—the man she'd wanted for the better part of a year, the man she'd fantasized about and lusted after—took her breath away. She wanted more, wanted to somehow get closer, and she made a soft whimpering noise as she rocked against him.

Hot, heady desire spiraled through her when she felt his

erection slide against her hip. So hard, so thick. God, he was huge. She shivered when he rolled his hips into her, sliding his hard cock against her a second time.

His hands slid from her back down to her ass, where he gave her cheeks a firm squeeze as he pulled her tighter against him. She clenched her thighs together, her clit throbbing and her panties wet as his mouth moved with increasing hunger against hers, the kiss morphing from warm and sweet to hot and demanding. She felt ready to burst into flame, everything inside her was so hot. She was kindling, and he was a match, sparking so much damn need through her she could barely stand it.

The door to the office opened, and Zack broke the kiss, still holding her against him. Joe stepped into the room and, as soon as he saw them, averted his gaze. She assumed Zack's plan was to make it look as if they'd snuck off to make out, diverting attention from where they were and why.

"I'm sorry. Uh…dessert is served." Joe quickly stepped out of the room but left the door open.

Zack's fingers flexed against her ass again, and she trembled. She'd never been kissed like that before. She was aroused. Awake. Hungry. She clenched her thighs together again, trying to soothe the throbbing ache simmering low in her core. Her blood pumped hot and fast, lust and need and want all pooling together and shimmering through her, intense and vibrant.

"Alexa." His voice was low and rough, and she forced herself to look up and meet his eyes. So dark they were almost black, they glittered down at her, and hot excitement swirled through her. "I've wanted to do that since the day I laid eyes on you. Fuck." He dipped his head and buried his face in her neck, sucking gently just below her ear. "You taste so damn good, princess. I can't stop." His tongue grazed her earlobe, and she gasped, feeling that sweep of his tongue as though he'd touched her clit. He growled softly against her and did it again.

"I don't want you to stop," she sighed out, tipping her head back and giving him better access, and although she'd said those words before, this was the first time she'd ever really meant them. His teeth scraped against her earlobe, and she jerked against him, his hard cock rubbing against her stomach. Somehow she managed to get her mouth to form coherent words. "This doesn't feel like pretending." Her voice was shaky, her heart fluttering in her chest as she waited for his answer. She didn't want to pretend. She wanted to be his, for real.

He raised his head and met her eyes, his hands caressing her face. "This was never pretend for me." At the intensity shining in his gaze, she knew he was telling the truth. That somehow Zack wanted her. There was no going back. Not now.

"Me neither."

In response he slipped his arms around her waist and brought his mouth back to hers, and Alexa moaned. His tongue stroked hers, the kiss hot and deep, and she felt as though he were claiming her. As though their shared admission had broken down all the barriers between them.

"Everything I said downstairs," he said, speaking the words against her mouth, catching her lips in small, nipping kisses, "I wasn't making any of it up." Her heart beat faster, and she could feel her pulse everywhere, her entire body becoming one giant throb. He caught her lower lip between his teeth and tugged gently, swiping his tongue to soothe the bite and then kissing her again, deep and slow, their lips and tongues finding an easy, promising rhythm.

His mouth felt so good, so right against hers, and she couldn't think anymore. She could only bask in how good he was making her feel.

She broke the kiss, needing desperately to tell him the truth, even though they were wading into complicated waters. "I've…It's been you, Zack. Since the day I met you, for me…it's only been you."

His eyes softened as his grip on her tightened. He pressed his forehead to hers. "I'm sorry."

Her heart practically shuddered to a stop. "For what?"

"For choosing wrong a year ago."

Up until now she hadn't realized that he'd seen her as a choice at all, and while she wanted to know about everything that had happened a year ago, now wasn't the time. Her heart resumed its rhythm, pounding so hard and so happily she thought it might shatter. The happiness filling her up was almost too much, so big and bright it hurt.

"You are so beautiful, Alexa. God, I…" He gazed down at her and then slipped his hands into her hair, kissing her again. She slid her arms around him, reveling in the feel of all those hard muscles hidden beneath his shirt. He groaned against her mouth as they tasted and explored, and she lost all sense of place and time as her entire world narrowed to Zack and his lips, his tongue, the warmth of his mouth, his body pressed against hers.

Her. He wanted her. He'd wanted her as much as she'd wanted him, this entire time. The realization felt like joy, except that joy wasn't a big enough word.

"What's going on here?" Her father's voice came from the doorway, and they broke apart. Zack dropped his arms and cleared his throat, glancing sheepishly at the floor. "Sorry, sir. I…we…got a little carried away."

Her father stared at them with his arms crossed and

his eyes narrowed. His gaze moved away from them and scanned the room. Once he was finished with his slow sweep, he returned his disapproving gaze to them. "Dessert. Downstairs."

* * *

Zack sat with his arm thrown casually over the back of Alexa's chair, although he felt pretty fucking far from casual at the moment.

He'd wasted a year not going after Alexa. A whole fucking year he could've been with her because she felt the same way he did about her. He'd wasted a year pretending he wasn't halfway in love with her.

He wasn't going to waste more time, that was for damn sure.

He smiled politely at something her mother said and shoveled some crème brûlée in his mouth, replaying that kiss. Again. Yeah, he'd grabbed her and kissed her to protect her, but the second his mouth had connected with hers, he'd been gone. Done. Game over. It had been fucking perfect and sweet and hot and a thousand times better than any of the hundreds of times he'd imagined it.

But he wasn't stupid. He knew that they didn't face a smooth, obstacle-free path just because they'd shared a hot kiss and admitted their feelings for each other. There was the complicated matter of her family situation. He had a feeling that the fact he'd dated Taylor would weigh on Alexa. He had his fight to focus on. Not to mention that it wasn't exactly kosher for a bodyguard to date his protectee. Despite the circumstances of how Sean and Sierra had gotten together, Zack knew Sean would boot him from the case if he thought their pretend relationship had crossed the line from fake to real. The idea of someone else taking over, of someone else protecting her, made him want to punch something. No. She was his to protect, and he wasn't letting that go.

Probably all things he should discuss with Alexa. Alone. Preferably naked and sweaty and sated after he'd made her come half a dozen times. Given that they were staying with Sean and Sierra, that scenario wasn't likely to play out in the immediate future, but he liked the fantasy all the same.

His still-hard cock jerked against his zipper, and he shifted slightly in his seat. Alexa reached up to where his hand sat on her shoulder and twined her fingers with his, tracing her thumb over his knuckles. They'd figure it out together. That much he knew for sure.

"Enjoy the tour?" Jonathan Fairfax leveled his gaze at Zack, his expression stony.

Doing his best to play the part of chastised boyfriend, Zack swallowed thickly and glanced down at his lap before meeting Fairfax's eyes, knowing he had to play this right. "You have an amazing house."

Fairfax's eyebrows inched up slightly, as though he was surprised by Zack's answer. After a second he tipped his head. "Mmm. Well. You didn't seem terribly interested in the architecture." Zack didn't have time to respond, because Fairfax leaned forward, his hands clasped on the table in front of him. "What do you want? Money?"

Alexa's eyes widened, and her grip tightened on Zack's hand. "Dad! I can't believe you!"

"Or are you just in it for the sex?" Fairfax took a healthy swallow from his tumbler, and Zack realized he might be a little bit drunk.

Zack shook his head and shot Alexa a reassuring smile.

"It's okay." He turned his attention back to Fairfax. "I'm in it because I think your daughter's a fantastic person. She's kind, and funny, and smart, and, yes, beautiful."

Fairfax rolled his eyes, and Zack ground his teeth as a wave of protective anger crashed into him.

"Well, honey, I think your acting skills are still intact, as you seem to have this one fooled." Fairfax turned to Zack, his eyes like ice. He was trying to scare Zack off, he knew. Knew and didn't care, because he wasn't going any-fucking-where. "Alexa is a weak-willed doormat. She's needy and not very good at much of anything. Her beauty is the only tool in her kit, and believe me, she's used it. Even if she was too stupid to see it as a tool in the first place."

"Jonathan!" Alexa's mother cried out, slapping her open palm against the table. "That's enough!"

Fury snapped up Zack's spine, his nostrils flaring, his jaw aching he was clenching it so hard. He imagined slamming his fist into Fairfax's sneering, corrupt face, but knew there was too much at stake. He wouldn't do anything to put Alexa's safety in jeopardy.

Alexa stared at her lap, and when she blinked, a tear slipped free and fell onto her skirt, leaving a small dark splotch. He didn't know if Fairfax was trying to bait him or was simply a nasty drunk, but it didn't matter. They needed to leave, and not just because Zack was dangerously close to killing him.

Zack stood angrily, tossed his napkin on the table, and helped Alexa to her feet, tucking her against him. "Thank you for dinner." Turning, he led Alexa back toward the front door as an argument exploded between Jonathan and Melanie Fairfax. Zack pulled Alexa out into the cool night air, shutting away the sounds of the argument behind them as the door snapped closed. Alexa pulled away from him and practically ran to the SUV. He scanned the courtyard as he moved, looking for anything suspicious while keeping an eye on her.

She leaned against the body of the vehicle, hugging herself, her shoulders shaking. Finally, she looked up, mascara streaking her pale cheeks. "At least we got the job done. And I feel ten percent less guilty. Timely reminder of what an asshole he is." She gave him a weak smile, and he brushed her tears away with his thumbs, aching for her. He kissed her on the forehead and then on the temple before pressing his forehead against hers, cradling her face in his hands.

"None of what he said is true. Not a fucking word of it."

Fresh tears escaped, and she blinked furiously. "You don't know that."

"Yes, I do. I absolutely do." He kissed her, softly and gently, wanting desperately to comfort her. "And I'll tell you every damn day that you're kind and smart and beautiful, inside and out, until you believe it. Until you know it like I do."

She laid her hand on his cheek, her fingers rasping against his stubble. "I don't deserve you."

"Shh. Stop. C'mon, princess. Don't do that." He kissed her again, a gentle caress of his lips against hers.

"What are we doing, Zack?" she asked, and slipped her arms around his neck, holding him close.

"Starting something, I hope. I know it's not simple. But I don't want to waste more time. Not now that I know how you feel."

She snuggled into him, rubbing her nose against his neck. "It's anything but simple. But I want it too. I can't…" She raised her head and met his eyes. "After tonight, I can't go back."

"I can't go back either." He kissed along her jaw, and she relaxed into him. "And I'll take hard and complicated and messy, if it's with you. But…" He tugged her earlobe with his teeth, and she pressed her hips into him.

Alexa has sensitive ears. He stored that bit of information. "If Sean finds out that this *isn't* pretend, he'll assign someone else to you. We're not supposed to be involved with clients, and he'll take me off the case. I don't want that. I need to be here. I need to protect you."

"I don't want someone else," she said, kissing lightly along his jaw. His cock jumped against his zipper, desperate for more. God, just the thought of her mouth on him was almost too much. "I want you." Her lips trailed down his neck, and he had to focus on what he was trying to say.

"Then as far as everyone else is concerned, we're still pretending." He didn't like it, but it was the way it had to be right now. He'd spent a year denying his feelings for Alexa. He couldn't do it anymore.

"Okay." She lifted her head, and her eyes were bright. "But what if Sean finds out? Aren't you risking your job?"

"I'd risk a lot fucking more than my job to be with you, princess." He dipped his head and kissed her neck, working his way back up to her ear.

"God, you make me feel so good." She tipped her head back and sighed. "You have no idea how much time I've spent thinking about you."

Satisfaction charged through him, lighting up his senses. "I doubt it's half as much time as I've spent thinking about you." He trailed his mouth over her skin, so warm, so soft. "Thinking about how beautiful you are. How good. How fucking adorable."

"What else?" she asked. The tears and tension were gone, and the knot between his shoulders loosened.

"What it would feel like to kiss you. To hold you. To wake up next to you." He pulled back and met her eyes. "To lose myself inside you."

She trembled. "The other night, after my dream, after we almost kissed, I went to bed and imagined what it would feel like to fall asleep in your arms."

An emotion too intense to name rocketed through him, almost tearing his heart right out. "Fuck, princess, I'm sorry."

"Stop apologizing." She pressed her hands against his chest, gently easing him away. "Let's go home. I don't want to be here anymore."

* * *

What kind of fucked-up cat-and-mouse game were they playing?

Jonathan rubbed a hand over his mouth as he eased back in his desk chair, sitting alone in the darkened library, listening to Frank Sinatra. He swirled the scotch in his glass, watching the amber liquid slosh around. He'd had a bit too much tonight, and he set the glass on the blotter on his desk, staring at it as though it could somehow explain to him what the fuck was going on.

As calmly as possible, he went over what he knew. Alexa had begun distancing herself months ago, moving out when he hadn't wanted her to. Then he'd found that damn earring here, in the library, after the dinner party, but there was no proof she'd overheard his conversation with Kramer. They'd searched her house and come up empty-handed, with no evidence she knew anything about the Golden Brotherhood. The break-in had spooked her, and she and her boyfriend, were staying with friends.

According to the tail Elijah had set on her, her daily routine was pretty much the same, with the addition of the boyfriend. She'd come when he'd asked her to, had brought the boyfriend when he'd asked her to, but something had been off tonight. And it bugged the ever-loving fuck out of him that he couldn't seem to wrap his mind around what it was.

The boyfriend, maybe. Something about him wasn't on the level, not at all. And he couldn't shake the feeling he'd seen him somewhere before.

He didn't know what Alexa knew, if she knew, or, if she did know, if that was the reason for how she'd been acting lately. He didn't know who this boyfriend was. He still didn't know where Crosby was.

And right now, what he didn't know could be very, very bad for the Brotherhood. And what was bad for the Brotherhood was dangerous for everyone else.

Including that damn bartender. Including Alexa.

CHAPTER 15

"How did it go?" Sean strode toward the front door as Zack and Alexa stepped inside, and although what Alexa really wanted was to slip her hand into Zack's, she didn't.

"Good, I think," she said, toeing off her sandals and letting her purse fall to the floor. "I was able to place all the devices and activate them. Morales texted me to let me know everything was working."

"We almost got busted at one point by one of the staff," said Zack, leaning back against the wall and crossing his arms.

"Oh yeah? What'd you do?"

Zack tipped his head at her, and she was impressed with how casual he was able to look. "I kissed her. Made it look like we'd snuck off to make out."

Sean nodded approvingly. "Good call. Glad it went to plan."

"I guess now we just wait?" asked Alexa, tugging off her denim jacket and hanging it in the closet.

"Morales will see what they can pick up with the bugs you planted, and yeah, we wait."

Sierra padded into the hallway, a bowl of popcorn in her hands. She passed it to Sean and wrapped Alexa in a hug. "You okay?" Sierra pulled back and rubbed Alexa's arm, and Alexa felt her throat thicken a little at Sierra's concern.

Swallowing, she managed a small smile and a nod. "Yeah. I'm okay."

"You know where you to find me if you want to talk or if you need anything. Yeah?"

"Yeah."

With a final nod, Sierra took the popcorn back from Sean, who followed her into the living room.

A shard of guilt dug into Alexa, right between her ribs. She'd brought her drama, her danger, to their doorstep and was completely encroaching on their space, not to mention lying to them.

Zack touched her lightly on the arm, and she felt that touch from her shoulder to the tips of her fingers, as though her entire body was sensitized to him. "I need to go fit in a workout, even though it's getting late."

"Oh." She felt oddly disappointed, although it wasn't as if they could curl up on the couch together and watch a movie or something.

"The fight's the day after tomorrow. You're gonna come, right?"

She nodded. "I wouldn't miss it," she said, although the idea of watching him in that cage had her stomach tying itself into knots.

"I'll be back, but not until later. After I work out, I need to swing by my place, pick up a few more things."

"I wish I could see where you live. What's it like?"

He smiled and tucked her hair behind her ear. He

glanced down the hallway, but the *Walking Dead* theme song echoed softly from the living room. "It's a studio apartment on Los Feliz. It's small, but it's nice." He leaned closer, his nose brushing hers. "God, I've thought of you in my bed so many times."

His words sent both lust and fear spiraling through her, because as much as she wanted that too, she knew she'd have to figure out a way to tell him about her past and what it meant. About how it affected her. She wasn't ready, but she knew she owed him the truth.

"I've thought about you too," she whispered, wanting to say something true. "Even when you were with Taylor."

That shard of guilt dug itself in deeper, and he slipped his fingers under her chin, tilting her face up. His eyes narrowed slightly, and it was as though he knew, as though he understood how she felt.

"Don't do that, princess. You haven't done anything wrong."

She nodded, although she wasn't too sure about that.

"I'll see you tomorrow. Sleep tight." He cupped her face and gave her a quick kiss, one that was far too fleeting and only left her wanting so much more. And then he was gone, the door closing behind him, leaving Alexa to head upstairs.

She closed her bedroom door quietly behind her and stripped her dress off, dropping it in a puddle of fabric on the floor. In her bra and panties, she moved in front of the floor-length mirror mounted on the back of the door. She studied herself, trying to look past the familiarities and see herself as Zack might. But all she could see was how *different* she was from Taylor.

They were both blond, but where Taylor's hair was long, thick, and the color of honey, Alexa's was baby-fine, just past her chin, and a silvery blond that looked almost white in harsh lighting. Taylor's eyes were a light sky blue, another similarity, but Alexa's had silver in them, dimming the blue. Where Taylor was tall, Alexa was petite. Where Taylor was lithe and toned, Alexa was soft and curvy.

Where Taylor was pretty much a sex goddess, Alexa was…unsure. Experienced, but in all the wrong ways. It wasn't that she didn't like sex. It was more that she didn't know *how* to enjoy it. She'd spent so much time just enduring and detaching that she wasn't sure how to proceed with Zack.

What if he found her lacking?

She closed her eyes, took a breath, and then opened them, looking again. She turned her head, examining the planes and angles of her face. The button nose and rounded cheeks. The soft, feminine slope of her shoulders. Reaching up, she skimmed her hands over her breasts, the pale pink of her nipples barely visible through her white bra. She teased her knuckles over her nipples, and they beaded beneath the lace. Cupping her breasts, she let herself feel the weight of them, imagining what Zack's hands would feel like on them.

She let out a soft sigh as she imagined his hands on her and slid her hands lower, over her stomach, her hips, wondering when she'd get to feel his skin on hers. Surprised at just how much she wanted that. She wanted him with an unprecedented intensity. Before tonight she'd yearned for him. Pined. Lusted from afar. But now that she knew what was between them, she *wanted*. With each breath, each heartbeat, she wanted.

She traced her fingers over the lace of her purple thong, pulling at it slightly. The fabric slid against her, and she moaned softly.

She was wet, the crotch of her panties slightly darker, soaked through with her arousal. She moved the fabric over herself again, her hips moving of their own accord at the rasp of pleasure caused by that small brush.

From Zack. Because of Zack. For Zack.

She walked toward the bed, yanking off her bra and panties as she went. Slipping under the covers, she spread her legs and rested her hand on her aching pussy.

Pussy. Such a dirty word, one she didn't really use, but right now, in this moment, it felt right.

She traced her fingers over her soft bare skin, teasing her lips apart. She couldn't remember the last time she'd been this wet. She slipped a finger inside herself and slicked her wetness over her clit, gasping at the bolt of pleasure flaring up her spine at that one touch. Her eyelids were heavy, and they fell closed as she moved her fingers in a slow circle over her clit, aching warmth pooling deep inside her.

Spreading her legs open wider, she let herself sink into a fantasy, pushing everything else away. No Golden Brotherhood. No Taylor. No string of men she'd never wanted to sleep with. Just her and Zack, and the things she wanted to do with him, and to him. The things she wanted him to do to her. The things she imagined she'd like, given the chance.

Words fell away, images flickering like a dirty montage as she rubbed her clit, firmer and faster now. Dropping to her knees in front of him and taking his cock into her mouth, his hands in her hair, her name falling from his lips. Zack's mouth on her breasts, his hand between her legs, touching her just like this.

She changed her rhythm as sweat gathered along her hairline, switching from circles to firm diagonal strokes across her clit, and she could feel that twisting deep inside her as the pressure built. She'd never come with a man, only like this, and she wanted to know what it would feel like to come with Zack inside her.

The image of Zack climbing on top of her and sliding inside her tight, aching pussy almost pushed her over the edge, and she stroked faster. God, she was desperate for it, not just for release, but for him. Her clit swelled, and she wanted…more. It felt good, but it wasn't nearly enough. She let out the breath she'd been holding as she imagined being spread out before Zack, her legs wide, her pussy dripping, her knees pressed to her shoulders as he filled her, over and over again. Stretching her and soothing the clenching ache deep inside her. His hands big and slightly rough on her hips as he stroked harder and deeper, getting caught up in the pleasure spreading between them like a wildfire.

So much that it almost hurt, she wanted to make him feel good. Wanted to please him. Wanted to be good for him.

She slid a finger along each side of her clit, pulling slightly as she rubbed, and she could smell how turned on she was. Sweat gathered behind her knees, under her breasts, in the crooks of her elbows, and she let her mind wander to beautifully dirty places. Zack fucking her from behind, his hand between her legs. At the idea of him pulling free and coming on her ass, marking her in such a primal way, she came, her hips bucking up off the bed, her legs shaking. Hot, heavy throbs beat through her body, her clit pulsing against her fingers, swollen and overly sensitive.

She pulled her fingers away and lay completely still, her heart pounding, throbbing in time with her clit. It wasn't the first time she'd thought of him while she touched herself. Not by a long shot. But it was the first time she'd felt that maybe she was allowed. That maybe she wasn't doing something wrong.

Maybe. It was hope tinged with guilt, and it crawled over her sweaty skin, dulling the buzz from her orgasm.

She'd come, but it hadn't eased the ache deep inside her, or the uncertainty that when she and Zack had sex, she'd be enough for him.

* * *

Although he'd hit the gym less than twelve hours ago, Zack was back at it the following morning. The fight was tomorrow night, and this morning would be his last workout before the fight, so that his body had time to recover.

Holding the medicine ball in front of him, he lowered his back to the floor. It was supposed to be a light workout, but God knew he had enough pent-up energy to keep going for hours.

He'd spent an hour reviewing tapes with Jenks, watching his opponent, memorizing the way he moved. Some guys didn't watch footage before a fight, but Zack found value in studying his opponent and coming up with strategies. It made him feel more prepared. Given his dyslexia, it was the only kind of studying he actually liked.

After reviewing the footage, he'd spent an hour in the cage, sparring with Jenks, working on various holds and defense techniques. Now he was focused on conditioning. Sit-ups, push-ups, lunges, all interspersed with rapid-fire jump rope.

He pulled himself up to sitting again, and Alexa's words

from the night before echoed through his brain, making his blood beat hotter and faster through him.

It's been you, Zack. Since the day I met you, for me...it's only been you.

And now he was in it with her, no looking back. No more excuses.

He let the medicine ball drop between his bent legs with a heavy thud as the truth hit him. Excuses. He'd used them with Taylor, and with the women who'd come before her, never letting himself get in too deep with anyone, insisting that he didn't have time for a relationship because of his commitment to fighting. He'd felt so sure that he didn't have room in his life for fighting and a relationship, felt so sure he wasn't looking for anything serious. Those excuses had felt so damn necessary, and not like excuses at all, but like the truth. But when it came to Alexa, he saw those reasons as the hollow excuses they were. He'd hidden behind those excuses because he'd never met a woman he was willing to make room for.

There were no excuses when it came to Alexa because the idea of not pursuing something with her...Yeah, it was impossible now that he knew how she felt about him. A year ago he hadn't pursued anything with her for a couple of reasons, namely doubt and intimidation. He knew he owed her an explanation. A wave of guilt and shame rocked him, a tingle spreading uncomfortably through his chest as he thought about what had happened with Taylor. The way he'd leaned on those excuses, had even believed them. But subconsciously he'd known that she wasn't the woman for him, as much as he might've cared about her.

It had only ever been Alexa, who was so sweet and warm and good. He knew that now, like he knew the sky was blue and fire was hot.

An elemental truth.

He reached behind him and peeled off his shirt, then wrung it out and watched as the sweat dripped from the soaked and bunched cotton onto the mat. With a sigh he pushed to his feet, his muscles trembling slightly. He grabbed his towel from a nearby bench and wiped at his face. Time to hit the shower and head back to Sean's, check in on Alexa. Make sure she was safe.

A chill worked its way down his spine, the magnitude of what was at stake rocking him. Alexa. Them. Her safety. His job, potentially. He didn't even want to think about what they'd be facing if her father, an incredibly dangerous man, found out what she'd done. Found out that Zack wasn't who he'd said he was.

So much hidden. But not his true feelings for Alexa. Not anymore.

"You heading out?" asked Jamie, who was just finishing up his own workout.

"Yeah. I should get back to Alexa." He flung his sweaty T-shirt over one shoulder, his towel over the other. Cool air brushed over his skin, evaporating some of the sweat.

"If I don't see you before, good luck tomorrow." Jamie said. "And don't forget the Rocky Rule."

"You know that rule's bullshit," he said, waving Jamie away. The rule, based on the famous quote from *Rocky* that "women weaken legs"—meaning a fighter shouldn't have sex right before a fight—had been disproven in all kinds of scientific studies that Zack hadn't read. But it still held major sway with a lot of fighters.

"Even if the science doesn't prove it, it's tradition." Jamie wagged his finger at him. "You don't mess with tradition."

Zack smiled and shook his head, crossing his arms over his chest. "Doesn't matter. Not seeing anyone right now."

The look on Jamie's face shifted from joking to serious, his smile firming into a thin line. "I heard what happened last night."

Zack frowned and swallowed, his mouth suddenly dry. "What do you mean?"

Jamie stepped closer. "You and Alexa. Natalie and I, we heard everything."

Oh fuck. The bugs. A weight pressed against Zack's chest. "You were with Morales."

Jamie nodded. "Sean sent me to check in with her, make sure everything was going okay with planting the listening devices. We were sitting at her desk when you…" Jamie tilted his head, letting his silence fill in the blanks.

Zack clenched his jaw, tension radiating through him. "Did you tell Sean?"

Jamie shook his head. "No." And then a smile spread across his face, his eyes twinkling. Fucking twinkling. "I *knew* it!" he said, clenching his fist triumphantly.

Zack felt his eyebrows slam together. "What the fuck do you mean, you knew it? You don't know shit."

Jamie blinked at him. "Dude, I have eyes. And a brain. And observation skills. Ever since you and Taylor split…" He shook his head. "Man. The way you look at Alexa. Anyone could see it."

"How do I look at her?"

Jamie laughed, and Zack couldn't help but smile. "Like she's this adorable little kitten that you want to hold and pet and protect from the world. Like you want to keep her all to yourself. Like you'd do just about anything to keep her safe and make her happy."

Zack arched an eyebrow. "You can tell all of that from a facial expression? Bullshit."

"Okay, so I'm putting my own interpretive spin on it, but…" His eyes met Zack's, and the asshole smirked. "I'm not wrong."

"You're a jackass."

"Oh, sure, but I'm also right."

Zack scoffed out a laugh and twisted his mouth into a scowl, letting his eyes roam over the gym, not sure what to say.

"And Alexa? She looks at you like she could drown in you and die happy for it."

"Okay, easy there, Shakespeare," Zack said, grabbing at the opportunity to rib Jamie and get himself out of the hot seat. "Are you going to tell Sean?"

"If I do, he'll turf you from the case."

Zack closed his eyes for a second, his jaw clenched so tight it hurt. "I know."

Jamie met Zack's eyes, his expression serious. "Do you think this will negatively impact your ability to keep her safe?"

Zack shoved a hand through his sweaty hair and tugged at the back. "Fuck no. And…God, Jamie, I need to be there. I can't get booted."

Jamie nodded slowly. "I get it. That's why I'm not going to say anything."

"You're not?"

"Nah. But if I think you're slipping, I will. Stay focused, De Luca."

Relief filtered through him. "I will." He headed toward the showers, slapping Jamie on the shoulder as he passed.

"Don't forget Mighty Mick's advice. It'd be a distraction you don't need right now, man. In a lot of ways."

Jamie's warning followed Zack into the locker room, and he knew he was right. He also knew he wasn't going to be able to stay away from Alexa. Everything was snarled up—he and Alexa, his need to protect her, his inability to walk away, the dangerous game they were playing with her father, the fact that tomorrow's fight was instrumental to his career. He stripped and cranked the shower on, letting the hot water pelt his tense muscles. He'd handle it. For Alexa, he'd fucking handle it.

CHAPTER 16

Alexa sat in her bed, propped up against the headboard, staring down at her e-reader but completely unfocused. Although it was early, not even nine, she'd crawled into bed almost an hour ago. Sierra had gone out for a drink with Taylor, and although she'd invited her, Alexa hadn't felt like joining, in part because she was avoiding Taylor. She had enough stuff to work through right now, and she could handle only so much at once.

She'd last seen Sean in the living room, a Dodgers game on the TV, his laptop open in front of him and a few folders spread over the couch, his bare feet propped on the coffee table. She hadn't wanted to intrude when he was clearly busy working and had headed upstairs.

Not that Sean and Sierra made her feel as though she were intruding. Not at all. She just felt so damn out of place, as though she didn't belong anywhere. Not even in her own life, so much of which had been a lie, apparently.

She'd thought that maybe today would feel different

somehow. After planting the bugs. After Zack. But it had turned into a nothing day, like so many other nothing days. The sky hadn't fallen, and it wasn't until she'd crawled into bed that she realized she'd spent the day waiting for just that to happen.

She'd barely seen Zack, as he'd been busy training, getting ready for his fight, and she hadn't left the house. Sierra had had meetings and been out most of the day, and Sean had been at the office. Ian had stayed in the house, keeping an eye on things, and, while she liked him, he wasn't much of a talker. She'd had way too much time to think and wonder and worry, and by the time she'd eaten dinner, her brain had been exhausted. She'd tried shutting it off with a movie but hadn't been able to focus. So she'd tried her book instead, but even the latest Nora Roberts—normally her favorite—couldn't hold her attention. Her mind was too busy devouring itself with everything going on.

A knock sounded softly at her door.

"It's open," she called, dropping her e-reader into her lap. She'd expected to see Sierra, but Zack poked his head in.

"Hey. Just wanted to check in on you," he said, stepping in and leaning against the wall, his arms crossed in front of him. She smiled, warmth infusing her at the sight of him. At the sound of his voice. Ever since she'd met him, she'd loved the sound of his voice. It wasn't deep or rumbly but still pleasantly masculine. Gentle, and almost quiet, with a melodic quality. Confident and friendly and warm. There was no hint of the violence he was capable of in his voice. He didn't sound like a guy who could choke someone out, who could make them bleed with his bare hands. But he was, quiet, friendly voice and all.

She shrugged. "I'm okay. I missed you today."

"Missed you too, princess. Busy day."

"Are you nervous? About your fight?"

He shook his head, his mouth easing up in a crooked smile. "Nah. I'm ready."

She nodded, and when his eyes met hers, a heavy silence hung between them. Alone, in a bedroom, the air practically crackling. "Do you…want to come sit with me?" Still holding his gaze, she patted the spot beside her on the bed. A question. An invitation.

His eyebrows rose, but he didn't say anything. He shut the door behind him but then returned to his spot against the wall, arms once again crossed over his chest. She traced the contours of all those battle-earned muscles with her eyes, the way the fabric of his dark-blue T-shirt clung to them. Dipping lower, she took in the black belt looped around his waist, his jeans, his sneakers. The hard, muscled length of him.

He cleared his throat softly. "I'm fighting tomorrow. We can't have sex." The word *sex* filled the space between them, the way a heartbeat fills a chest, taking up so much room and making its presence felt because it's *alive*.

She licked her lips, her heart galloping away in her chest, and then she smiled. "That thing from *Rocky*'s true?"

A smile worked its way across his face, and he tipped his head. "Not really. It's mostly just tradition and routine."

"How long before a fight do you abstain?"

"At least a few days, sometimes longer. Long enough to bring some pent-up energy into the cage."

Blood rushed to her cheeks at the thought of Zack's pent-up energy, unleashed and focused on her. Something hot surged up through her chest, and then she laughed, pressing a hand to her mouth, a sudden giddiness bursting free.

Zack somehow managed to smile with his mouth and frown with his eyebrows at the same time. "What?"

She laughed harder, her eyes watering. "I'm sorry. I'm just having kind of a surreal moment. Like it's totally normal for you and me to have this casual conversation about sex." She flopped back against the headboard and wiped the tears from her eyes. "I don't even recognize my life anymore."

He chuckled softly and then toed off his shoes. "I'm coming over there, but no funny business."

She laughed again, and God, it felt good to laugh. "You bring all that sexy over here, and I won't be held responsible for my actions."

He strode toward the bed. "So you think I'm sexy?" He sat down beside her, his back against the headboard, his legs stretched out in front of him. Slipping an arm over her shoulders, he pulled her in against him, tucking her head under his chin.

"Yes. So much that I don't know what to do with it." It was the truth, and it felt good.

He cursed softly and kissed the top of her head. Then he sighed. "Jamie knows."

She frowned but couldn't bring herself to raise her head. It felt too good to be nestled into him. "Knows?"

"He was with Morales while you were activating the listening devices. He heard us. I guess Morales did too."

She sat up, worry and guilt slicing through her and disrupting the peace she'd found snuggled against him. "Shit. Are you in trouble?"

He shook his head. "He's not going to say anything. I need to keep you safe, and he gets that." He stroked a hand up and down her back, and she sighed, relaxing back into him.

How was it possible that just being held felt so incredibly good? So incredibly right?

"You're risking a lot," she said, tracing a hand up the center of his chest.

"Worth it." He kissed her temple and slipped a hand under her chin, tipping her face up. "So fucking worth it." His brown eyes shone down at her, full of a dark, glistening intensity.

She raised her hand from his chest and stroked his cheek, his thick stubble rasping against her palm. "I need to ask you something." It was a question that had been bouncing around her brain all day.

"Anything."

She settled back down against him. Before anything else could happen between them, she needed to understand. "A year ago…why *did* you choose Taylor and not me?"

His chest rose and fell, a soft, steady movement against her cheek. "Because I assumed there was no chance in hell a woman like you would even be interested in me. You're practically Hollywood royalty, and you're gorgeous and have this amazing personality. It was intimidating." He paused, and she let it sink in. *Zack* had been intimidated by *her*. It felt…unbelievable, almost. He continued. "And you were so shy around me. I just thought…" He shrugged. "That I was right. That you weren't into me."

Alexa thought back to a year ago, and she wasn't sure if she wanted to laugh or cry. "I was shy around you because you're so hot and sweet and funny and normal, and I was pretty sure I didn't deserve all of that." At the time, still living with her parents, she hadn't felt worthy of a man like him. But things were different now. Her life might've been falling apart, but she felt more whole than she had in a long time.

"But you're amazing. Why would you think that?" Such a simple question, with such a complicated answer.

She shook her head, her insides glowing with his compliment. "I guess I was intimidated too. And then it was so obvious that Taylor did like you…"

"So you let it go," he said, finishing her thought. "If I'd known…" He let out a heavy sigh and held her closer.

"Don't," she said. "We can't change the past." God, did she ever know that.

"By the time Taylor and I broke up a few months later, you were dating someone else."

She nodded. She'd briefly dated Jesse Miller, another actor. Her mother had set them up, and Alexa had played along, just as she always had. "And you'd become my friend's ex."

"If I'd known that anything between us was possible, I wouldn't have let that stop me. I know it's messy, but…" He trailed off, and she raised her head from his chest to look at him. He traced his thumb over her cheekbone. "I've wanted this since the day I met you. I've never stopped wanting it. Never stopped wanting you and caring about you."

Zack acted as if it was so easy to care about her, when she'd spent her whole life being told the opposite. She didn't have words for the swelling in her chest, so she kissed him, a light, brushing sweep of her lips against his, wanting to give some of that sweetness back to him.

The enormity of everything at stake weighed her down, and she snuggled back into him, resting her hand on his firm, warm chest, the other curled between them. It was wrong for him to be in her bed. Wrong for her to pursue something with her friend's ex. Wrong for him to get involved with someone he was protecting.

And yet with his heart beating against her palm, it only felt right.

She pressed her lips against his throat, leaving a trail of soft, delicate kisses because she didn't know how else to convey everything she was feeling. Gratitude. Happiness. Fear. Worry. Doubt. Lust. And something bigger, deeper, thrilling, and terrifying, shimmering around them. It was as though the kisses the night before had dissolved the wall between them, and while everything was so new, there was also something comfortingly familiar about being with Zack.

He circled his arms around her waist, and suddenly she was in his lap, straddling him.

"No sex," she whispered, her breath whooshing out of her in a hard exhale when he sucked the skin right under her ear. His hands caressed up and down her back, and she closed her eyes.

"We're not having sex. We're making out." He kissed her neck, and she rolled her hips against him, unable to help herself. His cock was spectacularly hard and thick, even through his jeans.

God, it felt right. Real and hot and so, so right. She'd been drawn to him from the second she'd laid eyes on him, as though her body and heart had known something her brain hadn't wanted to acknowledge: that maybe, *just maybe*, he was meant for her.

He brought his mouth to hers and kissed her, slowly and deeply, as their hips moved together. His tongue stroked into her mouth, matching the rhythm of his hips, and she kissed him back, the slide of his tongue against hers sending hot shivers through her. She wove her hands through his soft, thick hair, and he groaned quietly against her mouth and then broke the kiss, his chest rising against hers.

"You see what you do to me? God, Alexa," he whispered, his voice hoarse, his cock pressed against her thigh. A surge of power charged through her, unlike anything she'd ever felt before, and she wanted to chase it, needing more. Tentatively, she rocked against him and was rewarded with a husky groan. "I should go," he said in a tortured whisper, just before he crushed his mouth to hers in a searing kiss, his lips hot and urgent against hers.

"I know." Her mouth moved against his as she slipped her hands under his T-shirt, tracing her fingertips over the ridges of his abs.

He pulled back slightly, his eyes dark and hooded. "Sean's home. We might get caught."

"We might," she agreed. His cock twitched against her, and she let out a soft sigh.

He kissed her, slow and teasing, cupping her ass and rocking her against him again, the ridge of his cock sliding against her, and even through her yoga pants and panties, she felt that slide like an electric shock.

"We should probably stop," she said, her voice a little shaky.

"Do you want me to stop?" he asked, his brown eyes holding hers. The air between them thickened, pulsing with tension, and she slowly shook her head.

"Ah shit," he ground out before kissing her again, a little harder, a little rougher than before, and she realized just how much he'd been holding back. He kissed her until she couldn't breathe, until she couldn't think, until she couldn't feel anything but him. Kissed her and kissed her and kissed her. Never in her life had she been so thoroughly kissed.

"But no sex," she managed to gasp out several minutes later.

"We're not having sex. We're making out." His voice was husky, and, with one arm wrapped around her waist, he caressed her breast, his knuckles brushing over her nipple through the cotton of her shirt. She arched into his touch, moaning softly, raw need spreading through her like a fire. He kissed her again, his tongue sliding against hers, sending heat spiraling through her and feeding the growing throb between her legs.

She felt as though she were about to burst into flames, everything in her body heavy and hot and aching for something more. It was intense and not anything she was used to. This gnawing hunger, the sensation of climbing toward something was almost too much to bear. And all they were doing was kissing and touching, fully clothed.

With a ragged breath, he broke the kiss. "Take your shirt off. I want to see you." He rolled her nipple through her shirt, and she jerked, hot pleasure arrowing through her body and feeding the pulsing ache between her legs.

"But no sex," she said, leaning back slightly and reaching for the hem of her T-shirt.

His jaw clenched. "Take your shirt off."

She did, pulling it off over her head and letting it fall to the floor beside the bed. As his eyes devoured her, he raised his hands and traced the curves of her breasts, studying them as though he'd never seen a naked woman before.

"Do you have any idea how beautiful you are?" he asked, his voice almost a whisper, his hands still moving so, so gently over her bare breasts. When he looked at her like that, with reverence and awe and lust, she *felt* beautiful in a way she never had before, especially with a man. It was a golden truth, and warmth radiated through her chest, a happiness almost too big to hold.

She cupped his face and kissed him softly. "You make me feel beautiful."

"God, Alexa. My God." He buried his face in her neck, still caressing her breasts. His thumbs traced over her nipples, and her breath came in sharp gasps. He caught her earlobe between his teeth and tugged gently, sending tingles of pleasure racing down her spine. She pulled impatiently at his shirt, and he leaned forward so he could pull it off and toss it to the side. She fell against him, her breasts pressed into his bare chest, and the sensation of being skin to skin with him almost overwhelmed her. The warm slide of his bare skin against hers felt like joy, felt like desire, felt like home. Something inside her was unraveling and tightening at the same time, and she needed more. Needed Zack.

They weren't alone in the house, and they weren't supposed to have sex, but she couldn't bring herself to stop kissing him, stop touching him. She'd wanted this—exactly this—for too long. She didn't care about anything but Zack and how good he felt. How good he was making her feel. And God, it felt good *not* to care about anything except feeling good.

His mouth trailed lower, and he kissed a path across one breast and then the other. He pulled her nipple into his mouth, sucking and licking and biting, holding her in place with an arm around her waist, his hand caressing her other breast as she writhed against him. Pleasure speared through her, and she clenched her thighs, feeling achy and empty.

"Oh God, that feels good," she said, and he responded with a low, growling moan, moving his mouth to her other breast.

"So damn beautiful," he said, his mouth moving against her.

Another surge of power zapped through her, and she slid her hand lower, over his gorgeously muscled chest, his firm, taut stomach, and down to his cock, hard and straining fiercely against his zipper. She ran the tips of her fingers over him, smiling when she felt his cock twitch as though jumping toward her touch.

"Jesus fucking Christ," he said, his voice barely above a whisper, and brought his mouth back to hers again. "We should stop," he murmured against her mouth, his thumb playing over her nipple as she stroked him, his other hand cupping the back of her head. He pulled back, and she wanted to beg him not to stop. It was a greedy, selfish thing to ask, and she should feel guilty, but she didn't. She was so wound up with wanting that she didn't have room for anything else.

But then his eyes, hot and dark, met hers. It was as though someone had lit a fuse, igniting the air between them, and she knew they weren't going to stop. Knew it and could've cried, she was so relieved.

For the first time in her life, she understood why everyone was so obsessed with sex.

He pinched her nipple, drawing a moan from her, and she brought her trembling fingers to his belt buckle, the hot, aching throb deep inside her growing more and more intense with each touch, every kiss. One hand still on her breast, he hooked a thumb into the waistband of her yoga pants, toying with them, teasing her as he slid his thumb against the fabric.

"Yes," she moaned, and he started to slide them down, easing them over her hips. She stood and kicked free of them, but then stilled, the tiniest twinge of guilt working its way through the haze of lust clouding her senses. "What about no sex before a fight? The routine? The tradition?"

Zack swung his legs over the edge of the bed, facing her, and he gently gripped her hips and pulled her into the cradle of his parted legs. He kissed and nipped at her stomach, and she shook a little. Shook with wanting and needing and feeling and falling.

His hands still on her hips, he looked up at her. Holding her gaze, he hooked his thumbs into her panties and started working them down. "Fuck tradition. I need to be inside you."

This wasn't a fantasy. This was real. Zack was actually saying these words to her, and she could tell from the intensity shining in his eyes that he meant them. Her heart burst open, its insides spilling everywhere like something hot and melty.

She whimpered, almost overwhelmed with the intensity of the moment. Of what they were about to do, and what it meant to her.

"Fuck, princess. Look at you," he murmured as her panties landed around her ankles. She blushed under the hunger of his gaze, heat crawling across her chest. He smiled and, as he kissed her hip, slid one finger between her lips, stroking lightly over her clit. "God, you're so wet."

"From making out," she managed to say, although the last word barely came out because he'd circled his thumb over her clit. She felt him smile against her hip, and then he eased two fingers into her. She clamped a hand over her mouth to stifle the loud moan that tried to escape.

"I want to go slow and taste every single inch of you," he said, looking up at her as he fucked her slowly with his fingers. "I want to spend hours finding all the different ways you like to be touched and kissed. Finding out what turns you on. What makes you come." He curled his fingers inside her, and her hips jumped toward him as pleasure shot through her body. He feathered his thumb over her clit, and she let out a tiny, gasping moan, trying desperately to be quiet. "But I can't. I can't wait. I'm about to lose my mind." His free hand palmed the flesh of her ass, and she felt his hand tremble slightly.

The idea that he was just as gone as she was sent lust swirling through her, and she clenched around his fingers. "I don't want to wait. I just want you."

He pulled his fingers free, and he stood. He was so tall, so broad up close like this, and she traced the contours of his chest, her pulse pounding in her ears, in the tips of her fingers, between her legs. The soft clink of metal drew her attention downward, and she watched his big hands as he undid his belt and opened his jeans. Watched as he pushed first his jeans and then his boxer briefs down. Watched as his thick, hard cock snapped free of his clothing.

She bit her lip, worry flickering through her. "Um…whoa." Tentatively, she reached for him and stroked him, his cock heavy and hot in her hand. She couldn't fit her grip all the way around him, and she swallowed, nervous anticipation fluttering low in her stomach. He was big. Really big. Gorgeously big. Thick and long and…*big*.

He flexed his hips, pushing into her grip. God, she loved how he felt in her hand, velvety soft skin covering his impossibly hard cock. When he slid his arms around her waist and kissed her, it was soft and sweet, and she knew he was trying to reassure her. "I'll go slow." He kissed her again and then kissed a path from her mouth to her ear, teasing her earlobe with his tongue. "But you're so goddamn wet that I don't think we'll have a problem."

Even though she could see the pile of their discarded clothes, could feel the air against her bare skin, could feel Zack's hands stroking up her back, his mouth on her neck—hell, his hard, naked cock was *in her hand* and she was *stroking* him—it still felt surreal. She was about to have sex with Zack De Luca.

Doubt seized her, and she bit her lip. Did he like how she was touching him? Did he like how her body looked? Felt? What if she disappointed him in some way? What if he found her lacking? What if he regretted breaking his "no sex before a fight" rule for her?

What if what if what if. The two syllables thrummed through her.

"Hey," Zack said softly, tipping her face up to his, "you're shaking."

"I'm nervous." It was a half truth, but all she could give, because, despite her doubts, she still wanted him. Wanted to be with him.

He cradled her face with one hand. "Don't be. Nothing to be nervous about." He ran a hand through her hair and stroked the other down her back, caressing her ass. "We've both wanted this." He kissed her, so slowly, so sweetly, that it was like honey flowing over her. "We both know this is right."

His words settled over her, and she stepped away from him, pulling him toward the bed. He smiled, that crooked smile that lit up his whole face. "Hang on." He bent and pulled his wallet from the pocket of his jeans to retrieve a condom. She sank down onto the bed as she watched, riveted, transfixed, unable to take her eyes away from him, completely fascinated by his body, by the way it looked and moved and smelled. He tore open the wrapper and rolled the condom on, and as he moved toward her, she scooted back on the bed, her heart fluttering in her chest.

He eased his weight down on top of her, and she wrapped her arms around him, never wanting to forget this moment. The brush of his skin against hers sent ripples of need coursing through her, and she arched up into him, wanting more. Wanting everything.

Supporting his weight on one arm, he reached between them and pushed slowly into her, only an inch, maybe less. Enough that she could feel him. Enough that she wanted more.

"God, Zack. Yes. I want you inside me," she whispered. He held her gaze as he slowly worked his cock into her, his eyes soft and full of emotion. Inch by inch, he stretched and filled her, and she felt like a spring, not coiled tight, but being stretched in opposite directions, everything inside her pulling and tightening. Pressure and warmth and throbbing that all felt so damn good she didn't have words for it.

He pulled all the way out and then slid back into her, burying himself to the hilt this time. She bit her lip to stop herself from crying out and wrapped her legs around his hips. He held completely still, and she traced her hands down his back, marveling at all the hard, rippling muscle beneath warm skin. He flexed his hips, somehow pushing in deeper, and she arched up into him, pleasure flaring through her.

Supporting his weight on his arms, he gazed down at her, his eyes so, so bright. "Alexa," he said, her name a hoarse whisper.

"I know." He stroked in and out of her once, and she held her breath, trying to be quiet. "I know."

She was in love with Zack De Luca. With his body

inside hers, she couldn't deny it—didn't want to deny it—any longer. He pressed his forehead against hers and pumped his hips, establishing a slow, steady rhythm, and something deep inside her started to build, hot, twisting pressure.

"You feel incredible," he said, gazing down at her with those smoldering brown eyes as he fucked her slowly, sweetly. "I've never…" He kissed her, and she kissed him back with everything she had, because she'd never either. Never and probably wouldn't for the rest of her life.

He rolled his hips as he slowly pulled out, and she gasped, pleasure slicing through her. "Do that again," she begged, whimpering when he complied. He kissed her again, and she shuddered, the drag of his cock inside her exquisite, igniting all her dormant nerve endings. His breath came harder as he set a new, faster rhythm, rolling his hips and stroking deep, urgent passion spreading between them and pulling them down like an undertow.

"Yes, Zack," she panted, over and over again, losing herself in the intense, glorious fullness of his cock inside her. He thrust into her harder, and she couldn't stop the surprised, gasping moan from escaping her mouth as an orgasm crested over her. Her body started to shake, and she clenched around him, her orgasm bursting through her in heavy throbs.

"That's it, sweetheart," he ground out, still pumping in and out of her as she pulsed around him. "Come."

She twisted her head and pressed her face into the mattress as he took her higher and higher with each stroke in and out of her drenched, throbbing pussy. Higher until she didn't know what she wanted or needed. Until she couldn't talk or think or breathe. She could only come, wave after wave of hot pleasure slamming into her.

His face pressed into her neck, he slipped a hand between their bodies and found her clit. One slide of his fingers over her wet, swollen flesh, and she clenched again, coming harder. She felt as though she'd burst open, and he thrust into her hard and deep several more times before every muscle in his body went rigid, and she felt the pulse of his cock inside her as he came.

A silence fell over the room, and for several seconds neither of them moved. Then, without a word, he pulled out of her and disappeared into her bathroom. When he returned he settled against the pillows and pulled her into his arms. She laid her head on his chest, trying to breathe against the turmoil of emotions surging through her.

He trailed his fingers across her back and kissed the top of her head. "Goddamn, princess," he said, his voice a little rusty sounding.

She smiled against his chest, her limbs boneless. "Goddamn yourself."

He tipped her face up to his and kissed her, lingering and tender. "Thank you. That was…" His eyes were once again soft with emotion. "God, that was fucking beautiful."

Her eyes stung, and she pressed them shut. She took a deep breath and then another, her chest squeezing as her throat thickened.

She felt good. Too good, and everything burned. Her mind spun clumsily, and her body hummed with the afterglow of what they'd just done. What *she'd* just done. She blinked and swallowed, holding everything back, but it was no use. He'd cracked the dam, and she wasn't sure she could contain it, what felt like magnitudes. Her shoulders trembled slightly, and Zack's arms tightened around her.

"Hey, you okay?" he asked, stroking a hand up and down her back.

"No. Yes. I don't know." She sighed and squeezed her eyes shut as she tried to find the words to say everything she wanted to say. A tear slipped free and rolled down over her cheek, landing on Zack's chest.

"Shit, Alexa, did I hurt you?" With an impossibly gentle touch, he nudged her face up, forcing her to meet his gaze. His eyes were dark, intense, and full of worry.

"No. Not at all."

He relaxed slightly. "Then what's wrong? Talk to me."

She chewed the inside of her lip. "I've never told anyone this before."

He stroked a hand over her hair. "You can tell me anything, princess. Anything."

It didn't matter that her skin was prickling, or that her stomach was churning, or that her brain spun with fifty million different versions of how this could go very, very wrong. Not only did she owe it to him—to them—to tell him the truth of her past, but she found that she actually wanted to let someone in for the first time.

"You asked me in the car, the other day, about how my father had hurt me."

The hand that had been stroking her hair stilled. "Yeah."

"When…God, I don't even know how to say it. It sounds so pathetic."

Zack didn't say anything, just kissed the top of her head. But she needed to tell him. She'd lived with it for so long, running from what had happened. She was exhausted from carrying it, from carrying the shame, the sadness, the anxiety, alone. And if they were actually going to do this, to start something together, she owed him the truth.

"When I was a teenager, he made me do things." She raised her head and met Zack's eyes. "He forced me to have sex with men." The words hung in the air, heavy and loud. It was her truth. She'd used her body, had done things she'd hated, and was still dealing with the fallout, both emotional and physical.

For several seconds Zack didn't speak. His brow furrowed and his nostrils flared, but he didn't say anything. It was amazing the kind of eternity five seconds could contain. Finally, he cleared his throat softly. "What kind of men?"

"Directors. Producers. Sometimes so I could get a role. Sometimes so he could. Sometimes just because one of his friends wanted me."

"Motherfucker." He spoke the words vehemently but barely above a whisper. "God, Alexa, I'm sorry. I'm sorry for what he did, and I'm sorry I didn't beat the shit out of him yesterday."

She swallowed, absorbing his words. He hadn't pushed her away. He knew what she'd done, and she was still in his arms.

"I'm not asking this to blame you, because clearly he's the one at fault here. You didn't do anything wrong."

You didn't do anything wrong. Such simple words, and although she'd heard them from her therapist, had even said them to herself in the mirror, she hadn't started to believe them until they came from Zack. As though a part of her had been waiting for him, all this time.

"Asking me what?"

"Did you ever try to say no?"

She nodded, and more silent tears slipped free. "When I was seventeen, I stood up to him. He broke my arm, and I still had to do it anyway. I didn't say no again."

"Son of a bitch." Another whispered curse, and his arms tightened around her. Holding her closer, not pushing her away. "Does your mom know about this?"

Alexa nodded, and she was unable to keep the resentment out of her voice. "Yeah. She knows." She tucked a strand of hair behind her ear, feeling lighter the more she talked. "I think that's why the Brotherhood stuff made sense to me as soon as I heard it. He controls everyone, and has a use for everyone. This was his use for me." She laughed sadly. "*Is* his use for me, if he thinks he can just give me to Kramer. To him, I'm not his daughter. I'm a convenient whore." Her voice broke on the last syllable, tears slipping free as she spoke the truth of how she saw herself.

"I'm so sorry," said Zack. He brushed his nose against her cheek, and when she looked up, he kissed her, his lips firm and warm against hers. "I'm so sorry he did that to you. I'm so sorry you felt trapped. I hate that he did that to you. I hate him for it." His voice shook with anger.

"A part of me feels so stupid that I didn't see what was happening around me. In hindsight I see it now. But I was usually too caught up in my own shame to look outside of myself."

Zack pulled back a little and traced his thumb over her cheekbone. "Don't you dare blame yourself for this. You didn't do anything wrong. He exploited you. The people who should feel ashamed are your father and those men."

She let his words wash over her, absorbing them and basking in them as she settled back down against him, her cheek pressed to his heart. Objectively, she'd known all this. But to hear it from someone she cared about, someone she'd been vulnerable with and opened up to…Somehow it meant more and gave her the courage to keep going. To keep opening up until her entire heart was stretched wide, all of it there for him to see. "I learned how to detach during sex. How to just kind of float away until whoever was on top of me was done. It was the only way I could get through it. It didn't feel good to me."

"*Fuck.* Shit, Alexa. I'm so sorry. I'm so sorry." He spoke the words against her temple. She'd told him her secret, the pain and darkness she carried deep inside, and the world hadn't ended.

"It's been lonely," she whispered, cracking herself open with more truth. But if she didn't open herself up, she couldn't let any light in.

"You don't need to be lonely. Not anymore."

She wiped at her cheek with one hand, the tears still flowing, slowly but steadily. "I've never come during sex before. This…this was the first time."

He was quiet, and she once again raised her head to look at him. He was smiling, big and wide. Not judging her, or leaving, or any of the horrible things she'd convinced herself she deserved. She laughed softly. Actually laughed, despite the scars she'd just shown him.

That was what he did to her. Orgasms aside, she felt so…God, she felt vibrant with him. Alive and happy and as if she'd found home. "You seem pretty pleased with yourself."

He arched an eyebrow, the huge smile still in place. "You're damn right I am." He kissed her forehead, and then her temple, and then her mouth, slowly and sweetly. "But not because of what it says about my skills. Because of what it says about how *you* feel about *me*."

She felt giddy and greedy and alive with the rush of relief coursing through her. "I never imagined that you and I could…I can't even…" She shook her head, and he kissed her again. She sighed deeply, inhaling his warm, faintly musky scent. She wanted to wrap that scent around herself.

Dipping her head, she kissed a slow path over his collarbone, ending at his shoulder, each kiss a tiny thank-you for understanding. For not judging. For having her back. She kissed the badly drawn dragon there, wanting every piece of him for herself.

He reached down and laced his fingers through hers, bringing their hands together over his heart. He knew the whole of her, and still wanted her. The surge of joy and relief that rushed through her was so powerful that she could've held up the moon.

"I don't know what to say, Zack. I've never felt like this before."

He rubbed his thumb over the back of her hand. "Me neither."

She wasn't sure how long they lay together in silence, twined around each other, basking in each other. In their connection. In the freedom of knowing the truth. It didn't matter, because it wasn't long enough.

"I wish I could stay." He raised their joined hands to his mouth and kissed her fingertips one by one as he spoke. "I wish I could spend the night making you come over and over again, until neither of us can move. I wish I could fall asleep holding you. I wish I could wake up beside you. I want all of that, so badly."

Her heart picked up its pace even though she hadn't moved. "I wish you could stay too." But he couldn't, and they both knew it. He'd already stayed too long.

With a heavy sigh, he slipped away and pushed up off the bed, then picked up the condom wrapper and shoved his legs into his jeans. He gathered the rest of his things and then padded barefoot to the door, listening. After a few seconds, he crossed back toward the bed and kissed her, hard and deep.

"Good night, princess."

He disappeared into the hallway and closed the door almost silently behind him. Alexa flopped down on the bed, feeling like a new person.

For the first time, she felt free and happy.

CHAPTER 17

The exterior of the Los Angeles Memorial Sports Arena glowed shamrock green in the night, two giant spotlights shining up into the sky and sweeping back and forth, crossing beams over and over again in a steady rhythm. In front of the arena, a lit-up sign flashed "Monsters of the Cage: Los Angeles Fight Night."

Alexa swung her legs out of Sean's SUV and touched her black pumps down on the pavement, grabbing Carter's massive arm to steady herself. Sean pulled away from the curb to park, and she waited with Carter. They'd pulled up to the back entrance of the arena, for both privacy and security reasons, and she could hear the excited buzz of the crowd out front. When they'd driven past, hundreds of people had milled about, filtering into the arena.

She'd agonized over what to wear tonight and had finally opted for a simple black sleeveless dress with a deep V-neck and a flared skirt that swished just above her knees. She'd wanted to look the part of his girlfriend, pretend or otherwise, although they weren't really in pretend mode tonight.

"Whoa," she said, glancing at Carter. "I don't think I realized how *big* this is." She gestured at the lights, the sign, and the swarms of people around them.

"MMA's pretty popular, and this is one of the biggest promotions in Southern California. Should be at least ten thousand people here tonight."

"Promotion?"

"It's just another name for the organization behind the fights. A league, kind of. The more high-level fighters, the more sponsors and revenue, the bigger the promotion, the bigger the payouts, the bigger the opportunities. Each promotion has a matchmaker, a guy who sets the fights based on what he thinks will bring in the biggest revenue. More crowds, more betting. It's a sport, but it's also prizefighting. Tonight's the light heavyweight championship, Zack's weight class. If he wins, he'll become the champion, and there's a good chance he'll be offered a contract with a much bigger promotion." Carter smiled at her as they made their way toward the back door. Her heart fluttered, nerves and worry flitting through her. "Over the past few years, he's worked damn hard to get here."

A surge of pride flowed through her. She knew what this meant to him, and she wanted so badly for him to win. Her heart thumped in her chest, anticipation swirling through her.

She smiled as Sean and Sierra caught up with them, and they made their way inside. Carter led them through a series of hallways and showed their passes to a security guard all in black. He pointed at a set of steps, and Carter led the way again, ushering them into a box that gave them a completely unobstructed view of the cage. The box wasn't luxurious, but it was private and comfortable. And they weren't alone.

Alexa smiled and nodded at an attractive couple in their early fifties who were already seated, realizing suddenly that they must be Zack's parents. A man, maybe thirtyish, sat beside them, and Alexa noticed he had the same brown eyes and the same mouth as Zack. He said something to his mother, and his voice bore an unmistakable resemblance to Zack's. His brother. They were his family. Here to support him and cheer him on. When was the last time her family had cheered her on? Supported her in any kind of loving, healthy way?

Never. There'd never been anything healthy or loving about her relationship with them. Nothing.

"Hi," Alexa said, smiling tentatively at them, not entirely sure what to say next.

The woman smiled warmly at her, honey-brown curls falling around her pretty face, and Alexa recognized Zack's brown eyes. "Hi. You must be Zack's friends."

"We are," said Sean, extending his hand. "I'm Sean, I work with Zack. This is my fiancée, Sierra, and Carter Davis, another member of the Virtus team. Should be a few others joining us soon. And this is Alexa."

Zack's brother looked at her, his eyes widening in recognition. "You're Alexa Fairfax," he said, his tone almost turning it into a question. Before she could answer, he stood and shook her hand. "I'm Chris, Zack's brother. I'm the older one, but I stopped referring to myself as his *big* brother about fifteen years ago." She couldn't help but laugh, and she felt herself relax a little. Despite the resemblance between them, Chris was at least six inches shorter than Zack. Although to be fair, at six foot three, Zack was taller than almost everyone.

"I'm Donna, Zack's mom," said the woman. "And this is my husband, Mark." The man stood and shook everyone's hand, and she noticed a definite resemblance to Zack. Studying his parents was like putting a puzzle together. He had his mother's eyes and mouth shape, but his father's hair, cheekbones, and square jaw. Zack definitely looked more like his father, who was tall and broad-shouldered, while Chris looked more like his mother, with softer features and the same light-brown curls.

"It's nice to meet you," said Mark, releasing her hand and slipping an arm around his wife's waist.

"And you," said Alexa, smiling at them, wanting to make a good impression. It occurred to her that she'd never actually been in this situation before, meeting the parents of the man she was…whatever it was she and Zack were doing.

Sean and Sierra moved to the other side of the box, settling in, and Alexa's chest tightened at the easy way Sean threw his arm over the back of her chair and she leaned into him. Sierra whispered something in his ear that elicited a smile, and he kissed her forehead.

"How do you know Zack?" asked Chris, glancing between her and Carter, clearly wondering if she was Carter's date for the night. Donna leaned forward, apparently interested in Alexa's answer.

"Oh, Zack and I…we…" She broke off, trying to figure out what to say. "We're friends, and right now I'm also his client."

"Oh yeah?"

"Yep." She smiled and shrugged, wrinkling her nose slightly. She knew she should say more because she could tell Chris was curious as to why Zack was working for her. But she didn't have the energy to make something up, nor did she want to get into the mess of her life with these people. She'd already dragged Zack into it, and that was bad enough.

Chris studied her for a second, warmth sparkling in his eyes. "So, you wanna hear some embarrassing stories about Zack?" He winked at her.

"Oh yes, please." She smiled, a bright warmth flowing through her, settling right alongside the jealous ache in her chest. Zack's family was so nice. So normal.

"Christopher Aaron De Luca, you will *not* tell stories about your brother tonight." Donna glared at Chris and flashed Alexa a smile. "They have a sibling rivalry that makes the Civil War look like a petty squabble," she said, shrugging in a "what can you do" way. Chris rolled his eyes and shot Alexa a mock-pained look, and she laughed, happy to be included in the joke.

"Do you have any siblings?"

Alexa shook her head. "No, it's just me."

"Ah well. With your movie career, I'm sure your parents must be very proud."

She swallowed uncomfortably. "You must be really proud of Zack," she said, flipping the topic around. "This is a huge deal for him."

Mark nodded, and yet another warm smile made its way to her. "We are. He's worked so hard to get here. I'm sure it means a lot to him that so many of his friends and coworkers have come to cheer him on."

"I'm so nervous for him," she said, glancing around at the arena again. "You must be too."

Donna shrugged. "Yes and no. We've been watching him fight for years. But that's very sweet of you to be nervous for him." Her eyes swept over Alexa, her gaze slow and appraising. "So you and Zack are just friends?" Her eyebrows rose, but there was nothing threatening or challenging in her tone. Alexa couldn't remember the last time she'd had a conversation with her parents that was neither threatening nor challenging in some way.

"Yes. We have a friendly, professional relationship," she answered, hating that she had to lie to his parents. But what the hell could she say?

So many lies. Lies on top of lies. This was her world now, apparently.

Donna frowned. "Mmm. Too bad. You seem lovely." She leaned forward slightly, a conspiratorial smile on her face. "Exactly the kind of woman I'd want my son to bring home to Sunday dinner."

"Oh, wow. That's…that's so nice of you to say," she said. Her eyes stung a little at the simple compliment, and her heart had taken off at a gallop at the idea of Zack bringing her home. She and Zack hadn't defined who they were to each other, but Alexa was hopeful Donna would get her wish.

Alexa and Carter settled into the empty seats beside Zack's parents and Chris, and her chest hurt a little. She was jealous of Zack's family and sad for herself at what she'd missed out on. But Alexa knew—better than most, probably—that you didn't get to pick your family, and all you could do was play the hand you were dealt. It just sucked that her hand was full of jokers and poker rules. Unwinnable, regardless of her luck or her strategy.

Ian entered the box, hot and grumpy as usual in a gray Henley and jeans, his reddish-blond hair curling around his ears and almost to his jaw. A waitress followed him into the box, ready to take drink orders.

"You want a beer?" Sean asked, and Ian scoffed.

"That swill they're sellin' for seven dollars for a shitty little plastic cup? No."

"I'm buying."

Ian's eyebrows rose, the only change in his expression. "Oh. Well. Aye, maybe I'll have one, then."

"You're lucky I like you, you cheap bastard." Smiling and rolling his eyes, Sean waved the waitress over and pulled out his wallet, apparently buying a round for everyone.

Ian sat down at the end of the row of chairs, not saying hello, not talking to anyone. Keeping himself apart, his face, his shoulders, everything about him tense and guarded. On edge. Alexa studied him for a moment, and she rubbed absently at her chest. Ian MacAllister was a man who carried pain around, pushing the world away. She wondered if anyone else saw it. Carter stood and went to speak to him.

Taylor dropped down into the seat beside Alexa, a beer already in her hand. Her leather jacket creaked against the chair as she leaned toward Alexa. "Hey, you," she said, poking her in the leg. "How you holding up?"

Alexa flashed her a quick smile and then glanced down at her lap, where her hands were clenched together. The waitress passed her a beer, and she took it, grateful for something to hang on to. She hadn't expected to see Taylor tonight, and she found she was having a hard time looking her in the face.

She'd had smoking hot sex with her friend's ex. She glanced at Taylor, and the vision of Zack above her, moving inside her as she came, seared through her. Blood rushed to her cheeks, and she took a big swallow of beer.

"Hey, you okay?" asked Taylor, leaning forward, her forearms braced on her legs.

"As okay as I can be, I guess. Yeah." She took another sip of beer.

Taylor stared at her, her head cocked slightly. She

narrowed her eyes, and Alexa fought the urge to squirm. Taylor's eyes swept down Alexa's body and then widened. "You had sex!"

Sweat broke out on Alexa's upper lip as she glanced down at her body, wondering what the hell Taylor could see. "What? What are you talking about?"

"I knew there was something different about you. You seem...I dunno, relaxed, despite everything going on. Your eyes are bright. You looked so damn sad last time I saw you, but now...you're glowing, babe." Taylor nodded wisely. "I know the signs of good dick when I see them."

Alexa opened and closed her mouth once, twice, a panicked guilt sitting like a weight on her chest. "I didn't...There's no one..." She stammered, her face hot.

Taylor threw an arm over Alexa's shoulders. "You're too cute. I didn't know you were seeing anyone."

"I'm not." She shook her head, her throat burning.

Taylor's mouth fell open, and she leaned closer, dropping her husky voice to a whisper. "Is it someone here?" She glanced around. "Carter? Ian? I bet Ian would be good. All that intensity. Mama." Taylor gave a little shiver.

"Um...aren't you newly married?"

Taylor eased back, a playful smile on her face. "Yep, and I'm disgustingly happy. But that doesn't mean I'm suddenly blind_or without imagination. And nice dodge."

"I'm not dodging anything. I think you're projecting all the, um, good dick you're getting onto me."

Taylor threw her head back and laughed. "I can't believe you said 'good dick.' I'm finally rubbing off on you."

Colt sat down beside Taylor. "I don't know what you're doing to her, but leave poor Alexa alone. Her face looks like it's gonna burst into flames," he said, shooting Alexa a wink. She didn't know Colt at all, but in that moment he was pretty much her favorite.

Carter sat back down beside Alexa, a bottle of water in his hands. As he was officially on duty tonight, there'd be no beer for him.

"I'm nervous," she said, her gaze roaming over the packed arena, the flashing jumbotron, and the official-looking people standing together in clusters near the octagon.

"You've come to his fights before, right?"

She nodded. "Yeah. But none of them were this big." And the last time she'd seen him fight was before everything had changed between them. Something deep inside her clenched as she remembered his last fight and the way he'd landed a hard punch, his gloved fist slamming into his opponent's face and sending him crumpling to the ground, blood gushing from his nose.

Sure, he could rip someone apart in the octagon, but there was a sweetness, a tenderness in the way he touched her, the protective way he held her. Brutal when necessary, but not a brute. All that power restrained until the exact right moment. All that controlled strength in her service. She wasn't sure if she should be embarrassed at how much it turned her on.

She'd seen how hard Zack worked, how much all this meant to him. And now that she understood just how huge tonight could be for his career, more than anything, she wanted to watch him kick some serious ass.

* * *

Zack fucking *De Luca*.

From his cushy leather seat in his private box in the

Los Angeles Memorial Arena, Jonathan stared out over the crowd, a crumpled piece of paper in his fist.

He'd known that motherfucker had looked familiar. And it was because he fought in Monsters of the Cage, the MMA promotion partially owned by the Golden Brotherhood.

It had been a long time since Jonathan had come to the fights, but he was damn glad he'd come tonight.

He hated being lied to, and his mind seized up. For several seconds he held perfectly still aside from the twitch in his cheek. As the arena's lights dimmed, he pulled his phone from his pocket and searched for Zack De Luca. The first hit was the Virtus Security webpage.

Zack De Luca was a bodyguard.

Alexa had lied about hiring a bodyguard. Alexa had brought someone into his house who'd lied to his face, and the reasons behind it could only be bad.

He dropped the crumpled list of fighters with their pictures, stats, and short bios to the ground. He'd deal with Alexa and her lying, her snooping, her whatever the goddamn fuck she was doing, later. Right now he wanted—no, *needed*—to crush De Luca like the insect he was. De Luca had no idea who he was fucking with. No one lied to him and got away unscathed. No one.

Jonathan scrolled to a number on his phone and dialed, then calmly raised the phone to his ear. Elijah and several others sat in the box with him. He had to handle this, and as quietly as possible. Always in control.

"Yeah?" the league's president answered.

"It's Fairfax. I want to make this title fight interesting."

A pause. "Interesting how?"

"Scratch Diaz. Put someone else in. What about Ferreira? Is he here tonight?"

"He's here, but he's a heavyweight, and he's suspended for steroid use."

Jonathan smiled. "Sounds pretty damn interesting to me. Put him in. Let's see what De Luca's made of."

Another pause. "Yes, sir."

"And you tell the ref to let them go. I'll pay a bonus if there's no stoppage."

Oh, it was going to be *fun* watching that lying bastard get beaten to a pulp. Ferreira was a roided-up maniac and had a good fifty pounds on De Luca.

"So you want De Luca to lose?"

Not just lose. Suffer. Bleed. "Make it happen."

CHAPTER 18

Zack sat on a bench in the busy locker room, adjusting his gloves and then taking a small sip of water from the bottle beside him. The roar of the crowd filtered through the cinder block walls, rushing over him, and his skin prickled hotly. He pushed off the bench and flipped his hood over his head, antsy to start his warm-up. To move. To burn off some of the nervous energy tensing his muscles. Other fighters worked with their trainers, shadowboxing or stretching throughout the locker room.

Jenks nodded at him and pulled on a pair of punching mitts. "Let's go, kid. Start with a one-two," he said, holding his padded hands up in front of him. Slipping into a loose orthodox stance, Zack threw several light punches, concentrating on his form. Nervous adrenaline pumped through him with each beat of his heart, but he knew from past experience that he needed to stay out of his head and focus on the physical. Punch, duck, weave, breathe.

Again.

Again.

If he let the mental take over, he'd lose control of the physical, and then awful things happened. Like getting knocked out with a kick to the head.

Jab. Hook. Elbow. Breathe.

Again.

He was grateful that he'd fought enough times now to know that the prefight nerves were normal. Part of the process. Because he knew that as soon as he got into the octagon, the nerves would vanish, and it would be go time, all that energy channeled into an intense focus that had seen him through sixteen professional MMA fights.

Jenks held a pad up, and Zack kneed it, imagining driving his knee into Diaz. Hitting him with punches, elbows, kicks. Pouring everything he had into the fight. He pushed away the bigger picture, not letting his mind wander down the road of what this could mean for him and his MMA career, and narrowing his world to his body and the pad, the only image in his mind Diaz and everything Zack was going to do to him.

Punch. Knee. Kick. Elbow.

Again.

Breathe.

"De Luca." Jim Donaldson, the referee for Zack's fight, stepped into the locker room, and Zack paused his warm-up. It wasn't unusual for the ref to chat with both fighters before they hit the octagon, but Zack knew Jim, and he had a strange, unreadable expression on his face. "Got some news for you."

Jenks lowered the pads and frowned. "What kinda news?"

"Still a championship fight, but it's catchweight," he said, using the term referring to matches between fighters of different weight classes. It was sometimes used when one of the fighters didn't make weight.

"No, it's not," said Zack, stepping toward Donaldson. "I'm two-oh-five. I made weight." He shook his head, confusion sending his mind racing in a way he didn't need right now.

Donaldson shook his head. "You're fighting Manuel Ferreira. President of the league made the decision just a few minutes ago."

"No, he's fucking not," said Jenks, throwing the pads down. "Ferreira's two fifty and was busted for juicing last month."

"He was reinstated," said Donaldson, rubbing a hand over the back of his neck, clearly uncomfortable with the situation.

"When?" Jenks spit out the word.

"I don't know. But he's cleared."

Jenks turned to Zack. "You don't gotta take this fight. This is bullshit. We'll file a complaint with CSAC. They won't stand for this."

"What happened to Diaz?" asked Zack. This didn't make any sense.

Donaldson shrugged, heaving a sigh. "Don't know. But he's out."

"You don't know much, do you?" said Jenks, his lip curled in disgust.

Zack dropped back down onto the bench, his heart sinking as disappointment settled over him. He could feel everything he'd worked for slipping through his fingers. The championship. The shot at a career. The chance to prove to everyone—to himself—that he could be the best at something, for once in his life.

He couldn't let that happen. He couldn't walk away. Not

now. The Zack from a year ago might've walked away, but things were different now. He was stronger. Smarter.

And it was Alexa. She'd opened his eyes to what he could have, had shown him that he was worthy of the things he wanted, if only he was willing to fight for them.

"No," he said, his voice calm and steady. Even though he might get the shit kicked out of him, he knew it was the right call. "I'll fight him." He met first Jenks's eyes and then Donaldson's, who nodded curtly.

"I was offered a bonus if I let the fight go as long as possible," said Donaldson.

Jenks got right up in Donaldson's face. "That's illegal! You can't do that."

Donaldson took a step back. "And I won't. I told you that to give you a heads-up. I don't know what the hell's going on, but something's up. I'm not going to let it turn into some kind of massacre out there."

Zack snorted and stood from the bench. "It won't. Ferreira's big, but he's slow and stupid. I can take him." He wasn't sure if he was trying to convince himself or the other men in the room.

Donaldson sighed and then shrugged. "It's your funeral, kid."

* * *

"What's going on? Who's Ferreira?" asked Alexa as she returned to her seat from the bathroom.

Taylor shrugged. "No idea. They just announced the change."

Colt looked up from his phone. "Fuck me. Apparently this Ferreira dude's two hundred and fifty pounds."

Alexa let out a small gasp. "What? I thought he had to

fight someone in his weight class. Zack talked about how he had to weigh in at two hundred and five pounds this morning."

"I guess it'll be a catchweight fight," said Carter, crossing his arms over his chest. "Between weight classes."

Colt shifted in his seat, leaning forward. "Damn. Two fifty. That's fucking huge." He tipped his chin at Carter. "You're the biggest dude in here. What do you weigh?"

"About two forty."

Alexa's eyes roved over Carter's massive frame, and her stomach twisted. The guy Zack now had to fight was even bigger than Carter, apparently.

Oh God. They'd broken his "no sex before a fight" rule last night, and now the odds were stacked against him. She sat there, staring at her feet, paralyzed with worry and guilt. Clenching her hands into fists, she laid them in her lap.

"What's going on with you?" asked Taylor, and when Alexa looked up, her blue eyes were filled with concern.

"Just thinking about all the shit with my dad," she said, which wasn't completely untrue. She seemed to be dealing in a lot of half truths these days.

Taylor looked as if she was going to say more, but then another fight started, drawing her attention away. All Alexa could do now was wait and worry and sit with her guilt.

* * *

As the opening strains of AC/DC's "T.N.T." echoed through the arena, Zack hopped from foot to foot, tapping his gloves together and huffing out a hard breath before starting his walk toward the octagon, the crowd screaming, the cheering swelling and washing over him, fueling the focused, intense excitement pumping hotly through his veins. He was here to fight, and to win, and it didn't matter who the powers that be put in front of him. Even if his opponent had fifty pounds on him.

He pushed his hood down around his shoulders as he approached Donaldson, then pulled off his hoodie and T-shirt in one swift tug. As Donaldson checked to make sure Zack's mouth guard and cup were in place, Jenks smeared a thin layer of Vaseline over his brows and cheekbones to help prevent the skin from splitting open when hit. Given the size and power of Ferreira, chances were good he wasn't walking away from this unscathed. His heart throbbed in his ears in time with the music, and he bounded up the steps and into the octagon. He jogged to his corner, then jumped on the spot to keep his muscles warm and to give his pent-up energy an outlet.

"You goin' night-night, pretty boy," taunted Ferreira from the other side of the octagon, tapping his massive fists together. Zack didn't say anything, merely stared and stretched his neck from side to side. Ferreira's head was huge and slightly misshapen, with a heavy brow and protruding jaw. He was about the same height as Zack, but built like a fucking Sasquatch. About as hairy and ugly as one too. With only the space across the octagon separating them now, Zack sized up his opponent, watching him. He smiled at Ferreira, not saying anything, bouncing his back against the cage.

"What you smilin' at, you male model–lookin' son of a bitch? I can't wait to fuck that face up."

Zack just kept smiling at him, not breaking eye contact, stretching his arms out to the sides and eating up Ferreira's taunts like a fat kid at an all-you-can-eat buffet. Despite his size advantage, Zack knew Ferreira was chirping because

.he was nervous. He probably hadn't trained much since his suspension and hadn't been expecting to fight tonight.

Donaldson signaled for the men to move to the center of the octagon and touch gloves.

It was time.

* * *

Alexa had to remind herself to breathe as she watched Zack and Ferreira charge at each other from their corners the second the referee signaled the start of the fight. Right away Zack landed a hard kick against Ferreira's side, the snapping crack of shin hitting ribs loud and visceral. Ferreira countered with a hard punch, connecting with Zack's face. He absorbed the impact and hit Ferreira with a right-left combination, sending him backward a few feet. Her heart leaped up and settled somewhere around her throat, fluttering in a rapid rhythm.

For the entire first round, they traded punches and kicks, circling around each other and stalking each other across the octagon. Zack's movements were fluid and athletic, his sleek muscles flexing powerfully as he executed punch after punch, kick after kick. Brutal yet graceful. Powerful yet controlled as he dodged out of Ferreira's way time and time again. Sweat gleamed on his tan skin under the arena's bright lights.

The horn sounded, signaling the end of the first round, and Zack and Ferreira retreated to their corners. Jenks crouched in front of Zack, offering him a bottle of water while Jamie held bags of ice against him, one on his chest, the other on his back, rubbing them back and forth. Jenks shook out Zack's arms and legs, loosening him up. Zack listened intently as he spoke, nodding occasionally between small sips of water. A red mark was emerging on his cheek where Ferreira had hit him, along with a few red welts on his legs where Ferreira had landed kicks.

The welts might as well have been on her skin, because she ached just looking at them.

"It's Zack, isn't it?" Taylor's voice was quiet as she leaned toward Alexa.

She whipped her head around, her hair fanning out as she moved. "What?"

Taylor arched an eyebrow. "The good dick. It's Zack."

Alexa sucked in a breath, and her throat thickened. She blinked furiously and stared down at her lap, shame tingling over her.

"Hey." Taylor gently laid a hand on Alexa's arm. "What's wrong?"

Alexa looked up, forcing herself to meet Taylor's eyes. "I'm so sorry, Taylor."

Taylor's eyes widened. "Oh shit. You think I'm mad?"

Alexa nodded, and Taylor threw her arm over Alexa's shoulders and pulled her in for a side hug.

"Honey, I'm not mad. Zack and I are long done, and I've moved on. I want you to be happy. I love you."

"But he hurt you, and you're my friend. I should put that first."

Taylor shook her head. "Zack and I are good. Clearly he wasn't the one for me." She glanced over at Colt. "But maybe he's the one for you. You know," she said, easing back into her seat, "I can see it. You guys would be good together."

"You're seriously not mad?"

"Not even a little." Taylor glanced down at Sean and Sierra. "Does anyone know?"

"Jamie does, and now you. But no one else. It's complicated."

Taylor nodded. "Yeah, I can see that. But really. Don't let the fact that Zack and I dated hold you back, okay? Stop being so damn nice. Go after what you want."

Alexa smiled, and the knot in her stomach started to dissolve, relief sinking in. "Thanks, Taylor. I…Your blessing means a lot."

Taylor held a hand over her heart. "I would never stand between a friend and good dick."

The sixty-second break between rounds seemed incredibly short, and as the fighters rose from their stools, Alexa's battered heart pounded against her ribs. As hot as it was to watch Zack fight, it was also nerve racking. He hadn't sustained any major damage, but her heart sank with the knowledge that there were still four excruciating rounds to go, and that the odds were stacked against him.

* * *

Pain exploded across Zack's face as Ferreira's elbow smashed into him, splitting open the skin above his left eyebrow. Blood trickled down the side of his face, warm and wet, and he shot his leg out, landing a hard kick against Ferreira's thigh. Using the opportunity to create some distance, he danced back a few paces, wiping away the blood running into his eye, pain throbbing from the gash. He glanced quickly up at the clock. Still two minutes left in the third round.

Fuck.

He didn't have the luxury of time or space to poke at the dread settling low in his stomach.

He couldn't allow himself to think, even for a second,

that Ferreira might beat him and take the belt. He couldn't allow himself to think or feel, period. There was only his body and his opponent. Nothing else. There was no room for anything but an instinct honed through years of training and dozens of fights.

They circled each other, trading a few more testing jabs, each looking for an opening. Seeing his chance, Zack charged, hooking his arms around Ferreira and slamming him into the cage. Ferreira struggled against the grappling clinch, grinding and working to get free. Zack kneed him in the stomach, trying to maintain his hold, but the dude was fucking strong. Using his sweat-slicked skin to his advantage, Ferreira began to slip free. Zack readjusted his grip, hooking an arm under Ferreira's leg and slamming him to the ground with a hard, echoing thud. But Ferreira was able to scoot his hips free, and he struggled to his feet, slipping out of Zack's grasp. He was so much bigger than anyone Zack had fought before, and Zack couldn't keep him pinned down.

Ferreira kicked at Zack, but he was gassed from the clinch, and the kick was sloppy and slow. Running on instinct and seizing his opportunity, Zack grabbed his foot and pulled him down once more to the mat. This time he didn't give Ferreira the chance to scoot free, and he moved into full mount, his legs tangled with Ferreira's as he unleashed a series of brutal hammer-fisted punches, his own blood dripping from the gash above his eye onto Ferreira's chest. He poured everything he had into breaking through Ferreira's defenses, his arms heavy and aching, his lungs on fire from the lack of oxygen.

Zack landed a hard blow to Ferreira's cheek, the skin splitting open and beginning to bleed almost instantly. Ferreira's head bounced off of the ground with the impact, and he flopped an arm out to the side. Fueled by a raw, primitive hunger, Zack laid into Ferreira again, pushing past his own exhaustion, the thrill of victory brushing at his fingertips. Close enough to feel. Close enough to touch.

But not close enough that it couldn't be snatched away by the sound of the horn. That primitive hunger still humming through his veins, Zack pushed up off Ferreira and stalked back to his corner.

* * *

"What's that metal thing?" asked Alexa, her eyes glued to Zack. Now that they'd stemmed the bleeding—God, he'd been bleeding a lot—one of the trainers held what looked like a small metal iron against the gash just above his eyebrow.

"It's called an enswell," said Carter. "It helps prevent swelling."

"Really? How?" The how didn't matter, but she needed something to focus on besides the anxiety of seeing Zack bleeding and bruised. She rubbed at her chest, trying to soothe the tense ache centered there. Her eyes scanned over the floor of the octagon, drops of Zack's blood visible against the pale gray.

"It's kept in a bucket of ice water, so it's chilled," said Ian, leaning forward, his forearms braced on his thighs. "The cold constricts the capillaries, which decreases blood flow. Decreased blood flow means less swelling."

Alexa nodded, still watching Zack. "Is he winning?" she asked, the words like sawdust in her mouth. Although he was bleeding, he'd landed several solid hits and takedowns against his opponent. The fight was close.

Carter shrugged his big shoulders. "Hard to tell. They're giving each other hell, though, that's for sure."

She wanted to stop watching the fight, to stop watching Zack get hit, over and over again, but she couldn't. She'd stay, for him, and watch, no matter what.

She also wanted to rip his clothes off, wanted to use her body to make him forget about the pain he must be feeling. A primal urge sank its teeth into her, and heat flared up her spine. She wanted Zack again with an intensity that made it hard to think, amplified by the fact that Taylor knew and wasn't upset with her. She was allowed to want him, and that made her want him even more.

She glanced over at Zack's family. They'd been just as confused as everyone else at the sudden change in opponents and had cheered him on—very, very loudly in Donna's case—but were now quiet as they waited for the next round to start. Mark's face was pale, lines etched around his eyes. Chris rubbed gentle circles over his mother's back. Alexa wanted to ask how they were doing, if they were okay, but she didn't want to intrude.

The fighters rose from their stools, and Alexa's stomach clenched, anxious sweat beading along her hairline. She hoped the fight was over soon. Brutal and primitive, and so, so hot, it was almost too much to take. She rubbed her sweaty palms on the skirt of her dress, trying to breathe around the tangle of nerves and lust that made her feel as though she could jump out of her skin.

* * *

Zack's fist slammed into Ferreira's face, drawing fresh blood as the cut on his cheek reopened. Ferreira grimaced but regrouped quickly and shot his leg out, hitting

Zack hard in the right side with a forceful, snapping kick.

Pain seared through his torso, and his vision blurred around the edges. He staggered back a step, fighting to keep his hands up, and his legs wobbled beneath him. He gasped, all the air sucked from his lungs as if by a vacuum. The octagon spun for a second, and he dropped to one knee, unable to stay on his feet. The kick had hit his liver, hard, and the pain was excruciating.

Ferreira's hips swung back, and Zack knew he was lining himself up to send his knee smashing into Zack's face.

Zack saw his chance, and he grabbed it, knowing it was a long shot.

He was out of options and had to cling to hope in order to push through the pain. With a surge of energy, he pushed up to his feet and launched into a spinning kick, as fast and hard as he could. Pouring all his strength and power into the movement, he went for Ferreira's head, his leg high in the air, pain screaming down his side. With a hard, wet crack, his heel slammed into Ferreira's jaw.

Ferreira's arms dropped to his sides and he fell to the ground like a cut tree.

It was as though the entire world had slipped into slow motion, and as he lowered his leg back to the ground, all Zack could hear was his own rapid breathing, his own heart pounding in his chest. Sweat and blood trickled down his face, drops earned in the fight. Sharp, hot knives stabbed at his side with each breath.

The ref pointed at Zack, and for a second all he could feel was shock that the kick had landed and done exactly what he'd wanted it to do. Relieved triumph surged through him, and he raised his arms, letting out a victorious yell. As he looked up, sweat dripped in his eyes, blurring the bright lights into something soft and glorious. He swallowed, his throat thick with the mix of emotions that came with living a moment he'd dreamed of and worked toward for so long.

As the crowd roared, he hauled himself up on the octagon, straddling the padded top, and once again raised his arms and let out a triumphant yell. His blood rushed through his veins in time with the crowd's screams, and a surreal incredulity settled over Zack.

He'd never felt more alive.

CHAPTER 19

The private nightclub in downtown Los Angeles was smaller than Alexa had been expecting, holding only a couple hundred people. A huge marble bar dominated the front, surrounded by a crush of people, many of whom Alexa recognized from Take Down. A row of curved black leather booths lined the wall facing the dance floor, with a cluster of tables off to the other side. At the far end, a DJ worked at a table, blue and yellow lights flashing over the mass of bodies moving in time to the music.

She followed Carter to the bar, letting him cut a swath through the crowd with his broad shoulders. She craned her neck, looking around. She knew Zack had to shower and get his wounds tended to and might not show for a while, but she looked for him anyway.

"Was that a hell of a fight or what?" asked Jamie, shouting over the music as he joined Carter and Alexa at the bar. He and Carter exchanged a back-slapping man hug.

"It was fucking incredible. I thought he was done, and

then he pulls that kick out. Unbelievable," said Carter.
"You want a drink?" he asked Jamie.

"Yeah, sure. I could use a tequila. Or five." He smiled at
Alexa.

"Can I get a mojito?" she asked, standing up on her toes
and shouting to make herself heard.

Carter nodded and signaled to the bartender. She rocked
back on her heels, eyes roving over the club again. She felt
kind of awkward, just standing there not saying anything,
but the music was so loud that conversation was almost
impossible.

"So Zack's okay, right?" she asked, shouting up at
Jamie.

Just as the bartender handed her her drink, she felt a pair
of arms slip around her from behind.

"You worried about me, princess?" Zack's voice slid
over her skin like silk, and she arched her back, his breath
warm against her ear. Setting her drink down on the bar,
she spun around, still in his arms. Even in the dim, flashing
lights, she could see that his left eye was black and
swollen, the skin an angry reddish purple. The gash along
his brow had been stitched up. More bruises colored his
left cheekbone, but, battered as he was, he was standing in
front of her, solid and warm with an adorably cocky smile
on his face. He was wearing a light-blue button-down shirt
tucked into a pair of dark jeans, the collar open and the
sleeves rolled up to his elbows.

Unable to help herself, she slid her hands up his hard
chest, and she felt a rumble against her fingers. His grip
around her tightened, and he hauled her off her feet and
kissed her, his mouth hot and urgent against hers. She knew
people were probably staring at them, and she didn't care.
As if she could care about something like being stared

at when Zack's tongue was stroking against hers, sending liquid heat pooling low in her belly. She'd wanted this, exactly this, from the second he'd set foot in that cage.

After several seconds he set her down, her body sliding along his. She wobbled slightly on her heels and looked up to see that Carter and Jamie were, in fact, staring at them.

Zack shrugged, cocky smile back in place. "Adrenaline. Sorry."

Carter shook his head, smiling. "Yeah, you look real sorry."

Zack laughed and shot Alexa a wink before signaling to the bartender and ordering a gin and tonic.

She tugged on Zack's arm, and he dipped his head so she could shout into his ear. "Of course I was worried about you. What happened? Why did you have to fight that guy instead of Diaz?"

He shook his head slowly and shrugged. "I don't know. Nothing like that's ever happened to me before." The bartender set his drink down in front of him, and he picked it up and took a healthy swallow. Already, sweat was beading on the outside of the plastic cup, and she retrieved her own drink.

"It didn't seem fair that he was so much bigger than you."

"It wasn't." He shrugged again and then smiled, that cocky pull of his lips. "Didn't stop me from winning, though."

She ran a hand up his arm, so hard and solid beneath her fingers. "It was hard to watch, but I'm so proud of you."

He clinked his cup against hers. "Thanks, princess."

She took a sip of her drink and glanced up at him. Tentatively, she reached a hand up and traced the tips of her fingers over the bruises on his cheek. "Does it hurt a lot?" she asked, biting her lip.

"Nah. It looks worse than it feels." He moved a bit closer, and his breath was hot against her as he spoke directly into her ear. "I want to kiss you again, right now, so damn bad."

Heat flushed through her, and it had nothing to do with the mob of people around them. She caught his earlobe in her teeth and nipped slightly. "Watching you fight…God, Zack, it was so *hot*."

"We're going to dance," he shouted to Carter and Jamie. He didn't give her a chance to say anything before he set their drinks on the bar, grabbed her hand, and pulled her toward the dance floor.

* * *

Zack was only half-aware of the high fives, fist bumps, and shoulder slaps he received in congratulation as he tugged Alexa farther into the club. He needed an excuse to put his hands on her, to hold her close, to do *something* with the adrenaline pumping hot and fast through his veins.

He felt as though he'd been floating ever since he'd knocked Ferreira out, defying the odds and winning the championship. He'd been floating when the league's president had slapped that big gold belt around his waist. Floating when he'd answered the journalists' questions after the fight. Floating when he'd emerged from the arena, his championship belt—later sent home with Jenks for safekeeping—slung over his shoulder. Even the creeping sensation that the fight had somehow been rigged hadn't been able to bring him down. For tonight he'd push that aside. Tonight was for celebrating.

And then, with Alexa's body pressed against his, her voice in his ear telling him he was hot? Yeah, definitely floating.

Tonight. Fuck, tonight was everything.

They reached the dance floor, and he slid his arms around her waist and slipped his leg between her thighs. Immediately, they fell into a rhythm, hips rocking from side to side in time with the music pounding through the speakers. He pressed his thigh more firmly into her, and she ground against him, her dress riding up her thighs. He could feel the warmth of her pussy through his pants, and his cock twitched in response. He trailed his hand up her arm and then wove his fingers into her hair, tilting her head back. The cut above his eye was throbbing, and his side, where he'd taken the kick, was tender and almost burned, but he didn't care. Not with Alexa, so beautiful, so sweet, grinding against him the way she was.

"You feel so fucking good, princess," he said into her ear before kissing her, their tongues sliding together, matching the rhythm of their hips, the music, the thrum of his pulse. When he broke the kiss, he could feel several sets of eyes on him, and he glanced over his shoulder. A group of women had danced closer, watching him as he danced with Alexa. Watching him, not her, and one glance down at Alexa told him she'd seen it too.

Still in his arms, Alexa did a sexy half turn, pressing her ass into his hips, writhing against him in time with the music. Claiming him, showing every other woman in there that she was his, and that he was hers. She leaned forward and circled her hips against him, raking her hands through her hair, and he slid a hand up her spine, imagining how good it would feel to fuck her like this, her ass bouncing against his hips as he lost himself inside her.

Alexa leaned back against his chest, and as one song blended seamlessly into the next, they kept dancing, swaying together, hips grinding, hands stroking. He lowered his head and caught her warm scent and, unable to help himself, kissed her neck, sucking and nipping at her skin. She arched her back and raised one of her arms, spearing her fingers through his hair. His heart pounded harder as he moved his hips against her in time with the music. Even though he should've been exhausted from the fight, he was riding an adrenaline high, and the feeling of Alexa's body against his as they moved to the music was only pushing him higher.

Everything—the danger her father posed, his need to keep her safe, how incredible she'd felt beneath him last night, winning the fight—seared through him, and he scraped his teeth along her earlobe. He couldn't hear her gasp, the music was too loud, but their bodies were pressed so tightly together that he felt it.

He didn't know how long they'd been dancing. Three songs? Four? All he knew for sure was that as much as he was enjoying it, it wasn't enough. He felt so big, so alive, so awake that he craved more. "I need you." Three little words that contained so much. She turned in his arms, still swaying against him in time to the music. There was no way she couldn't feel how hard he was, pressed together and grinding the way they were.

"You can have me, champ," she said into his ear, her breasts pressed against his chest. "Any way you want me. I'm yours."

Mine. The word flashed through him, and he grabbed her hand, holding on to her as they wove their way through the crowd on the dance floor. He'd been to this club before as a bodyguard, so he knew its layout well. Well enough that he knew there was a hallway that ran along the back, containing bathrooms, an office, and, at the very end of the hallway, a small storage closet.

It wasn't ideal, but the storage closet would have to do, because if he didn't get inside Alexa within the next five minutes, he was going to lose his damn mind.

Alexa let him lead her down the hallway, and as soon as he was sure the coast was clear, he tried the door leading to the closet. He thanked every deity he could think of that it was unlocked. Alexa followed him inside, the door slamming when he cupped her ass, lifted her, and backed her up against it. He fumbled for a light switch, and a dim bulb flickered to life above them. Her pale skin seemed to glow in the faint light, and warmth radiated through his entire body. That warmth was so many things. It was need and hope and joy and…Fuck yeah. He was in love with her.

He kissed her, more gently than he wanted to, trying not to be too rough with her. He was ready to burst out of his skin, adrenaline coursing through him. She bit at his lower lip, and he groaned, kissing her harder, deeper, his hands gripping her ass. She writhed against him and let out a shuddering moan.

"Tell me no, princess. Tell me to stop," he said, because he knew he wouldn't be able to be gentle or tender with her. Not right now. He pressed his face into her neck, kissing her warm, slightly salty skin.

"Please don't stop. Please don't, Zack. I want this. I want you. Now." Her fingers fumbled with the buttons of his shirt, slipping them clumsily free.

"I'm too wound up. I need it hard, maybe even rough. Tell me no."

"Please don't stop," she said, her voice shaking. He

raised his head and pressed his forehead to hers, struggling with what he wanted. Struggling with what he needed.

She met his eyes. "Please," she whispered, and it was that tiny plea, so quiet it almost disappeared in the rumble of bass through the walls, that dissolved the last of his control.

He closed his mouth over hers and ground his hips against her, flattening her arms between them. His shirt hung open now, and she raked her nails down his chest. The sharp sting felt good, a kiss of pain that only heightened his senses, and he set her back down on her feet.

"Take your panties off." He backed away from her, only a half step, but enough to give her room to move. Holding his gaze, she slid her hands up her thighs, taking the fabric of her dress with her. She hooked her thumbs into her black thong and slid it down her legs, then stepped out of it and let it drop to the floor. Zack rubbed a palm over the bulge in his pants, his cock throbbing, his pulse pounding in his ears.

"Good. Now turn around, princess. Put your hands on the door." She did as she was told, and he closed the distance between them. Roughly, he gripped her hips and pulled her against him, causing her to step back and lean forward. He pushed the skirt of her dress up around her waist and palmed the flesh of her ass, caressing and then squeezing.

"I'm going to fuck you just like this," he said, her cheeks filling his hands, the skin impossibly soft against his palms. He nudged her feet apart with one of his and dipped one hand lower. Slick heat greeted him, and he slid a finger inside her. "Holy shit." He couldn't stop the words from falling from his mouth, she was so hot and wet around him. His balls tightened, the need to get inside her obliterating everything else.

She glanced up over her shoulder at him, her cheeks pink and her eyes bright. "That's what you do to me. That's how much I want this."

He added a second finger, stretching her, not because she wasn't ready but because he didn't want this to be over. And he knew he'd be gone soon after he got inside her. Pumping his fingers, he stroked her clit with his other hand, and she arched her back, moaning.

"Could you come like this, princess? You're so wet and swollen. Do you want to come on my hand?" She clenched around him as he spoke, and he pumped his fingers harder, curling them as he circled her clit.

"I think…Maybe…Yes…Oh God, please…," she panted out, working her hips against him. He added a third finger, and her legs started to shake as she clamped down on his fingers, coming hard. She let out a low, throaty moan, and he circled an arm around her waist to keep her upright as she shook and came and shook and came. He gave her a second to ride it out and then slipped his fingers free. Palms still against the door, she glanced up at him, her face gorgeously flushed.

He sucked one of his fingers into his mouth and let out a groan. Her eyes widened, and he smiled. "You taste so damn good."

She didn't say anything, only heaved a heavy sigh and returned her gaze toward the door, arching her back and stepping her legs farther apart in silent invitation.

Hell fucking yes.

His hands shook a little as he wrenched his belt open, tugged down his zipper, and freed his cock. He pulled a condom from his wallet, then tore the foil open and slid it on in record time. Desperate for her. Chasing the adrenaline.

"Alexa." It was all he said as he gripped her hips and slammed into her. She was soaked, and he slid deep with one thrust. He knew he should go slowly at first, give her at least a second, but every cell in his body screamed *go*, and he pulled his hips back and plunged into her again, hard and deep. She was hot and tight and so damn wet around him. He thrust again and again, fucking her hard, his hands rough on her hips. With each thrust she pushed back against him, and for a second his vision faded in and out, euphoria cresting over him like a wave. Like a fucking tsunami. Her fingers curled against the wood of the door, and she moaned with each fast, hard slide of his cock inside her. Bass thumped through the walls, swallowing her sounds, and he pulled all the way free, taking a second to memorize the gorgeous sight in front of him. Alexa, sprawled against the door, back arched, ass on display. Pretty pink pussy wet and swollen. Dress around her hips.

And she'd said she was his.

The thought seared through him, and he pushed back into her, fucking her harder. The metal of his belt buckle clanked rhythmically, punctuating each thrust. Sweat trickled down his temple, stinging his swollen eye. Heat flared down his spine, and he cried out, his grip on her hips too hard, too rough, but he couldn't stop. He came, hard.

King of the goddamn fucking world.

With his heart racing in his chest, his skin tingling, his muscles finally loose, he leaned forward and laid his hand on the door beside Alexa's. Her hand was so small, so pale and delicate next to his, and his heart clenched when she inched that hand over and placed it on top of his. She wove their fingers together, knotting them against the door.

He bent over her and kissed her shoulder, her neck. For several moments neither of them spoke, and he stayed buried inside her, still hard. The music vibrated through the walls, female laughter erupting in the hall as a group made its way to the ladies' room. The pipes above them made a chugging noise. The sounds of life happened around them, but the only thing that mattered was Alexa. Beautiful, sweet, lovely Alexa, who he'd just fucked fast and dirty in a supply closet.

Some of the haze started to clear, and he kissed her shoulder again. "I'm sorry."

She turned, causing him to slip free of her body, and he missed her instantly. She raised a hand and cupped his cheek. "No. Don't. It was perfect."

He kissed her, slowly and sweetly this time, basking in her. The way she felt, and tasted, and sounded, and smelled. Every piece of her.

"Nobody…" He swallowed against the thickness in his throat and blinked, shaking his head. Jesus. The words pushed up through his chest, into his throat, filling his mouth until they spilled out. "I love you." He'd never said those words to a woman before, and he knew it was because none of those women had been Alexa.

His heart beat frantically in his chest, and she laughed, her entire face lighting up. "Because I let you fuck me in a storage closet?"

He smiled. "No. Because it's impossible not to love you. Because you're everything I never even realized I wanted, or needed. Because I can hardly breathe when I look at you, you're so damn beautiful. Because it doesn't matter that I was just inside you. It's not enough. I've never felt like this about anyone, ever, and I can't imagine ever feeling like this about anyone else, and it's because of the thousands of tiny things that are you." He took a deep breath, his chest heaving. "It's you."

God, did the truth feel good.

She blinked, and a tear fell, slipping down over her still-flushed cheek. "I've been in love with you for a year, Zack. A whole damn year. From the first day we met, I was done."

He brushed her tear away, his hand trembling. His thoughts scattered in a million different directions, past, present, and future coming together in a flashbang of emotion. Regret and lust and happiness and love.

"Taylor knows," she said. "She knows, and it's okay." A smile broke out across her face, and he could see the relief in it. Could almost taste it.

"I'm glad, but even if she hadn't been, I couldn't have walked away." He brushed his lips against hers. "I can't. And no matter what happens with your father, with this investigation, I'm not going anywhere."

They stood together for several moments, touching and looking, basking in the afterglow of hot sex and the truth. But they couldn't stay, just like the other night.

"We need to do this in a bed," he said, and she giggled, stuffing her thong into her discarded clutch. He disposed of the condom in the small garbage can in the corner and then buttoned his shirt and buckled himself back up. He pressed his ear to the door, listening. But the music was too loud, and he couldn't hear much except for the booming beat. After giving her a once-over to make sure she was decent, he took her hand and pulled the door open, and they stepped out of the supply closet.

Alexa's father stood in the hallway, his back against the wall, his arms crossed over his chest. Protective instincts kicking in, Zack moved in front of Alexa, sheltering her from her father. From this monster of a man who'd abused her in horrible ways.

Jonathan sneered at Zack, his gaze lingering on the gash above his eyebrow. Pushing off the wall, he strode toward them, moving with a cocky swagger. White-hot rage coursed through Zack's veins, and the only thing that stopped him from decking the asshole was concern for Alexa's safety. As badly as he wanted to make him suffer for what he'd done to her, he couldn't.

"I have to say, I quite enjoyed that fight, *De Luca*," Jonathan said, his voice dripping with anger. "Even if the wrong man did win." He raised his hand toward Zack's injured eye, and Zack jerked his head out of the way, his mind reeling.

He'd been at the fight. He knew Zack had lied to him. He knew who Zack was. Zack shifted in front of Alexa, keeping her behind him.

Jonathan dropped his hand. "Alexa, *honey*," he said, his voice cold and commanding, "come here. I have a present for you."

Zack didn't move and stared Jonathan down, not wanting Alexa to get any closer to her father. Logically, Zack knew he should be scared, but all that mattered was Alexa and keeping her safe.

Jonathan got right in Zack's face, and he didn't move, didn't even flinch. "You have no idea who you're fucking with, De Luca. Move."

"No." Zack was amazed how low and calm his voice sounded, because the protective anger beating through him was making it hard to breathe.

Jonathan moved his hands to his hips, holding his suit jacket open and flashing the gun stowed in his waistband. "Move. Right. Fucking. Now."

"No."

But before he could stop her, Alexa stepped out from

behind him. She didn't say anything, but she held her head up, meeting her father's gaze. Zack's eyes darted from Alexa to her father's hands to the fire exit down the hall. Visualizing all the ways this could go wrong and all the ways he could protect her. Every muscle in his body tensed; he was ready to do whatever it took to keep Alexa safe.

Jonathan reached into his pocket and handed something to Alexa. A diamond earring. She gasped, and her fingers trembled as she closed them over it.

"I don't know what you think you're doing, but this is your one and only warning, you stupid little bitch."

Zack's temper flared, and he took a step toward Jonathan, his fists clenched at his sides. His jaw ached, tension and anger and the need to protect her twisting everything tight.

Jonathan flashed the gun at his hip at Zack again with a flick of his suit jacket, and stepped farther into Alexa's space. "You'd better run, little girl. This is the only chance you're gonna get." He turned his sneering glare on Zack. "And if I see you again, I'll kill you. I'll blow your goddamn brains out." He stepped back, slipped his hands into his pockets, and turned to walk away. "Enjoy the rest of your evening."

Zack stared at Fairfax's back, torn between wanting to go after him and needing to stay with Alexa to protect her. To comfort her. He stared until Jonathan disappeared into the crowd, and Alexa sagged against him. His arms came up around her as wave after wave of protective anger crashed over him.

The game had just changed, big time.

CHAPTER 20

The sun's yellow glow was just visible on the edge of the horizon where the mountains met the sky. Alexa traced the shadowed, rocky outline of the mountains with her eyes, watching as the band of gold around them grew slowly. She let her eyes wander up, the gold fading into a soft peach color, and then a delicate pink, and finally a seemingly endless stretch of lavender sky. The underbellies of the clouds glimmered a vibrant coral. Scrubby little bushes dotted the sides of the two-lane road.

Dawn in the desert.

Alexa shifted in the backseat of Morales's car, watching the desert landscape as they headed north, away from Los Angeles. Away from her father, and the Golden Brotherhood. Away from the threats and the danger and what she'd done.

She hadn't known what to do after the confrontation with her father yesterday, but Zack had insisted on leaving the after-party and had taken her right to Morales, who'd met them at her office after Zack had called her. He'd filled her in on what had happened, and she'd made several phone calls. The terms *safe house*, *protective detail*, and *intelligence unit* had filtered through the fog of Alexa's mind. She realized now, in hindsight, that she'd been in shock. Despite everything she'd known about her father, a part of her still hadn't expected him to come after them like that. Hadn't even expected him to find out.

Sean had met them at the LAPD offices, two duffel bags in his hands, one for her and one for Zack, packed with clothes and toiletries. Alexa knew Sierra had packed her bag for her because she'd found the note inside. She'd started to cry, tracing her fingers over Sierra's recognizable, loopy scrawl.

I love you. Be safe.

Ian had volunteered to come with them for extra security, and Morales had taken him up on the offer. He now sat silently in the front seat beside Morales.

Until everything with the Golden Brotherhood blew over, they had to disappear.

Alexa didn't want to think of what it meant for her and Zack if things didn't blow over. Would they have to go into some kind of witness protection program, starting over in a new city with new identities? Would they be allowed to stay together? What would she do with her life? What about Zack's fighting career? What kind of future did they have? She didn't want to spend her life looking over her shoulder.

After the four of them had made all the necessary arrangements, she, Zack, and Ian had piled into Morales's car, not a police vehicle but her own, and she'd driven north into the desert, not taking the highway but small, deserted side roads. The safe house was in a city called Palmdale, about two hours away from Los Angeles. Two officers from what Morales had called "Special Ops" would meet them there and provide security.

Safe houses and security details. This was her life now.

Zack reached over and intertwined his fingers with hers, his thumb rubbing circles over the back of her hand. The swelling around his eye had gone down, but the skin had darkened to a nasty purplish black, and it looked even worse than it had yesterday.

Yesterday. Twelve hours ago his fight hadn't even happened yet. God, had only a handful of hours passed? It felt like so much longer.

She felt as though she'd aged a year, at least, over the past few days.

Once, when she was a little girl, she'd imagined that life was measured in heartbeats. A person was given so many heartbeats at birth; some got more, some got less. But when they were gone, they were gone, and your time was up. If her childish theory was true, she'd spent a lot of her heartbeats over the past few days. She'd spent them being scared, worried, anxious, and upset. Wasted heartbeats. But she'd also spent them on Zack. At least those heartbeats had been worth it. She knew she should feel guilty about dragging him down with her, but she didn't. She couldn't bring herself to feel anything but happy and relieved that he was here with her.

Morales turned into the driveway of a completely normal-looking house on a quiet street. Light-beige stucco. Sage-colored garage door. Matching shutters framing the windows. Small front lawn with a cottonwood tree right in the middle. Morales pulled the car into the garage, and, bone weary, Alexa followed her into the house, Zack and Ian behind her. Morales pressed her phone to her ear, checking her messages as she did a sweep through the house, shutting curtains and checking the locks on all the doors. Zack set their bags down by the stairs.

The garage led into the kitchen, which, again, was completely normal. Light-gray tile floor. Oak cabinets. A table and four chairs by a set of sliding glass doors that led to the backyard. The kitchen opened onto a living area with a large sectional sofa, a small gas fireplace, and a flat-screen TV mounted to the wall. Built-in bookshelves flanked the fireplace. Everything clean and tidy. It could've been any family's home. And for who knew how long, it'd be hers.

"I know it's been a long night, but we need to debrief and go through house protocol. Then you can crash," said Morales, tucking her hair behind her ears. "We'll do protocol first." She looked at Alexa. "I'm sorry we took your phone away, but it's a way for the Brotherhood to trace you, and bringing it here could compromise the location of the safe house. You have your burner?" she asked, and Alexa nodded. Sean had brought both her and Zack prepaid phones so that they'd have a way of communicating, if need be. "Good. You might've noticed that this looks just like a normal house, and that's because it is. The main reason this location is secure and safe is because the Golden Brotherhood has no way of finding its location. That being said, we do have safety protocols in place.

"First, my car will always be in the garage, with the keys in the ignition, allowing for ease of access if we need to bolt on short notice. It will also always have a full tank of gas. If something happens and you need to use it, do it.

"Second, there will always be someone on watch duty. We'll rotate shifts between the five of us—me, De Luca, MacAllister, and the two Special Ops officers arriving later today. Once everyone's here, we'll work up a schedule."

"I can take first watch," said Ian. "You lot need sleep. I'm relatively fresh, in comparison."

Morales nodded. "Appreciate that. Third, the house is equipped with a security system, motion-detecting flood-lights, and security cameras. These do not feed to a security company but to LAPD Special Ops.

"Lastly, the idea is to stay out of sight. The backyard has high fences and is private-ish, but avoid it if you see others outside. Especially you, Alexa. You're a public fig-ure and easily recognizable. Anything you need—clothing, medicine, toiletries, whatever—one of the Special Ops guys can do a run."

Alexa slumped back into the sectional, struggling against the waves of exhaustion pulling at her. "I understand. I guess you have no idea how long we'll be here, right?"

"I can't make any promises, but I do have some new information that makes me hopeful it won't be long. The bugs you planted worked exactly the way we wanted them to, and I know the FBI are getting ready to move in. They don't have enough on your father yet, but they do have enough—in conjunction with other investigations they've been running—to start making some arrests. The other piece of news is that, thanks to you, Crosby is safe."

Relief flickered through Alexa, along with a sense of pride that she'd helped to save someone's life. "Who is he?"

"A journalist investigating the Golden Brotherhood. We found him before they did, and he's in protective custody now."

Alexa nodded, too tired to do anything else. "Good. I'm glad."

"Which leads me to an another point. Alexa, when the time comes, you'll have to testify against your father."

She sighed and then nodded. "I know. Honestly, I don't really have anything to lose at this point. If I can help, I will." It didn't matter that he was her father; she knew him for exactly who he was now, and her guilt was gone. He was a corrupt, power-hungry, violent man, and even though he'd given her life and raised her, he wasn't her father in any real sense of the word. He never had been, if she was honest with herself.

"Good. You're a key witness, and any testimony you give will only help the case when we get there." Morales pushed to her feet. "Any questions? No? Let's assign bedrooms and crash, then."

Without a word Zack picked up their bags, and they followed Morales up the stairs.

Home sweet home.

* * *

"There are five bedrooms. One of the bedrooms has two single beds, so we should have enough that no one's sleeping on the couch," said Morales.

Zack adjusted his grip on the bags in his hands. "We'll only need four rooms," he said, and Alexa and Morales both turned to look at him. "Alexa and I will be sharing."

"You'll be…Oh. Right." Morales arched an eyebrow, studying them for a second. "I…heard. Well, take the master, then. It has an attached bath." She pointed at the first room on the left and gave them a once-over again but didn't say anything. "I'll be down the hall. Get some sleep."

Zack couldn't remember the last time he'd been this tired. He felt worn down and was running on empty. But one look at Alexa and all he wanted to do was take care of her. His own shit—the exhaustion, the pain in his face and ribs, the fear and the anger—didn't matter.

He opened the door to their room and ushered her inside, closing it behind him. A queen-size bed sat in the center of the room, a nightstand on either side. The only other pieces of furniture in the room were a dresser facing the bed and a freestanding mirror in the corner.

Alexa sank down onto the bed. She was pale, dark circles coloring the skin beneath her eyes. Zack stepped into the adjoining bathroom, which had both a glassed-in shower stall and a jetted tub nestled under the window.

The first bed that he'd ever share with Alexa was in a safe house. Not exactly the most romantic setting, but it didn't matter. She was safe, and he was here with her. Everything else was details.

He pulled open the shower door and turned on the water, running it until it was warm but not hot. He stepped back into the bedroom and found Alexa exactly where he'd left her, still staring at her lap. With gentle pressure on her elbows, he urged her to stand and started undressing her.

"Zack, I don't think…Right now…" She shook her head even as she raised her arms above her head and let him pull her dress up and away.

He trailed his hands down her arms and unhooked her bra. It slipped down, and he kissed her forehead, smiling against the sweetness of her skin. "I know. I'm too tired too. Let's have a shower and go to bed. Okay?"

She smiled, a real smile, and he returned it. This, right here, was exactly where he was supposed to be. With Alexa. Making her smile, taking care of her.

She bent to take her shoes off, and he undid the buttons on his shirt, then tossed it to the floor, toed off his shoes, and shucked his jeans and boxer briefs. He watched Alexa's cute naked butt as she padded into the bathroom.

"I found towels," she called, and poked her head back into the bedroom. Her gaze softened as she looked at him, her eyes doing a slow caress up and down his body. She stepped back into the bedroom and grabbed shampoo, conditioner, body wash, and one of those girly sponge things from her bag, and this time he followed her into the bathroom.

She opened the shower stall's door and stuck her hand in, testing the water before stepping inside. He followed her in, the door snapping shut behind him. He pulled her into his arms and nestled her against him, kissing the top of her head as warm water pattered against them. He didn't ask if she was okay, because he knew she wasn't. He didn't ask how she was feeling, because he knew she was too tired and overwhelmed and wrung out to even know. He didn't do anything except hold her, wishing he could shoulder it all for her. Wishing he could kiss it better, and knowing he couldn't.

But he could comfort her. He could take care of her. He could protect her. So he would.

God, he would, until his heart stopped beating, he would.

"I love you," she said, her voice echoing softly off the tiles. She pressed a kiss right over his heart, and it thumped against her lips in response. "I love you, and I'm so sorry."

"You have nothing to be sorry for, princess." He kissed her, gently and slowly. "I love you too. We'll get through this." He eased her away from him and scooped up the shampoo bottle she'd set down in the corner. "Turn around."

She turned and raised her face to the spray, letting the water wash over her. When her hair was wet, he squeezed a small amount of the shampoo into his palm. The smell of coconuts filled the air, and he smiled. The first time he'd ever held her, when they'd danced at Sean and Sierra's engagement party, her hair had smelled like coconuts.

He rubbed his hands together, slicking the shampoo over his palms and fingers, and then started massaging her scalp, working his fingers in slow circles.

She let out a soft, sighing moan. "Oh God, that feels good."

He smiled and worked the shampoo through her hair, massaging her scalp for several minutes. He turned her around, rinsed the shampoo out, and repeated the massage with conditioner.

"You have the best hands," she said, her eyes closed, her shoulders relaxed, and a sense of possessive satisfaction took root in his chest.

"They're yours," he said, a thickness filling his throat. Everything he had was hers.

She reached behind her and circled her fingers around his wrists, guiding his hands down her body, over her breasts, stopping when his hand was over her heart. "Yours," she said, echoing him.

His blood hummed in his veins. Happiness and possession and the need to keep her safe all sang through him. He rinsed the conditioner from her hair and then squirted a bit of her body wash onto the purple puff. It lathered up quickly, and he worked the puff over her skin in gentle circles, watching the soap and water slide over her skin, over the curve of her neck, the delicate slope of her shoulders, the straight line of her spine. Her full breasts with those pink nipples. The flare of her hips, the roundness of her ass.

She was so beautiful that it almost hurt to look at her. So beautiful and sweet and strong.

Unable to help himself and grateful he no longer had to fight what he wanted, he pulled her against him and kissed her, trying to pour everything he was feeling into the kiss. "I know it's fast and things are crazy, but I'm *so* all in with you, princess."

She cupped his cheek. "Me too. God, Zack, me too." With a contented sigh, she rinsed the soap from her body and took the puff from him, then washed him in turn, her touch so sweet, so gentle. She frowned slightly as she worked the soap over the bruise on his right side where he'd taken that kick. "I'm so proud of you, for the way you fought yesterday, but it's hard to see you hurt."

He laid his hand over hers, holding it over the large bruise. "I'm okay."

She nodded and started moving her hand again, trailing more soap across his skin, washing him as thoroughly as he'd washed her. She yawned, and he rinsed off quickly and then shut off the shower. He grabbed the towels she'd laid out and passed one to her, and they dried off in sleepy, contented silence. But she seemed a little less tense, a little less sad, than when they'd first stepped into the safe house.

As soon as she was dry, he scooped her into his arms and carried her to the bed, then pulled back the covers with one hand. He laid her down and climbed in beside her, the sheets cool against his skin.

She snuggled into his arms, her eyes already closed. "I'm glad you're here with me," she whispered, and he stroked a hand up and down her back. She smelled like coconuts and home.

"There's nowhere else I'd be, princess. I belong with you."

She murmured the word *belong* and then fell asleep in his arms.

CHAPTER 21

ell me what you like."

Alexa set down the fantasy novel she'd chosen from the bookcase downstairs. She hadn't wanted to read about real life, craving the distraction of dragons and wizards and magic.

Zack, finished with his watch shift, sat down on the edge of the bed, his eyes on her. On her and hungry. Her stomach fluttered, and her heart gave a little jolt.

This day, of nothing and waiting and whiling away the hours, was the new normal. But at least she was safe. And at least she was with Zack. She was immensely grateful for both of those facts.

She played with the hem of her T-shirt. "What I like?"

Zack's eyes tracked the movement of her fingers, and another hot flutter stole through her. "Yeah. In bed. We haven't talked about that."

She swallowed, suddenly very aware of every tick of her pulse in her throat. "Is that something people do? I don't really have a good frame of reference here."

"Yeah," he said, smiling crookedly. "Couples talk about sex. Or, at least, they should."

She chewed her lip, uncertainty creeping in. She met his eyes and gave a half shrug. "I…I don't really know. I've never…" Another half shrug as blood rushed to her face. "It's never mattered."

He moved up on the bed, sitting in front of her. "It matters to me."

"I don't know what I like. I wish I knew what to tell you."

Her fingers were still playing with her T-shirt, and he took her hands in his. "Do you ever make yourself come?"

Her face heated even more, but despite her embarrassment she didn't feel the need to hide from him or to lie. "Yeah, I do."

He glanced at the mirror in the corner and then returned his attention to her. "Will you show me?"

She was amazed that her face hadn't burst into flames. "You want me to touch myself?"

He smiled, wolfish and slow. "Yeah, princess. I do."

A flood of heat coursed over her skin. A throb settled between her legs, and she clenched, surprised at how turned on she was at the idea of touching herself in front of Zack.

With slow, deliberate movements she undid the button of her jeans and slid the zipper down, arching her hips up off the bed to wiggle free. Zack tugged his shirt up over his head and let it fall to the floor, and she did the same. He undid his belt but didn't undress any further. No, instead he stood and walked to the corner and dragged the mirror toward the bed, placing it right beside her.

"So we can both watch," he said, and then dipped his head and caught her mouth in a hot, deep kiss. His tongue stroked hers, and she squirmed slightly, in both anticipation and nervousness. She'd never, ever done anything like this before. But she didn't want to stop.

He kissed her and kissed her and kissed her, and his jeans hit the floor. So did her bra. Finally, when she felt as though her heart were about to burst from beating so hard, so fast, he broke the kiss. The mattress dipped under his weight as he climbed onto the bed, moving behind her. He held her so that her back was to his chest, and he angled them toward the mirror.

"Take your panties off," he said as he trailed hot, open-mouthed kisses across her shoulders. She did, tossing them to the floor, her entire body on fire. Not with shame, but with how much she wanted this. Needed this. He kissed her neck and then raised his head, meeting her eyes in the mirror. "Look how beautiful you are. How fucking sexy. God." He licked up her neck and nipped at her skin, sparkles of pleasure dancing over her. His hands gripped her hips, and she could feel his cock, thick and hard, pressed against her lower back. "Spread your legs, sweetheart," he whispered as he nipped at her ear. "Show me how you like to be touched."

She eased her legs apart, and he hooked his ankles over hers, holding her open. But she didn't feel trapped, or vulnerable, or exposed.

She'd never felt so desirable in her life. Zack made her feel beautiful, made her feel sexy in ways she'd never even imagined. His hands moved from her hips to her inner thighs, his fingertips feathering over the sensitive skin there. Her own fingers trembled slightly as she slid her right hand down, resting her palm over her bare mound. But they didn't tremble because she felt unsure, or ashamed, or worried she wouldn't please him. They shook only because of how much she wanted this.

Zack kissed her shoulder and then met her eyes again in the mirror, his gaze slowly sweeping down her body. She dipped her fingers lower, barely touching her clit, which was already swollen and throbbing. With a soft moan, she slipped a finger inside and then rubbed her clit in a slow, firm circle. She watched as it moved beneath her fingers, and she shifted her hips. Zack's grip tightened on her thighs, and she inhaled sharply when she saw the dark, intense lust shining in his eyes.

"Does that feel good?" he asked, his voice husky.

She alternated her strokes in her favorite pattern, slow circles and diagonal flicking brushes. "Mm-hmm."

"What do you think about when you touch yourself like this?"

His fingers inched higher on her thighs, almost at the seam now. One finger brushed the outside of her lips.

"You."

He smiled against her skin and trailed more kisses over her neck as she continued to massage her clit.

"What about me?"

"Everything. God, everything. What it would feel like to kiss you. What your skin would taste like. What it would feel like to have your hands on me. Your mouth. To have you inside me. How good you'd feel and smell and taste and sound."

He caught her earlobe in his teeth and tugged gently. "Fuck, princess. Me too. The night after Sean and Sierra's engagement party, I had the sexiest dream about you. Do you want to hear it? Should I tell you my fantasy while you touch yourself?"

"Yes, please," she sighed out, rubbing her clit, her hips rocking a little.

In the mirror she could see how wet she was. Could see

that Zack's eyes were glued to her hand between her legs. He shifted against her, his hard cock hot and thick.

"I dreamed that you'd come home with me after that party, and that the second we were alone in my apartment, you were on your knees, and my cock was in your pretty mouth."

"I want that," she said, her clit throbbing. "Then what happened?"

"I couldn't take any more, and I fucked you up against the wall, hard and fast, and you came so hard that you screamed my name." She shifted her hips restlessly and whimpered. "Then we moved to the bed. And then the shower. And then the floor. Over and over again, until neither of us could move."

"I want all of that too," she murmured, her skin slightly damp with sweat.

"When I woke up, it only took me a minute to get myself off, and I came so fucking hard, thinking about how much I wanted you."

"Oh God, Zack," she moaned, arching against him. His words seared through her, exhilarating and surreal.

"Look how wet your pussy is," he said, and she moaned again, louder this time. "Do you like it when I talk dirty to you, princess?"

She managed to nod. "Mm-hmm. I do."

"What do you like about it?"

A week ago she wouldn't have known the answer to his question or had the confidence to answer it, but things were different now. *She* was different now.

"Because *you* want to do those things to *me*, and I want all of it. I love you, and I want all of you. The sweet parts and the dirty parts. The strong parts and the soft parts."

"I don't have any soft parts right now," he said, moving

his hips against her, and she smiled, feeling light and free and happy despite everything. "Alexa." He kissed up her neck, his mouth hot and sweet against her skin. "I love you." He laid his hand over hers and started moving with her, and after a second she drew her hand away. His hand was so much bigger, his skin so much rougher than hers, and the contrast was delicious. The sight of his fingers moving over her clit was almost unbearably hot, and her insides pulled and tightened. Heat licked down her spine and settled between her legs, adding to the throb there.

"Like this?" he asked, touching her the way she'd just done, his strong fingers moving against her clit in alternating circles and firm strokes.

"Yeah," she sighed out. "Just like that." Her hips started to shake, and he took his hand away.

"Not like this. I want to taste you." Before she could say anything, he'd moved off the bed and onto the floor in front of her. He tugged her hips to the edge of the bed, and she eased onto her back. She watched him in the mirror, the muscles in his back flexing as he settled himself between her legs. Burning pleasure shot through her as he closed his mouth over her throbbing, aching pussy in a hot, openmouthed kiss, swirling his tongue over her swollen clit.

Her hips jerked, and her back arched off the bed. "Holy fuck! God!" she cried out as she fisted her hands in the sheets. She pressed up onto her elbows, her eyes darting between Zack in front of her and their reflection in the mirror. Splotches of red dotted her skin from her neck to her breasts.

His teeth scraped gently over her tender flesh, and he moaned. "You taste so damn good, sweetheart. Fuck." He bit out the last word before closing his mouth over her again, sucking and licking. She couldn't think. She couldn't move. All she could do was feel and watch as he worked his mouth against her, his big hands on her hips, the muscles in his arms and back taut and gorgeous. His stubble rasped against the sensitive skin of her inner thighs, adding another layer of sensation.

He moaned against her, and the added vibration coiled everything inside her into hot, glowing knots. His tongue swirled over her again, and he sucked her clit into his mouth. She broke, all those knots unraveling as she came against his mouth, her hips bucking, his name falling from her lips over and over again, and her entire body felt like a heartbeat, pleasure throbbing outward from her core.

Zack nipped at her thigh, and she ran her fingers through his hair. He smiled up at her. "I think we found something else you like."

She flopped down onto the mattress, her limbs shaking. "Uh-huh." Closing her eyes, she let herself bask in the golden afterglow filtering through her veins. He kissed his way back up her body, trailing his wonderfully talented mouth over her stomach, her ribs, her breasts—lingering over her nipples—her neck, her ears, and finally her mouth. He kissed her, and she could taste herself on his tongue. Fresh arousal rolled through her, and she cupped his face, his stubble rough against her palms.

"Thank you. That was amazing," she said, threading her fingers into his hair.

He kissed her again. "You're welcome, but I'm not done with you yet, princess." He pulled her up to sitting and stood, shucking his boxer briefs. A bead of moisture pearled at the tip of his cock, and she licked her lips, surprised at how badly she wanted to put her mouth on him.

As though he could read her mind, he smiled, that cocky

half smile that melted her insides. "Another time." He picked his pants up off the floor, then retrieved his wallet and pulled a condom out.

"I don't want to use that," she said, and he stilled, his hands dropping to his sides, the foil square still in one hand.

"You don't?"

She bit her lip and shook her head. "I don't want anything between us. I just want you. I've never done that before, but I want to with you."

"Are you sure?" he asked, and his voice came out strained, almost rough.

"I'm on birth control. So unless you have a reason why we can't…" She trailed off and shrugged.

"I'm good. I have to get tested all the time. For fighting."

"I want you, just you, inside me. Skin to skin. Just us."

He took a deep breath and dropped the condom, just letting it fall to the floor. "God, yes." He closed the distance between them and kissed her, hard and deeply and urgently. And then he was behind her on the bed again, urging her forward. "I want that too, and I want to watch." He moved them to the edge of the bed, directly in front of the mirror, and she knew what he wanted. What they both wanted. Rising up onto her knees, she straddled him, her back once again to his chest. He lined up his cock with her soaking wet entrance, slicking himself through her folds. With his other hand, he exerted gentle pressure on her hip, urging her down. She sank onto him, moaning as he filled her. She watched, fascinated, awestruck, as his bare cock disappeared into her. Both of his hands settled on her hips as she sank all the way down, loving the tight fullness of him inside her. Loving that there was nothing separating them. Loving him.

"Oh God, princess." He ground the words out, his forehead pressed to her shoulder. "You feel so good. So perfect. God."

She rocked her hips against him, reveling in the sight of him buried inside her. "I love how you feel, Zack. So big and so damn good."

He made a quiet growling sound and, with his hands firmly on her hips, guided her up and then down again. She couldn't tear her eyes away from the mirror, from them, from the intensely erotic sight of his cock sliding in and out of her, over and over again.

He kissed her neck and rolled his hips, and she tipped her head back against him. "Look at you, sweetheart. Look," he said, his voice barely above a whisper.

She raised one arm and curled it around his neck, threading her fingers into his hair. He was so gorgeous it almost took her breath away to look at him. His thick brown hair a mess. His eye blackened and a little swollen. "Look at *us*."

"Us. I fucking love that there's an us."

She never, ever wanted to forget this moment. The sight of her and Zack twined together, his gorgeously thick, naked cock moving in and out of her in sure, steady thrusts. The pleasure of his body inside hers. This gorgeous man, who was kind and sweet and strong, who loved her.

"Me too. God, me too."

He moaned and picked up the pace, his grip harder on her hips. "I'm gonna come inside you. Yeah?"

She wasn't sure why, but the idea turned her on so much that she started to come around his cock, pleasure shimmering through her blood. She clenched around him as her orgasm rocked her, obliterating everything except the beautiful fullness of his cock inside her, the fullness of her heart, the fullness of them.

"I love you. Fuck, Alexa, I love you." He pushed himself deep, and she felt each pulse of his cock as he came inside her.

She slumped against him, her heart racing, sweat slicking her skin. He kissed a lazy path from her shoulder to her neck, and she closed her eyes. "I love you too."

CHAPTER 22

Glasses clinked, and dull, mindless chatter filled the air around Jonathan and Elijah. Jonathan pushed his salmon around on his plate, but everything he ate seemed to taste like ash.

"So you have no idea where she is?" Elijah asked, sawing into his chicken.

"No, but I told her to run. For her sake, and for Melanie's. And it's Alexa. I don't think she knows much, otherwise she would've gone to the police, and we don't have any proof she's done that."

"I'll have our guys inside the LAPD keep digging, find out if anything more happened when she filed the break-and-enter report."

Jonathan nodded and sipped his water. "I think she knew something, though," he said, thinking out loud. "Why else would she snoop? Why else would she hire a bodyguard and lie about it?"

Elijah took a long, deep breath and then shook his head. "I don't know. I wish I knew what to tell you. Sucks that it's your daughter we're talking about, or this would be a hell of a lot simpler."

Jonathan nodded and set down his knife and fork. His chest hurt, and he'd lost his appetite. He'd barely slept the night before, his mind churning with scenario after scenario, none of them good. He rubbed a hand over the back of his neck, trying to ease some of the tension there. His temples throbbed.

He took another sip of his water, and as he set his glass down, he noticed a commotion near the front of the restaurant. Several men in navy blue jackets with bright-yellow letters spelling out "FBI" were headed straight for his table. He pushed to his feet as they approached, but they were focused entirely on Elijah, who'd gone pale. He adjusted his glasses and set his knife and fork down with a clatter.

"Elijah Todd, you're under arrest for the attempted murder of Christopher Crosby, acting as accessory to the murder of Jeff Astor, extortion, accessory to fraud, blackmail, accessory to drug trafficking, political corruption, money laundering, coercion, and nineteen counts of assault." The lead agent reached behind him for a pair of handcuffs and, with one hand on Elijah's shoulder, turned him around before slapping them on his wrists. All the other agents surrounded the table with their hands on their holsters.

Jonathan watched, helpless, as Elijah was read his rights, and a desperate anger pushed up through him, making him want to scream, to smash things. But he didn't. He stood completely still and made a list in his head of all the people he needed to call. Lawyers, and politicians, and cops.

Another agent stepped toward him, a stern expression

on his craggy face. "Mr. Fairfax, I'd caution you not to leave town at this time."

"Am I under investigation?" he asked, his lip curling.

"If you leave town, you will be."

"Is that a threat?"

"Advice." He turned and followed the rest of the team out, Elijah almost invisible in the middle of the group. All eyes in the restaurant were on Jonathan, and he sank back down into his chair. He rubbed his neck again and swallowed. For a brief second, he imagined an invisible noose tightening around his neck, cutting off his air. Cutting off everything he and his father and his grandfather had built.

Acid burned his chest, and he tossed his napkin down on the table. He threw money down and walked out of the restaurant.

The Brotherhood was bleeding, and he needed to find a way to stop it.

* * *

Zack stared down at the series of text messages from Jamie on his burner phone, not sure what to feel. What to think.

Everything he'd worked for was just sitting there, waiting for him, and he couldn't act on it because of the messed-up situation he'd gotten himself into with Alexa and her father. And while it sucked to have to put his life on hold, he didn't regret the choices he'd made, the ones that had brought him here, because nothing meant anything without Alexa, and right here with her was where he was supposed to be. Waking up beside her every morning. Curling up on the couch with her, watching TV or a movie. Cooking together. Making her come, over and over again, until she couldn't even keep her eyes open. Talking into the small hours of the night, about anything and everything.

Zack reclined in the mesh-backed patio chair and tipped his head back, staring up at the darkening sky, stars sparkling against the dusky purple. A particularly bright one shone directly overhead, and he wondered what star it was. Hundreds of thousands of tiny lights, hanging in the sky, millions of miles away. Entire galaxies reduced to dusty, twinkling specks. Zack studied them, centering himself and inhaling a deep breath.

The sliding glass door opened, and Alexa poked her head out. "Hey. Getting some air?" she asked, stepping out onto the patio. She'd done as Morales had asked and avoided the backyard for the most part. But the neighboring houses were dark and quiet, so it was safe right now.

"Yeah. Come here." He extended his hand to her and pulled her into his lap, breathing in the coconut scent of her hair, the sweet warmth of her skin, fighting back the disappointment welling up in him. For several moments he just held her against him, and the longer he held her under those hundreds of thousands of stars, the less the fight contract seemed to matter. *She* was what mattered, this beautiful, sweet, brave woman in his arms.

"Are you okay?" she asked, her breath warm against his neck.

"I had a text from Jamie. The UFC offered me a three-fight contract. Hopefully it's still waiting for me when this is all over."

She hugged him tighter. "I'm sorry."

"It's not your fault. And it's not the end. It just means putting things on hold."

"I know, but you've worked so hard for this, and now to have it happen when you can't do anything about it…I know what this means to you, and I'm sorry. I'm grateful you're here with me, but I hate that you have to put your own dreams on hold because of everything."

"It's disappointing, but I'm okay. This is where I need to be."

She played with his hair, and his scalp tingled. "Natalie thinks this will be over soon. I hope she's right. Apparently the FBI arrested my father's right-hand man today."

"They're closing in."

"Yeah, sounds like. Hopefully soon they'll arrest him and shut down the Brotherhood, and then we can come out of hiding. It'll be safe then. And then you can take that contract and pursue your dream."

He took another deep breath. "I need to talk to you about that."

She pulled back slightly and met his eyes in the darkness. "About fighting?"

"Yeah, and about us. About the future."

She frowned. "Okay. What about us?"

He took one of her hands and threaded his fingers through hers, holding their joined hands against his chest. "Fighting's not an easy career. I'll probably have to leave LA to train at a higher level. There are good gyms around the country, places like Florida and New Mexico. I'd understand if that isn't the life you want," he said, his heart beating painfully in his chest.

But she smiled and kissed him sweetly, and his heart settled back into place. "You, Zack De Luca, are the life I want. I don't really know what my future holds—I don't have a job or a family, really, anymore—but I have you. So you do what you need to do, and I'll be right here beside you, cheering you on, no matter where you go. Deal?"

"Fuck yeah, princess." He kissed her again, relief

filtering through him. He'd felt it was only fair to warn her about what she might be getting into. After several seconds he broke the kiss and tucked her against his chest. Together they gazed up at the stars as the sky darkened from deep purple to soft black. "What do you want to do when this is over?" he asked quietly.

She shrugged, her slender shoulders moving against him. "No idea. I'm just taking everything a day at a time. I know I don't want to act anymore." She sat up a little. "Hey, maybe I'll go to college. I've always wanted to."

He smiled, stroking her hair. "What would you study?"

"I'm not sure. I think I'd maybe like to do something in the nonprofit sector. Public health? Economics? Something to do with international development? I like the idea of helping people." She paused and tilted her head back, looking up at the sky. "Maybe if I do some good, I can atone for some of the bad my father's done. Maybe I can try to make it right."

He kissed her forehead. "You don't need to make up for your father's crimes, Alexa."

"I know I don't have to. I want to. I can't change what he's done, but I can try to make the world a better place. That matters to me."

He traced his thumb over her knuckles. "So I'll fight, and you'll save the world. I like this plan. What else do you want?"

"It's probably way, way too soon to say this, but our situation isn't exactly normal, and…although we've only been together a short time, I feel so close to you. Like I've known you forever."

"I get that. Lay it on me. What else do you want?"

"I really, really want kids. At least two, maybe more. I hated being an only child."

The sudden image of Alexa pregnant with his baby flashed through his mind, and he kissed her again. *Hell yes.* "Honestly, I've never thought much about kids or a family, I guess because I've been so focused on fighting. But yeah. Kids with you sounds pretty damn amazing."

"Zack," she whispered, and kissed him, slowly and tenderly, her tongue caressing his. His arms tightened around her, and his cock stiffened, heat throbbing through him. Heat, and the need to keep her safe, to make sure she had the future she wanted. The future she deserved.

She ran her hands over his chest, tracing the contours of his muscles. He wove his hands into her hair, tilting her head back slightly and deepening the kiss. She rocked gently against him and moaned softly, and he broke the kiss, nipping at her lips with his teeth. "Let's go upstairs. I need to be inside you."

She made the soft, whimpering noise that always drove him crazy, and she kissed him again, a playful sweep of her tongue across his. She wiggled off of his lap and grabbed his hand, tugging him eagerly into the house. The first time they'd had sex, the night before his fight, there'd been a shyness there. An uncertainty. That shyness was slowly disappearing, and he loved that she felt comfortable enough with him to open up and be vulnerable.

Mac sat at the kitchen table, nursing a cup of tea, watching the laptop that served as the main monitor for the house's security system. He smiled at them, but it was small and sad, and he returned his attention to the computer screen without a word.

They reached their bedroom, and the door had barely latched behind them before Alexa's hands were under his shirt, pushing it up. He reached behind him and tugged it up over his head, then tossed it to the floor. She slid her hands up his stomach and over his chest.

"You are so gorgeous. I can't believe you're mine," she said, and kissed a path across his chest, her lips soft and warm over his heart.

Mine. He closed his eyes, savoring the word. So much contained in four little letters, because he was hers. Fully and completely. Had been for a long time.

He pulled her shirt up over her head and cupped her breasts, his thumbs playing over her nipples through her bra. "I'm yours, and you're mine." He unhooked her bra and let it fall to the floor and pulled her against him, needing to feel her skin against his. He kissed her and backed her toward the bed, needing to get inside her. He tumbled her down to the bed, and her legs came up around his hips. Breaking the kiss, she stilled and took one of his hands, guiding it to her heart. It beat steadily against his palm, and she placed her own palm over his heart. Several heartbeats elapsed before she spoke.

"Ours. Us."

His throat thickened, and he kissed her. He'd never believed he could have something like this, especially not with someone like her. He felt so damn alive, as though his eyes were open for the first time in his life. He'd spent so much time fighting, but now he knew what it felt like to have something worth fighting for.

He slipped a hand between them and into her yoga pants, dipping into her panties while he kissed a path from her mouth down to her breasts. As he sucked a nipple into his mouth, he slipped a finger inside her. She was hot and wet around him, and he groaned as she clenched around his finger. He added a second finger and fucked her slowly as she moaned under him. When he pulled his hand away, his fingers were slick, and she shoved her yoga pants down, then began fumbling with the button on his jeans. He rose just enough to ditch his jeans and boxer briefs. He fell back down on top of her, and she took his cock in her hand, stroking him.

Bracing one hand above her head, he lined his cock up and pushed into her, going slow, not because he was afraid of hurting her but because he needed to savor every second of this. She wrapped her legs around his waist, urging him deeper, and he gave in, sliding in to the hilt. Her back arched up off the bed, and she moaned out his name. She slipped her arms around his shoulders, pulling him closer.

"When will it be enough?" she asked, her eyes shining and full even in the semidarkness.

"Never, Alexa." He slowly pulled out and then just as slowly pushed all the way back in. She was so deliciously wet and tight around him, but he wanted this to last. Nothing was ever enough with her.

She reached up and stroked his cheek. "Mine," she sighed out as he thrust in and out of her again, and he pressed his forehead to hers as he established a slow, steady, deep rhythm.

"Always, princess."

He reached up and took one of her hands, lacing their fingers together and pressing her arm into the mattress, her hand above her head. Bracing his weight on his other arm, he bent his head and kissed her as he moved in and out of her. Her nails scraped lightly down his back, and he started to move faster. He rolled his hips in the way he knew she liked, and when she pulsed around him, he did it again and again and again until she started to shake and he felt her pussy clench around his cock as she came.

"God, Zack, yes!" she cried out, so loud that the entire house probably heard her, but he didn't care. Throbbing heat flared through him, radiating outward from the base of his spine, and although he didn't want it to be over, he knew he couldn't hang on much longer. She felt too damn good. He fucked her harder, losing himself in the intense pleasure of her body around his, and he pressed his face into her neck as he came, emptying himself inside her. Giving her everything.

He collapsed down on her, his entire body heavy with release, with how fucking good she made him feel.

With happiness and hope.

CHAPTER 23

Jonathan held the small black square in his shaking hand. His temples throbbed painfully, and he clenched his teeth. Pain shot through his jaw and down his neck as he stared at the piece of plastic.

Slowly, he closed his fingers over it, tightening his fist until he felt the plastic give, accompanied by a satisfying crack. He sucked in a deep breath through his nose, fighting back the wave of panicked nausea licking at the back of his throat.

"*Fuck!*" he screamed, and threw the shards of black plastic down onto his desk, watching them bounce and scatter. He sank down into his chair and looked around the library—once his sanctuary—and ground his teeth again. His sanctuary had been violated, and he pulled his phone out of his pocket. Scrolling quickly through his list of contacts, he found the one he was looking for, and he waited impatiently as it rang. Finally, it was answered, and he didn't even wait for a greeting before he spoke, using as few words as possible in case the call was being recorded.

"Get over here. Bring the equipment. Now." He disconnected and made a second call, to one of his LAPD guys.

"It's me. I need to know where my daughter is."

"On it." The line went dead, and he tossed his phone onto the desk.

Alexa. She'd done this. She'd planted these fucking bugs. Her and that stupid fucker, De Luca. Was she working with the LAPD? The feds? What did she know? How long had she known?

His phone started vibrating on the desk, and he picked it up, swiping his finger roughly across the screen. "What?" he barked out.

Kramer cleared his throat. "I talked to Elijah's lawyer, and it's not looking good. You might want to get out of town."

His grip tightened on his phone. "I need to take care of a few things first." Alexa and her fucking bodyguard would pay for what they'd done. It didn't matter that she was his flesh and blood. He couldn't let her get away with this.

"Like Alexa," Kramer said matter-of-factly, and Jonathan frowned.

"What about her?" How the hell could Kramer know about her betrayal?

"Elijah's lawyer said he has it on good authority that she's been working with the feds."

Jonathan's blood turned to ice in his veins, and a chill worked its way down his spine. Fury gripped him, and he kicked at the wastepaper basket under his desk. "I'll take care of it. Make sure Elijah has whatever he needs."

"You got it, boss."

All this was her doing. That stupid, ungrateful, conniving bitch. He'd given her so much. Money, and opportunity, and an extravagant lifestyle most people only dreamed about. And she'd repaid him by betraying not just him, but the family legacy he'd worked so hard to build and protect.

He wouldn't let them get away with this. She and De Luca, they would pay. With blood, and pain, and silence, they would pay.

* * *

Alexa smiled as she knotted her favorite blue scarf around Zack's wrists and threaded it through the slats in the headboard, securing it in place. She'd been thinking about this for days, wanting to explore him. To revel in his body and make him feel as good as he made her feel.

She sat back on her heels and let her eyes take a leisurely stroll down his naked body. His hair was messy, sticking up in places because she'd been running her hands through it while they'd kissed and kissed and kissed earlier. His black eye was healing; all the swelling was gone, and the bruising had faded to a light brownish yellow. The muscles in his arms flexed as he adjusted his grip on the headboard, moving his head against the pillow propped behind him. The masculine lines of his chest, his pecs, his abs, all that gorgeous skin, beckoned to her, and she swung her leg over his hips, straddling his lap. The hair on his thighs bristled against her skin, and she leaned forward, scraping her teeth over one of his nipples.

She looked up and met his eyes, and he smiled that heart-melting half smile, the skin around his eyes crinkling. When she'd told him what she wanted, he'd offered himself up willingly, letting her take what she needed from him.

He flexed his hips up, and his hard cock brushed against her thigh. Her clit throbbed, and a dull ache took root in her core, but this, right now, this wasn't about that. This was about giving and claiming at the same time. About power, and trust, and adoration.

She moved down his legs, took his cock in her hands, and stroked him lazily, watching as a tiny bead of moisture formed on the tip. Still stroking him, she bent her head and kissed that bead of moisture, swirling her tongue over the head of his cock once and then sitting back again and licking her lips.

He shifted his hips impatiently. "You know I'm going to make you pay for this, right?" His voice was strained, and she smiled.

"I'm counting on it." She winked at him and then bent forward again, her bare breasts brushing over his chest. He groaned and strained against the scarf, the headboard creaking slightly. When he was still, she kissed a path down his chest, taking her time over his abs, kissing each defined muscle, licking and nipping at his skin, sliding her hand over his cock in slow, teasing strokes. She worked her way lower, licking the cut lines along his hips and then down.

She traced her tongue over his balls, and he groaned, his hips moving again against the mattress. She did it again and then feathered kisses up his shaft, rubbing her lips over his hot, smooth skin.

"I love your cock," she said, and slowly licked up the entire length of him. "I love how it looks, and how it feels, and how it tastes." The headboard creaked again, and she looked up.

His eyes were dark, his brow furrowed. "Show me how much you love my cock, princess."

"Mmm." The sound she made was half moan, half hum, and she wrapped her hand around the base. Smiling, she met his eyes and pressed the head of his cock to her lips. She flicked her tongue out and licked him, and his body jerked, his wrists straining against the scarf.

"God, Alexa. Please," he ground out, and she stroked him with her hand again.

"Tell me what you want me to do."

His hips rose up off the bed, toward her. "Put my cock in your mouth. Now."

She smiled and moved away, and he groaned. She settled back down on top of him, straddling him again. This time she slicked her pussy over his cock, rubbing her throbbing clit against him. They moaned in unison, and she did it again, rocking back and forth over the hard ridge of his cock, sliding easily because she was so aroused it almost hurt.

Pleasure—need and lust and love—licked over her skin, and he pressed up into her, his hips working. She threw her head back, high on arousal, and rocked her hips, back and forth, back and forth, and as he ground up into her, the throbbing in her clit stopped and then restarted again at double time as she came. She fell forward against him as she moaned out his name, her entire body shaking.

Zack slammed his head back against the pillow, his chest heaving. "Holy shit," he panted out, and her eyes fluttered closed for a second as she rode out the aftershocks of her orgasm. Once she caught her breath, she kissed her way down his body again, but with no teasing this time. Wrapping one hand around the base of his cock, she took him into her mouth, sucking and licking and moaning as she tasted herself on him. She swirled her tongue over and around his head, and she could taste how turned on he was.

A surge of power flowed through her, and she pumped her hand up to meet her lips, taking as much of his thick cock into her mouth as she could. She felt the head nudge the back of her throat, and her eyes watered.

"Jesus fucking Christ, princess. Holy fuck," he growled, pushing his hips up to meet her mouth, and she swallowed a little bit more of him. Slowly, slowly, she eased back and stroked him with her hand, slicking her saliva over him. She kissed the head, licking at him, sucking and teasing before once again taking him deep into her mouth. This time she found a steady rhythm, working his cock in and out of her mouth, slicking her tongue over his head with each pass. His hips jerked, and she let him slip free of her mouth, trailing the tip of her tongue over his hot, smooth skin. She stroked him and kissed his swollen head, looking up at him.

Her heart almost stopped, he looked so fucking ravenous. His eyes were dark, the cords in his neck straining. She kissed his cock again, still working him with her hand. "Do you want to come in my mouth?" she asked, and his cock twitched in her hand. For the first time in her life, she was enjoying this, and it was because of him.

"Please," he moaned, and she smiled as she once again took him deep, working him with her mouth. Another creak from the headboard, and his hips flexed up off the bed. "Alexa!" The first salty spurt of his come hit her tongue as the headboard gave way with a loud crack. He pumped his hips up to meet her mouth as he came, and she greedily swallowed down everything he gave her.

Slowly, she eased his still-hard cock out of her mouth and looked up at him. His eyes were glazed, and his hands were by his sides. The scarf was still wrapped around his right wrist, along with a slender piece of wood. One of the headboard's slats had snapped free.

"You made me break the headboard," he said, his voice strained, his chest heaving. And then he started to laugh, his shoulders shaking, and, as she sat up, she couldn't help but join him. She laughed and laughed until her stomach hurt and tears filled her eyes, and then she fell into his arms.

For the first time in her life, she knew what real happiness felt like.

* * *

Zack's eyes flew open, and he sat up in bed. Alexa slept beside him, sprawled on her stomach and wearing one of his T-shirts, her arms above her head. He frowned as he listened.

Something was wrong.

He pushed the covers back and slipped out of bed, careful not to wake her. He grabbed his gun from the nightstand and moved silently through the room, then turned the doorknob slowly so it wouldn't squeak. He stepped into the hallway and listened again, wishing his heart weren't beating so damn loud.

A car door slammed somewhere down the street. He made his way down the stairs, his gun cradled in his hands. The house was dark save for a faint light in the kitchen, and he made his way toward it.

Mac stood in the room, his Browning Hi Power in his hand, his head cocked. "You hear that?" he whispered.

Zack nodded, checking the clip on his M&P9. "Car door. Anything on the cams?"

Mac nodded. "Two vehicles by the curb a few houses down. Can't see the occupants; it's too bloody dark."

"Let me see if I can see anything through the front windows. I'll whistle if I do."

Mac nodded, and Zack hurried into the room at the front of the house. Just as he eased back the curtain, the window shattered. Sharp, stinging pain seared across his bare arms and chest, and he ducked, shielding his face with his arms instinctively. The alarm started blaring, and Zack ran toward the stairs. He had to get to Alexa and protect her.

At least eight men, all wearing ski masks, poured in through the shattered bay window, guns in their gloved hands. Locklin and Rowe, the two Special Ops officers, came charging in, guns drawn. Gunfire exploded through the house, and Zack dove behind the leather sofa, belly to the ground. The sofa wouldn't stop those bullets, and he needed to get to Alexa. As cautiously as possible, he peeked up above the top of the sofa, taking aim and shooting at the attackers.

Morales stood at the top of the stairs and, with deadly accuracy, aimed and took out three of the armed intruders. She moved quickly down the stairs, but more men swarmed into the house. Rowe lay on the floor, an ominous red puddle around him. It would be several minutes before backup of any kind reached them, and they were outgunned and outnumbered.

Knowing he needed to take this chance, Zack stayed as low as possible and ran. A bullet whizzed by his head, splintering the wood of the banister as he neared the stairs. He could hear the men moving farther into the house, and he grabbed at the banister. Morales had run into the fray, and the staircase was now unguarded. Panic flooded him, and he pushed up the stairs.

A hand closed over his ankle and yanked him down. Pain exploded across his ribs as they made contact with the hard wood of the stairs, and he swore. He kicked free of the grip and turned to face the man, who started to raise his gun.

Zack aimed a high kick, connecting with the weapon and sending it skittering across the floor. From the front of the house, shouts, bangs, and grunts echoed, but all he could focus on was the man in front of him. Zack would do whatever it took to stop him from getting up those stairs.

The man lunged at Zack, but he was ready for him and threw him off easily, landing a punch and a kick before shoving him back into the wall. He pinned him there and brought his knee into his stomach, and then threw him to the floor. He'd dropped his gun when the man had grabbed his ankle and was without a weapon. But the bullet that had narrowly missed him had broken the banister, leaving a couple of spindles loose.

As fast as he could, Zack grabbed two thick wooden spindles and brandished them in front of him. The man got up off the floor, and Zack struck out with one of the spindles, connecting with the man's temple. He slumped to the floor just as second man charged at Zack, intent on the stairs. Zack threw his elbow into the man's face, and the sickening crunch of elbow meeting jaw filled him with a grim satisfaction. Howling, the attacker stumbled backward, and Zack raised his leg and kicked him hard in the stomach.

A scream pierced the night from upstairs, and Zack's heart stopped.

Alexa.

He turned and ran up the stairs, and fell to his knees when he found their room empty.

* * *

Alexa fought and struggled, trying desperately to use any of the self-defense techniques Zack had taught her, but it was no use. She was outnumbered, and each of the men was much, much stronger than her. She could hear gunshots and yelling downstairs, and she knew her father had somehow found where they were hiding.

The two men who'd crashed in through her window held her pinned between them. They dragged her across the room, then made their way through the smashed window and out onto the roof. A desperate panic jolted through her, and she struggled harder, letting loose a scream. One of the men backhanded her, and she stumbled forward, stunned by the pain. Her mouth filled with blood, her eyes with tears as her mind spun with what to do. Going with them would mean only terrible things; she knew that much.

The men wore harnesses, and one of them crushed her against his chest, holding her in place as the other man clipped both men to the ropes attached to the house with grappling hooks. She squirmed against his iron grip, his meaty fingers digging painfully into her arms. Once both men were secured, the other grabbed her and began rappelling down the side of the house. This time she didn't fight, too scared of falling to the ground twenty feet below and breaking her neck.

In under a minute, they were on the ground, and the men began roughly ushering her toward a car several feet away. Alexa wanted to scream, to fight, to run, but a terrifying numbness had taken over, and she felt as though she were watching everything from high above. None of this could possibly be real. More gunshots rang out.

Please let Zack be okay. Please.

They threw her into the backseat of a car and before she could fight, had secured her wrists and ankles with a thick layer of duct tape. The men who'd grabbed her didn't get into the vehicle, and the car door slammed, locking her inside. Her heart raced so fast that she thought it might explode. Her arms and legs shook, and she looked back at the house, looking for signs that Zack was all right. Trying not to think about the fate that awaited her.

Her father sat in the front passenger seat, and he turned to face her, a sneer on his face. She shivered but forced herself to sit up straight and meet his gaze.

"Hello, Alexa. You have a lot of explaining to do." He turned to the driver and gave a sharp nod. "Let's go."

CHAPTER 24

I have to go after her." Zack picked up his gun from where it had fallen and shoved it into the waistband of his jeans. They'd taken out the intruders, but Rowe was seriously injured. Mac was on his knees beside him, his hands pressed to Rowe's shoulder as he stemmed the bleeding.

"Go," said Locklin, his phone pressed to his ear. "I'll stay with him, wait for backup, and deal with this mess."

"I'll come with you," said Mac, standing as Locklin took over. His hands were red, stained with blood, but he didn't seem to notice.

"Then let's go," called Morales as she strode toward the garage. In under a minute, they were in her car and on the road, speeding after the vehicle holding Alexa. The team had been able to grab an image of the vehicle and its plates from the security cam, and Morales had radioed it in. Aerial assistance was currently on the lookout for them.

"Detective, we have a location on the vehicle," came a tinny voice, and Zack held his breath as he waited.

"Go ahead," she said.

"They're moving north on Highway 14. Not sure where they're headed, but they're about ten miles ahead of you."

"Got it." Morales hit the gas, and her car shot forward. From his vantage point in the front seat, Zack watched as the road slipped by, forcing himself to suck slow, steady breaths in through his nose. If he didn't, he'd puke, or break things, or shout and swear until his throat was raw.

Visions of what might happen to Alexa—what might've *already* happened—swam through his mind, and he closed his eyes, trying to push them away. Trying to prevent his mind from going there.

He'd get her back. He had to.

* * *

The sun began to peek over the horizon, casting a pink halo around the mountains as the car moved farther into the desert.

"Where are we going?" she asked, shifting against the seat, trying to stop the shivers racking her body. Nobody answered her, and she wanted to scream and cry in frustration. All she had on was Zack's T-shirt and a pair of panties, and the interior of the car was cool. Goose bumps dotted her arms and legs, and she curled into the seat, trying to get warm.

She dipped her head and caught Zack's scent from his T-shirt, and her eyes stung and welled. A hundred questions burned through her mind. Where was her father taking her? Was he going to kill her? Was Zack okay? Was he coming after her?

What if he wasn't okay?

She closed her eyes, not wanting to go down that road. Not wanting to think about horrifying possibilities.

"Are you going to kill me?" she asked. She wasn't even sure she wanted the answer, but the silence in the car was making her crazy.

"I haven't decided yet. I want to," her father said casually from the front seat. "Your mother would be upset. That's the only reason I haven't yet." He turned in his seat. "What do you know?"

She met his eyes and didn't say anything. She knew there was nothing she could say that wouldn't land her in more trouble. He wouldn't believe her if she denied she knew anything, and she refused to tell him what she did know. Her father sneered, a look of disgust on his face as he studied her.

They'd yet to pass another car on the road, an eerily quiet stretch of desert highway, and she knew she was going to die, probably out here, alone in the desert. Before today she'd loved coming out into the desert, loved the soaring freedom of the sky, the wide-open spaces, the peace and the solitude. Today, the emptiness of the place weighed on her, the heavy bleakness of isolation. She felt trapped, confined, not by the lack of space but by its abundance.

"Shit, I think they caught up to us," said the driver, his eyes narrow slits as he stared in the rearview mirror.

Her father looked away from her and out through the rear window, and then he smiled. Her skin crawled, and she thought she might be sick at the sight of that smile, because it was one that promised pain and violence.

* * *

The engine of Morales's car roared, and her knuckles were white around the steering wheel. "Yes! I got taillights!" she said, nodding once. Zack stared at the tiny red lights in the distance, the only other vehicle on the long, lonely stretch of desert highway they'd been speeding down for nearly thirty minutes.

Thirty of the longest fucking minutes in his entire life.

"They're probably going to start shooting at us. Mac, De Luca, get ready to return fire if necessary. Go for the tires, and avoid the body of the car if you can. They've probably got Alexa in the trunk or the backseat. When I get close enough, I'll PIT the vehicle. It's not the prettiest solution, but it's all we've got right now."

Zack glanced over his shoulder, and Mac nodded, his expression grim.

Adrenaline and fear and anger all beat through Zack's body, his stomach churning. He felt as though they were upside down and underwater. He wouldn't be right again until he knew Alexa was safe. And if Fairfax had hurt her…so help him God, he couldn't promise he wouldn't kill him.

The gap between the vehicles continued to close, and the first spray of bullets hit the front of the car. Zack ducked, his gun clutch in his hands. Although she'd crouched down, Morales didn't waver from the road, maintaining speed.

A second volley of bullets bit into the car, and as much as he hated the thought of shooting at the vehicle holding Alexa, Zack knew they needed to return fire. They'd be no good to her if Morales's car left the road, or if one of them got shot. "We're going too fast for me to shoot through the side window. I need to take the windshield out," he said, ducking down as a third round of bullets pelted the car.

"Do it," said Mac and Morales in unison, and he raised his weapon. He leaned back in his seat and aimed his gun low on the windshield, keeping himself shielded and out of the way of the glass about to shatter. He squeezed the trigger and fired off four rounds, the sound exploding through the interior of the car. The tempered, laminated glass shattered but collapsed into sticky petals and, thankfully, didn't fly apart into shards. Leaning back farther in his seat, Zack raised his foot and kicked the spiderwebbed glass out of the way. Cool, dry air washed into the vehicle. Sitting up a little, he took aim again, going for the tires as Morales urged them closer and closer. He hit the rear driver's side tire, and the car wove, careening from one side of the road to the other. Another few shots came from the car in front of them and then stopped suddenly, even though they were gaining. The car careened across the road and then went into a sickening roll, flipping over twice before lurching to a halt.

"Fuck!" Zack's breath whooshed out of him as he shouted. The car had crashed because *he'd* shot out the tire.

His fault. His fault. His fault.

And if she wasn't okay, he'd never forgive himself.

Morales slammed on her brakes, and the three of them rushed out of her car, approaching cautiously, weapons drawn.

Zack's heart thundered in his chest, every muscle in his body coiled and ready. He needed to get eyes on Alexa, and then maybe he'd be able to breathe again.

* * *

Alexa groaned and fumbled for the door handle. The impact had slammed her against the interior of the car, and she could feel a warm, wet trickle down the side of her head. She struggled against the bindings on her wrists, trying to get her fingers to cooperate enough to open the door.

The driver was unconscious, but her father wasn't. He was moving, shifting in his seat, but he was stunned, just as she was, and she knew that this was her chance to escape. She blinked rapidly a few times, trying to clear the fog of fear and pain and concentrate on just getting the door handle to work. Everything felt so difficult, as though she were on another planet where the same rules of gravity didn't apply.

Finally, she closed her fingers around the door handle and pulled it the right way. The door gave, and as she tumbled out of the car, she realized it was upside down. She slammed into the pavement, shards of glass and metal digging into her skin. Those tiny points of pain woke her up, and she tried to get her feet under her, wanting to get away from the car. But her ankles were bound, and she couldn't seem to haul herself up. Blood seeped from her knees, biting pain clawing against her skin.

"Alexa!" She heard Zack's voice before she saw him, and she sucked in a breath, hoping that this wasn't some kind of cruel nightmare or trick of the pain screaming through her body. But then he was there, his hands on her shoulders as he helped her up. And then Mac was there too with a knife, cutting her wrists and ankles free. She threw her arms around Zack, her entire body shaking.

A scrape of movement behind her, and Zack stiffened. She turned, and it was as though everything slipped into slow motion. Her father emerged from the car, his gun drawn and leveled at her.

Zack shoved her away and moved in front of her just as her father fired, the crack of the gunshot echoing against the mountains rising up in the distance. Zack's gun fell from his hand, and he dropped to the pavement, landing on his knees and then falling over sideways. Blood bloomed against his gray T-shirt, welling up impossibly fast. His eyes glazed over, and his head fell to the side as more blood pooled from the gunshot wound to his chest. He didn't move. Bleeding and bleeding and bleeding.

"No!" she screamed and dove for Zack's gun. She'd never fired a gun before, but it didn't matter. She picked it up and aimed at her father, pulling the trigger without hesitating. He'd taken so much from her; she wouldn't let him get away with taking Zack. He grunted and grabbed his shoulder, then dove behind the wrecked car for safety. Her palms buzzed, and her arms vibrated with the recoil.

Ian moved forward, his gun trained on her father while Natalie scrambled for her radio, screaming for a medical evac and backup. Zack made a horrible gasping, choking sound, and Ian dropped to his knees beside him.

Her father started to emerge from behind the car, and Alexa raised Zack's gun again, her heart beating so fast it felt as though it were shaking in her chest. But her hands were steady, as was her voice. "Don't move, you son of a bitch!"

But he still saw her as she used to be, and not as the person she'd become. He smiled, shaking his head as though he were about to chastise her, and took a step toward her.

She pulled the trigger again, putting everything she hated about him into that small, controlled movement. He jerked and clutched at his throat, blood spurting from between his fingers as he gasped and sank to his knees. His mouth opened and closed, his eyes wide and frantic as he tried to breathe. The bullet had pierced his throat, blood spilling down over his chest.

She moved forward and kicked his gun away, leaving him to bleed out in the dirt. Maybe it was cold, but after everything he'd done, it was better than he deserved. On shaking legs, she turned and sprinted to where Zack lay, his eyes closed.

God, there was so much blood. So much.

Natalie made her way to the crashed vehicle to check on the driver. "He's dead," she called out, sounding shaken. "They're both dead."

Ian gently eased Zack up and glanced at his back. "It's not through and through. Let's try to stem the bleeding. It's the best we can do until the evac gets here." He took his knife and cut Zack's T-shirt open. The bullet had hit a few inches below his left collarbone, and the skin from his neck to his abdomen was an angry red. Ian's hands moved quickly as he examined Zack, checking for other vitals. Natalie dropped to her knees beside them and began applying pressure where Ian directed her.

"Multiple rib fractures below the wound. Damage to the chest wall."

Zack's chest moved up and down in short, shallow breaths, his face a sickly white, and Ian swore. He bent his head and listened for a second. "We're dealing with a pneumothorax." He raised his head and met Alexa's eyes, and she could see the fear in them. "His lung's collapsing because of the air seeping in through the chest wound, and he's losing too much blood."

"What can I do?" she asked, dropping to the pavement beside them.

Ian took her hands and guided them onto Zack's chest, right beside Natalie's. "Steady pressure. We're losing him. I have to try something." He scrambled away, and Alexa blinked furiously, knowing she had to stay calm.

"Please stay," she said, his heartbeat feeble and slow under her hands. She swallowed, her throat thickening and her eyes stinging as the future she'd planned with him slipped through her fingers before it had even begun.

Her father had robbed her of everything. Her innocence, her freedom, her happiness, and now the love of her life. An anger like she'd never known ripped through her, and she swallowed down the urge to scream.

Ian returned with the med kit he'd retrieved from Natalie's car, and Alexa couldn't do anything but pray as she watched him, feeling helpless as Zack struggled for air, lying in a crimson pool of his own blood. In the distance, she could hear the rhythmic chopping of a helicopter approaching, along with sirens.

Ian tugged on latex gloves and began pressing on Zack's chest, below the wound. After a second he nodded and coated the area with iodine. "Prop him up," he said, and Alexa maintained pressure while Natalie moved around behind him, shifting him into a reclining position. "Hold his left arm behind his head." Natalie took Zack's arm and propped it behind his head, and Ian felt below the wound again. Alexa focused on Zack's face as Ian cut into him and inserted a chest tube.

Zack took a deep, shuddering breath and then slowly let it out. She leaned forward and pressed her forehead to his. "Stay with me, Zack. Please, don't go."

His chest rose and fell once more, and then he stopped moving.

CHAPTER 25

Zack felt as if he were floating and sinking at the same time, unable to make sense of the sounds around him. Voices. Black. A beating of air. Flashes of blue sky. Wind.

Pain.

Cold.

Black.

Alexa crying.

He tried to open his eyes at that sound, to move, but nothing would cooperate, and every time he tried, all he got was more black.

Flashing lights, people shouting. Beeps and the sounds of footsteps echoing down a hallway. A sickly antiseptic smell.

More pain. More black.

No air.

He struggled, to breathe, to open his eyes, to do something, anything, to get back to Alexa, to tell her he was all right.

Another wave of pain.

Black. Black. Black.

* * *

Seafoam green was the color of nausea, Alexa decided. The scrubs of the doctors who couldn't tell her anything, who told her not to hope. The ugly walls of the surgical waiting room at Bakersfield Memorial. The vinyl of the chair she hadn't moved from since she'd sat down almost six hours ago, except for the one time she'd gotten up to vomit in the bathroom.

A giant clock hung on the far wall, ticking away the seconds. Zack was fighting for his life as the surgeons worked to save him, and she was sitting in an ugly green chair, staring helplessly at a clock.

Guilt sat like a rock on her chest. Not over shooting her own father, but over Zack, and the life-threatening injury he'd sustained protecting her from that bastard. He'd taken a bullet for her, sacrificing himself to keep her safe.

The medical evac had brought them here, and the only reason Zack had any chance at survival at all was that Ian had successfully inserted the chest tube. But the wound had caused a lot of damage, and he'd lost a lot of blood. She knew he'd crashed more than once. And still she sat, surrounded by seafoam green, waiting. Helpless. Powerless. Lost.

"Do you want anything, lass?" asked Ian, who'd been pacing the room, his arms crossed, his face grim. "Coffee? Water?"

"I could go to the cafeteria and get you something to eat," offered Sierra, who'd arrived with Sean, Taylor, and Colt a couple of hours ago.

"No, thank you," she said numbly, shaking her head. Donna, Zack's mom, sat beside Alexa, her hand on her thigh.

"He'll be okay. He's strong," Donna said, and Alexa wasn't sure if she was trying to convince herself or Alexa.

"I love him," she whispered, and pulled the sweater someone had given her tighter around her shoulders. She'd had her own wounds seen to, the scrapes and cuts from the car crash, and had been given a pair of seafoam green scrub pants to wear so she wasn't half-naked. They'd tried to take Zack's T-shirt from her, but she hadn't let them. She was numb, watching, not really absorbing anything. Distantly, she knew she must be in shock, but she couldn't seem to rouse herself from it. Maybe she didn't want to. Didn't want to face the reality that she might lose Zack. That she'd shot and killed her own father. That everything was a giant, colossal fucking mess.

"I know," said Donna, patting Alexa's hand. "I saw the way you watched him fight."

"This is my fault." Guilt weighed down on her. She was the one who'd involved him in her fucked-up situation in the first place.

"No, it's not," said Sean, crouching down in front of her. "He was doing his job, and he was protecting the woman he loves. It's what any of us would do."

Colt looked at Taylor and nodded solemnly, and Mark kissed Donna's temple. Natalie sipped her coffee, staring down at the floor. Ian and Chris paced. The clock ticked.

"I've seen guys survive a lot worse," said Colt. "He'll pull through."

"He will," said Taylor.

"He will," said Sierra.

Alexa nodded, and her heart vaulted in her chest when one of the surgeons stepped into the waiting room. He pulled the mask from his face, and she felt a little light-headed when he smiled.

"We were able to repair the damage to his lungs without having to remove the lower left lobe, which was badly damaged. We removed the bullet and all fragments and were able to stabilize him with the help of a blood transfusion. He's in recovery now, and still sedated. He's on a ventilator, and we've left the chest tube in place for the time being to evacuate any air and residual blood that may accumulate. We've got him on an antibiotic drip and a heavy dose of pain meds. The next twenty-four to thirty-six hours are critical, but I'm cautiously optimistic."

Zack's mom ran forward and hugged the surgeon. "Thank you. Thank you," she said, and he patted her back. "When can we take him home?"

"Barring any complications, we'll likely keep him for a week."

"Will he make a full recovery?" asked Zack's dad.

The doctor nodded. "Again, barring any complications, with physical therapy and hard work, he should be back to normal in a few months."

Alexa started to shake, overwhelmed with relief.

* * *

Zack opened his eyes, and for a second everything was blurry. He blinked, trying to clear his vision, trying to figure out where he was. Everything ached, from his shoulders to his hips, and he felt as though his limbs weighed a thousand pounds each. He blinked again, and the hospital room came into focus.

The curtains were open, revealing the night sky, and he wondered how long he'd been here. He closed his eyes again, trying to remember.

The car chase. The shoot-out. The gun leveled at Alexa. His heart rate picked up, the beeps from the monitor coming faster than before, and he tried to sit up. An intense wave of pain rocked him, and he looked down. A tube emerged from the side of his chest, just under his left pec, and more tubes came from his arm. He moved the fabric of the hospital gown aside and traced his fingers over the large gauze pad covering a hefty portion of the left side of his chest.

He remembered shoving Alexa out of the way, the bang of the gun going off, the searing pain burning through him, and then not much of anything. Flashes here and there, but nothing concrete. Carefully, he pulled himself up to a sitting position, his eyes scanning the empty room, quiet except for the machines surrounding his bed.

What if he hadn't saved her? The thought sent panic spiraling through him, and he had to force himself to calm down because it fucking hurt to take deep breaths. Everything hurt, but the pain would be nothing compared to the knowledge that he'd failed to protect her.

The door opened, and Alexa stepped inside, a Styrofoam cup in one hand and her phone in the other. She didn't look at him as she entered, her attention on her phone. A few scrapes lined her arms and her face, but she looked otherwise uninjured.

Joy radiated through him like sunshine, and he suddenly didn't give a shit about the pain in his chest anymore. She was alive, and safe. That was all that mattered.

"Hey, princess," he said, his voice rusty. Her head jerked up, and she dropped her cup. Brown liquid splattered on the floor, and the scent of coffee filled the room, chasing away the sterile, medicinal smell.

"Oh my God," she whispered, and ran to the bed to

throw her arms around his neck. "Oh my God, Zack. I was so scared."

He could feel her shaking, and even though it hurt, he managed to wrap his right arm around her. "Nothing to be scared of, sweetheart. I told you I'd protect you."

She cried harder, and he swallowed over the lump forming in his own throat.

"I thought I was going to lose you." She pulled back, settling on the edge of the bed. Raising a trembling hand, she cupped his face. "You saved my life. You got shot, and it's my fault. I'm so grateful, and I'm so sorry. God, Zack, I'm sorry."

He felt his stubble rasp against her palm, and he knew he'd been out for a day or two based on the growth. "None of this is your fault." He tipped her chin up, and she met his eyes. "I love you, and I'm glad I was able to keep you safe. I got shot because I was protecting you, and I'd do it again."

The corner of her mouth turned up, a hint of a smile. "You'd better fucking not."

He laughed and then winced, pain dancing across his ribs. "What happened? Tell me."

She sighed and took one of his hands in hers. "My father tried to shoot me, and you pushed me aside and got hit. I…" She bit her lip. "I picked up your gun, and I shot him. Twice. He's dead."

"Oh God, princess, I'm sorry." He carefully settled her against his right side and stroked her hair. "I'm so sorry it came to that."

"Me too, but I did what I had to do. For you. For us."

His arm tightened around her and she continued. "After I shot him, Natalie radioed for help, and Ian saved your life. He put a tube in your chest because you couldn't breathe properly, right there in the middle of the highway. It was pretty badass."

Zack glanced down and gave his head a slow shake. "Holy shit. How long have I been here?"

She glanced at her phone. "Almost three days. We're in Bakersfield. You were airlifted here and had surgery to remove the bullet and repair your lung. I think they're hoping to take your chest tube out tomorrow. They should let you go home in a couple of days."

"Come here," he said, and kissed her softly and gently, just needing to feel the warmth of her lips on his.

She laid her forehead against his. "Thank you for saving me," she whispered.

He winced again as he raised his hand and stroked her hair. "Anytime, princess."

"The doctor said you have a lot of physical therapy ahead of you. I don't know what that means for training and fighting, or for your contract."

"It doesn't matter, because without you none of that means anything. You're what matters, and you're safe. That's all I need."

"I love you so much. So much," she said, nestling her face into his neck.

"I love you too, Alexa."

She sighed and snuggled against his good side, and they fell asleep, safe and whole.

EPILOGUE

Six months later

Alexa arched her back up off the bed and moaned, her hands pinned above her head, her orgasm shimmering around her. Zack circled his hips, fucking her exactly the way she loved and sending her over the edge. Her hips bucked and jerked, and she called out his name, so loud that the neighbors could probably hear them. He kissed a path down her neck, and after a few more hard, deep thrusts, he buried himself inside her, panting her name.

He let go of her wrists, and she slid her arms around his shoulders, pulling him close and kissing him, her legs still around his hips. He stayed hard inside her, and he flexed his hips. Her muscles clenched around him in response, and he deepened the kiss.

"Aha! Hahaha!" His laugh was loud and high pitched, and he squirmed slightly above her. "Someone's licking my toes."

She laughed and pushed up onto her elbows. Sure

enough, Schroeder, the black-and-tan dachshund they'd adopted a month ago, stood at the foot of the bed, poking his head up over the edge like the world's cutest prairie dog.

"Hey, puppy," she cooed, and he gave an excited little whine. She lay back down and pushed her hair out of her eyes. "We'll have to save round two for later. I think someone needs a walk."

Zack kissed her once more and then pulled away, moving to the edge of the bed to pull on his jeans. She came up behind him and kissed the Japanese characters on his back. *Honor. Loyalty. Bravery. Strength.*

He'd inked those values onto his skin, and she watched him live by them every single day. She reached forward and traced her fingers over the scars, one from the bullet wound, the other where Ian had saved his life.

She still wasn't sure what she'd done to deserve him, this amazing, selfless, gorgeous man. But she knew she never, ever wanted to let him go, and so she tried to be worthy of him, every single day.

He gently pulled her hand away from his scars and raised it to his mouth to kiss her fingertips. He stood and then pulled a shirt on, moving to the window. Huge fluffy white flakes fell from the gray Montreal sky.

"Hey, look, princess," he said, and she rose from the bed and pulled her sweater and jeans on. He tucked her against him as they watched the very first snowflakes of the winter fall. They'd moved here in September, once Zack had finished his therapy and been given the go-ahead to ease back into training. They'd both been ready for a change of scenery, so when he'd been offered the chance to train at one of the top gyms in North America, they'd jumped at the chance to start fresh somewhere new.

Schroeder barked, and they both smiled. "Okay, okay," she said. "We're coming." He scampered toward the front door of their apartment, tail wagging so fast that his entire back end moved with it. As Zack tugged on his boots, she retrieved Schroeder's leash from the hook by the front door, and he danced in a circle. She pulled her coat on, waiting while Zack went back into the bedroom to get his phone. When he came back, he pulled her against him and kissed her, sweetly and gently. He kissed the tip of her nose, her temple, her forehead, and then opened the door. Cold, damp air swirled in around them, and she stepped outside, awestruck by the simple beauty of the falling flakes. For several moments they stood on the front stoop of their walk-up, watching as the snow drifted lazily from the sky. Even though their street was a busy one, there was something peaceful about the snow.

"You want to go up to the lookout?" he asked, referring to one of her favorite spots in their new city, and she nodded. She slipped her hand into his, and they started off, Schroeder trotting happily beside them. Taking their time, snowflakes falling prettily around them, they walked down Sherbrooke to Peel and then into Mount Royal Park.

"How was class today?" he asked as they walked, their breath puffing out in little white clouds.

She smiled. "Good. I'm nervous, but I think I'm ready for exams."

"You're gonna kill it, princess. You've been working so hard."

She'd enrolled at McGill University and was taking courses in anthropology, psychology, and communications while she figured out what she wanted to major in. It was everything she'd hoped it would be, and while she'd endured the curious stares of her classmates for the first couple of weeks, everyone seemed to have accepted her as just another student now.

"You've been working hard too," she said, and stretched up on her tiptoes to kiss his cheek. "I'm proud of you."

He smiled. "It feels good to get back in there again."

After being shot, he'd spoken with a representative from the UFC, and the organization had left the offer on the table, waiting for him when he was ready. She'd been there, right beside him, when he'd signed the contract last month, and she knew he was hoping to book his first fight by summer. She knew that he missed being a bodyguard sometimes, but it was a small sacrifice to make to chase his dreams. And she was happy to cheer him on every step of the way.

They reached the lookout, and she sighed happily. It was a flat, open area that provided a breathtakingly beautiful view of the Montreal skyline. A fine dusting of snow sat on top of the concrete railing, and she trailed her gloved fingers through it, watching the flakes scatter like fairy dust. Schroeder sniffed at the snow and then sneezed, a few white flakes still clinging to his little black nose.

The Montreal skyline twinkled in the falling dusk, and the park's lights came on, including the colorful Christmas lights strung through the bare branches of the trees. Dozens of people milled about, couples and families and people walking dogs. A gust of wind swirled the snow around them.

"Hey, aren't you Alexa Fairfax?" asked a man who'd approached them.

She plastered a smile onto her face. "Yeah, I am."

"Oh, wow. Can I get a picture with you?"

She nodded and rolled her eyes at Zack when the man wasn't looking. The story of the Golden Brotherhood, her father's death, and her mother's imprisonment had been huge news, and she'd spent more time in the spotlight in the months following last summer's events than she ever had during her career as an actress. Her mother had been devastated by Jonathan's death, and had vowed never to speak to Alexa again, which, frankly, suited Alexa just fine. She was ready to put that part of her life behind her and move forward without the darkness of her family hanging over her. She'd found a new family with Zack and the De Lucas, who were making the trek to Montreal in a couple of weeks so they could all spend Christmas together. Sierra, Sean, Taylor, and Colt were all coming up for New Year's Eve. She loved her new life, but missed her friends, and was looking forward to seeing them.

Once the man was satisfied with the selfie he'd taken, she took Schroeder's leash back from Zack. "You know, some days I'm really sick of being Alexa Fairfax."

He smiled, and something about the gleam in his eye sent her heart racing. "Mmm. Maybe I can help with that."

"What do you…" But the rest of her question died on her lips as he pulled a velvet box from the pocket of his coat. He flipped it open, revealing a simple round-cut diamond ring. Beautiful and perfect, just like the snowflakes falling around them.

"I think Alexa De Luca has a nice ring to it, don't you?" he asked, and her heart flew into her throat, fluttering madly.

"Are you asking me…" Once again she couldn't finish her question. Her eyes were stinging, her throat clogging, and her heart was trying to escape her body. Probably to fly into his waiting hands.

He sank to one knee, the ring box still extended in one hand. "Six months ago today, I kissed you for the first time, and I knew right then that I loved you. I couldn't remember what it was like to not have you in my life, couldn't understand how I'd lived without you. I don't ever want to find out." He pulled the ring free and held it clasped between his thumb and his forefinger. "I bought this the week we moved here. I was going to wait for Christmas Eve, but screw it." He dropped the ring box and took her shaking hand. "Alexa Elizabeth Fairfax"—he looked up and held her eyes with his—"will you marry me?"

She blinked rapidly, tears slipping free as her heart beat a happy, fluttering rhythm in her chest. God, her world made so much sense with him in it, made sense in a way it never had without him. She nodded, warmth radiating through her despite the snow falling around them. "Yes," she whispered.

He stood, and she threw her arms around him, kissing him. He kissed her back, and she could taste the promised happiness of the next sixty years on his lips. Breaking the kiss, she tore at her gloves impatiently, juggling them and Schroeder's leash, wanting the ring on her finger.

"There's an inscription," he said, and she took it in her trembling fingers, tilting it to see the words.

Yours. Mine. Ours. Us.

She slipped it on and repeated the words, kissing him after each one. "Yours. Mine. Ours. Us."

He pulled her tight against him and kissed her temple. "Always, princess."

When her home is vandalized, Hollywood star Sierra Blake knows it's time to bring in the experts. But from the moment she sets eyes on her indecently sexy new bodyguard, Sierra's thoughts are anything but professional…

An excerpt from *Necessary Risk* follows.

CHAPTER 1

Sierra Blake glanced up at the bank of lights, and tiny dots danced in front of her eyes. People didn't often realize just how hot stage lights could be. The expression "basking in the spotlight"? That stray *s* had to be a typo, because it was more like "baking in the spotlight."

"Sierra, what do you think separates you from other child stars?" The 90's Con panel moderator directed the question at her, smoothing a hand down his tie as he glanced at the index cards clutched in one hand. She took a breath, the prickling threat of sweat teasing along her hairline. God, was she relieved she didn't have to do this daily anymore. She smoothed her hair over her shoulder and ran her hands over the skirt of her cream-colored silk dress. Hundreds of eyes locked onto her, and a zing of adrenaline shot down to her toes.

She bit her lip and fingered the shooting star pendant at the base of her throat. "You mean, how did I avoid living 'la vida Lohan'?"

Laughter bubbled up from the audience, and she relaxed

a little. Although it was par for the course at events like this, she'd always hated that question and the quagmire of emotions it dredged up.

She took a deep breath and dove in. "Quite frankly, being a child star is pretty messed up. You're working with adults, keeping adult hours, making adult money, and trying to live up to the expectations of everyone around you. Any kid would find that kind of pressure confining. And that's where the rebellion comes in. Drinking and drugs and sex. And all of this is happening when you're trying to figure out who you actually are. How are you supposed to do that in that environment?" She paused, contemplating how much to share.

"But you didn't go down that road," prompted the moderator.

"I didn't. I think part of the reason is that *Family Tree* was an ensemble show." She looked across the stage at her former costars, smiling warmly. "There wasn't one star carrying everyone else. We were a group, and the older actors looked out for the younger ones. I think the shock of suddenly being in the spotlight was easier to absorb when it was shared between all of us."

"That's definitely true," interjected Rory Evans, one of the other stars of the show. "We all bonded in that environment, and we became a pretty tight-knit group. We were a support system for each other without really even realizing that's what we were doing."

"Totally." Steven Simmons nodded. "We were a crew. No one had pressure on his or her shoulders to make the show a success. I think part of the reason it was a success was that the bond Rory mentioned shone through on the screen. We were all friends."

"We're all *still* friends," said Rory, taking a sip of his

water. And it was true. Rory was a good friend, who'd seen her through the loss of a parent, through a change in career, from her teens to her thirtieth birthday just a few months ago.

"For sure," said Sierra, grateful that she hadn't had to shoulder the question on her own. "I can't speak for everyone else, but I think if I'd started in movies instead of on a TV show with the cast we had…" She shrugged. "Well, I don't know. I might've given Lindsay a run for her money."

"We all might've. In fact, some of us tried," said Steven, looking around innocently and drawing laughter from the audience. Although he had it together now, the antics of his early twenties were well documented.

"We did," said Sierra, her fingers once again straying to her star pendant. Rory reached over and squeezed her knee, giving her an encouraging nod. "You know the drinking, and the drugs, and the sex that I just referenced? All of that was true, at least for me. There was a period, between when *Family Tree* ended and when I started working on *Sunset Cove*, that I…" She trailed off, her fingers knotted together. "I lost control. I was seventeen, and my dad was dying of cancer. I was trying to figure out…well, everything, I guess. I was lost. Scared. So I drank, and I partied, and I hooked up with boys, trying to find a way to quell the fear that my world was about to end. Keep in mind that I also lived in a world that completely facilitated this behavior. It didn't matter that I wasn't legal, I had no issues getting into bars, finding someone to sell me pot, or getting boys' attention. That whole Hollywood world was so toxic. I didn't realize it at the time, but it was. Especially for a scared, lost kid. Everything came crashing down when my dad died, and then I had a pregnancy scare."

She forced herself to take a breath, and Rory gave her

knee another squeeze. "I'm telling you all of this to partly explain that in some ways, I'm not so different from other child stars. I was messed up. And that toxic environment is why I'm not really in that world anymore.

"When I thought I was pregnant, I went to Choices. For anyone who doesn't know, Choices is a nonprofit organization that provides confidential reproductive, maternal, and child health services at low or no cost, and has centers across the country. I didn't know where else to go. I didn't want to tell my mom. I didn't even know if I was pregnant, and I was too chicken to go buy a pregnancy test. What if someone recognized me?

"I was able to take a test there, and it turned out that I wasn't pregnant, which was a relief because clearly I would've been ill equipped to deal with an unplanned pregnancy at seventeen. I didn't have my own life together. How could I even think about a baby's life? The support I received at Choices played a huge role in turning my life around. They offered me counseling, birth control, and support at a time when I felt alone and scared. So after I finished working on *Sunset Cove*, I went to college, and now I work for Choices. I'm proud to be their spokesperson, because I know firsthand what a difference they can make in someone's life. Frankly, I—"

"Shut your fucking mouth, whore!" A male voice erupted from the crowd, and stunned silence fell over the audience. Sierra froze, her mouth still open. A chill ran up her spine as feeling of naked vulnerability engulfed her, pinning her in place. Rory's hand tightened on her knee and she scanned the crowd, but with the bright stage lights, she could see only the first few rows of people. Everyone else was hidden, shrouded in the shadows and beyond the reach of the lights. She glanced at Rory and the panel moderator, unsure what to do next. She'd spoken about Choices in public dozens of times, and no one had ever hurled obscenities like that at her.

And that's when something heavy, soggy, and cold slammed into her chest. It was as though someone had hit the slow-motion button on her life, and she felt as though she were suddenly underwater, dizzy and unable to get enough oxygen. Slowly she looked down, and all she could see was red, blooming in large patches on her dress, soaking it through. She ran her trembling hands down her torso, trying to figure out where all the blood had come from. But there was no pain, and the blood was cold.

Not her blood.

Shaking, she stood, and that's when she saw it, crumpled at her feet. A diaper with an exploded red dye pack. It was supposed to look like a bloody diaper. And someone had thrown it at her. A boiling anger ate at her chest, and her cheeks burned with humiliation. She clenched her jaw against the hot, stinging tears prickling her eyes.

"Oh my God, are you OK?" Rory's hands were on her shoulders, and the slow motion of the moment morphed into fast-forward. She shook again, a shiver racking her as a wave of dizziness washed over her, making the room tilt nauseatingly for a second. She nodded, her chest tingling hotly as her mind scrambled to make sense of what had just happened. The overwhelming urge to get the hell out of there took over, and she spun, almost tripping over the chair she'd just been sitting in. Shoving it aside, she ran offstage, needing to get away from the lights, away from the exposure.

Just away.

* * *

Sean Owens pulled his sunglasses from his face, squinting against the bright Los Angeles sunshine as he strode toward the back entrance of the convention center, slipping them into the pocket of his suit jacket. He scanned the small aboveground employee parking lot, on the alert for any unusual activity, but nothing stood out. The standard perimeter check complete, he reached into another pocket for his phone, ready to check in with De Luca, the new guy on his team, before heading back to the office.

Before he could send the text message, the nondescript door at the back of the convention center flew open, slamming against the brick wall with a sharp bang, and he tensed, his hand edging toward the Glock 19 in the shoulder holster under his suit jacket. A woman came rushing out, one hand clutched to her chest, her face pale.

She was covered in blood.

Ten years of training and carefully honed instinct kicked into high gear, and he rushed toward her, his legs kicking into motion before he even had time to think about it. He raked his eyes over her tiny body, trying to figure out where all the blood was coming from, and if it was hers. She wasn't moving as though she was injured. She almost collided with him, but he anticipated her and braced his hands in front of him, his fingers curling lightly around her upper arms to steady her. She gasped and looked up, and a pair of bright-green, terrified eyes met his. Immediately he looked behind her, trying to determine if someone was pursuing her.

"Are you hurt? Is this your blood?" he asked, keeping his voice calm as he held her steady, his eyes still scanning the area for potential threats.

She shook her head, the ends of her golden-brown hair brushing against his fingers.

"No," she said, her voice strained. "It's dye."

He frowned and once again scanned the area behind her as he swapped places with her, putting himself between her and the door.

"Are you all right? You're not hurt?"

She laughed, the sound shaky and hollow. "Am I all right? Not really. But I'm not injured."

Sean's heart eased out of his throat from where it had leaped at the sight of a woman covered in blood running out of the convention center. But only slightly.

She pulled away, moving back a little. "I need to go."

He nodded, wanting more than anything to help her. "Where? I can drive you."

She took another step away from him, one eyebrow arched, a frown on her face. "Yeah, I don't get into cars with strange men, but thanks for the offer." A bit of color returned to her cheeks, making her green eyes look even brighter.

"Understandable. My name's Sean, and I'm a security expert." She eyed him warily, and he continued. "A bodyguard. I'm here at the convention to check on a new member of my team, see how he's doing with a client." He slipped his hand into his pocket and fished out a business card, handing it to her, wanting to earn her trust. Even though she was uninjured, his instincts told him that she needed him. She studied the card with narrowed eyes for a second before crossing her arms over her chest.

"This doesn't prove anything. You could've had these made."

He bit his lip, trying to suppress the smile he knew wouldn't get him anywhere. But he couldn't help it. Not only was she cute, she was smart.

"I just…" She toyed with his card, running it back and forth over her knuckles. "I just need a minute."

"Why don't you sit down?" He gestured to a bench several feet away. She glanced from him to the bench before finally nodding. Still keeping himself between her and the door, he let her lead the way. She sat down heavily, her elbows on her thighs, her face in her hands. He eased down beside her, sitting so as to block her from view of the convention center's back door. He watched as she took several deep breaths, and his chest tightened slightly. She was scared, and upset. Even if she didn't trust him, he could protect her from whatever had her so upset, and no way in hell was he going to leave her on her own. He couldn't. Not only was it his training, but there was something about this woman. He couldn't put his finger on it, but he felt drawn to her. Wanted to protect her and look after her.

The parking lot was quiet except for the distant rush of traffic from the front of the convention center, the rustling of the leaves of the trees lining the parking lot, and a bird chirping softly somewhere above them. Her slender shoulders rose and fell as she took several deep breaths, and he said nothing, giving her space. After a few moments, she straightened and leaned back against the bench, smoothing her hands over her stained dress that had once been white or yellow. It was so ruined, he couldn't tell for sure. Her eyes raked over him, and he let her look, hoping to put her at ease. Finally her eyes met his.

"What happened?" he asked, needing to know so he could keep her safe.

She sighed heavily, and her shoulders relaxed, easing down from around her ears. "I was speaking at the convention," she said, gesturing to the building behind them, "and someone threw a diaper full of dye at me."

"Someone attacked you with a diaper?"

She nodded, her bottom lip caught between her teeth. She looked up, her eyes once again meeting his, and there was that tug in his chest again. That pull.

"Why would someone do that?" he asked, propping one ankle on his knee and threading his fingers together, forcing his body into a relaxed posture to hide the tension radiating through him.

"I guess because I have some unpopular opinions."

"About?"

"Equal access to birth control and family planning. I'm a spokesperson for Choices, the women's health non-profit." She looked down at her splotchy dress and sighed again, rubbing a hand over her face.

"Ah. Explains the diaper." The knot between his shoulders loosened just slightly. Chances were this was nothing more than idiot protesters, looking to make a point by embarrassing her. He looked back at the door again, but there was no sign of anyone following her.

Her lips moved, a tiny ghost of a smile. "I'm sorry I kind of accused you of…lying, or whatever. I didn't mean to be rude. I'm just…"

He held up a hand. "No apology needed."

She glanced down at his card, still clutched in one hand, now slightly crumpled. "I've heard of Virtus," she said, referring to the security company he ran with his father. The blue-and-gray logo was emblazoned across the top of the card he'd given her. She extended her hand across to him. "I'm Sierra, by the way."

He nodded. In the back of his brain, he'd recognized her almost immediately, but his concern for her had taken precedence over everything else. "I know. I'm Sean." He enveloped her small, delicate hand in his, and a warm, electrical tingle worked its way up his arm. Slowly she pulled her hand back, and damn, the friction of her skin against his felt good.

"I know." She held up the card.

He rubbed a hand over his cheek, his closely cropped beard bristling against his fingers. "Right. So, any idea who might've attacked you?" He scanned the quiet parking lot again. No way in hell was anyone getting close to her right now.

She blew out a slow breath and shook her head. "Not a clue." Some of the color dropped out of her face again, and he knew he needed to keep her talking. The urge to comfort her was nearly overwhelming. He couldn't change what had happened to her, but he could try to make the present suck a little less. He wanted to ask her about her own security, if she had anyone working for her, but thought that might come off like too much of a sales pitch, and that wasn't what she needed right now. So he headed in another direction.

"Were you on a panel?" he asked, tipping his head toward the convention center.

She nodded. "Yeah. *Family Tree* reunion. We do it every year for 90's Con."

"I remember that show. You were cute."

She smiled, fully and genuinely this time, and that smile aimed in his direction felt just as good as the slide of her hand against his. "Thanks. It was a long time ago. I'm surprised people are still interested in it twenty years after the fact, to be honest. Surprised, but glad."

He tilted his head, considering. "People grew up watching that show. I know I did."

Her eyebrows rose, and she leaned toward him slightly. "You did?"

"Sure."

"I guess I thought…I don't know. That it was mostly dweebs who watched it. It was kind of a goody-goody show." She shrugged, wrinkling her nose. Fuck, she was cute. His chest tightened again, but this time there was something else there along with the protectiveness.

He arched an eyebrow. "Who's to say I wasn't a dweeb?"

She laughed. "I seriously doubt that." Her eyes skimmed down over his body again, this time leaving a trail of heat in their wake.

"And why's that?" His eyes met hers, and a flush crawled up her neck and to her cheeks. Her eyes dropped to his mouth, just for a second, and something hot and thick pulsed in the air between them. She tucked a strand of hair behind her ear, and his fingers itched to repeat the motion.

Damn. She wasn't just cute. She was gorgeous.

"You don't look like a dweeb," she said softly.

Several feet away the door swung open again, and Sean leaped to his feet, putting himself between whoever had emerged and Sierra. She stepped out from around him and into the arms of Rory Evans, her former costar and…what, exactly?

"I've been looking for you. Are you OK?" he asked as he held her.

She nodded, and Sean was surprised at the jealousy swirling through him at the sight of this woman—who was pretty much a stranger—in someone else's arms.

"I'm OK. I just needed some air."

Rory smoothed a hand over her hair, completely ignoring Sean. "The police are here, and they want to get a statement from you about what happened."

She nodded again, and started to walk back toward the convention center. Turning suddenly, she laid a hand on

Sean's arm, giving it a squeeze. She smiled up at him and it was as if someone were squeezing his heart with a fist.

"Thank you, Sean." Her hand lingered on his arm for a second, the air between them once again thickening.

How good would it feel to pull her into his arms the way Rory had just done? At least there she'd be safe. "You're welcome. Listen, if you ever…need anything, give me a call." He pointed at the card still in her hand, reluctant to let her go, but knowing he needed to get back to the office. Trying to reassure himself she'd be all right, with her *friend*, or whatever the hell Rory was to her, and the police. "You sure you're OK?" he asked, wishing he could go back inside with her to keep an eye on her. Not wanting to let her go. It felt…wrong.

Another fierce tug yanked at his chest.

"Yeah. I am." Her eyes held his for a second, and then she turned, slipping her arm into Rory's.

Sean pushed a hand through his hair as he watched Sierra walk away, his heart punching against his ribs as she glanced back over her shoulder at him one last time before disappearing back into the convention center. He took a deep breath, and then another, and then he walked back to his SUV. He looked back over his shoulder, contemplating going inside, just for a few minutes, just to make sure everything was under control…yeah. It couldn't hurt. He'd taken a few steps back toward the convention center when his phone rang, vibrating in his pocket.

"Owens."

"Who are you sending on the Robinson job?" his father asked, no greeting, just a barking question. Typical.

"Davis and Anderson. Why?" Sean's jaw tightened, tension seeping down his neck.

"You don't think it needs a third?"

Sean shook his head, irritated but not surprised that as usual, his dad was questioning his judgment. "It's a pretty standard job, so no. I think Davis and Anderson can handle it just fine, and keeping it to two keeps it within Robinson's budget."

"Uh-huh," said his father, sounding unconvinced. "This goes wrong, it's on you."

"It'll be fine. They've got it, and I'll check in with them regularly," said Sean, yanking open the door to his SUV and dropping into the driver's seat. He rubbed a hand over his mouth, used to his dad's blaming him for everything that went wrong. But just because he was used to it didn't mean it went down any easier.

Especially the blame he deserved. After all, it was his fucking fault his mother wasn't around anymore.

Phone jammed between his ear and his shoulder, he pressed the ignition button and tugged his seat belt on.

"You check on De Luca?"

Sean grimaced. "Didn't get the chance. Something else came up, but I'll check in with him by phone. I'm sure he would've made contact if there were any issues. I'm on my way back to the office now. Did you get the proposal I sent about the revised marketing plan?"

His dad sighed heavily. "It's a waste of fucking time. Not to mention money."

Sean leaned his head back against the seat, his jaw clenched tight. Nothing was ever good enough. "Let's talk about it back at the office."

"Fine. But it'll take a lot to convince me you can pull it off."

Sean almost snorted. Story of his fucking life, right there.

Fall in Love with Forever Romance

STARLIGHT BRIDGE
By Debbie Mason

Hidden in Graystone Manor is a book containing *all* the dark little
secrets of Harmony Harbor...including Ava DiRossi's. No one—
especially her ex-husband, Griffin Gallagher—can ever discover the
truth about what tore their life apart years ago. Only now Griffin is back
in town. Still handsome. Still hating her for leaving him. And still not
aware that Ava never stopped loving him...

Fall in Love with Forever Romance

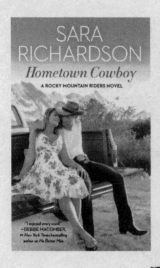

HOMETOWN COWBOY
By Sara Richardson

In the *New York Times* bestselling tradition of Jennifer Ryan and Maisey Yates comes the first book in Sara Richardson's Rocky Mountain Riders series featuring three bull-riding brothers. What would a big-time rodeo star like Lance Cortez see in Jessa Mae Love, a small-town veterinarian who wears glasses? Turns out, *plenty*.

THE BASTARD BILLIONAIRE
By Jessica Lemmon

Since returning from the war, Eli Crane has shut everybody out. That is, until Isabella Sawyer starts as his personal assistant with her sassy attitude and her curves for days. But will the secret she hides shatter the fragile trust they've built? Fans of Jill Shalvis and Jennifer Probst will love with Jessica Lemmon's Billionaire Bad Boys series.

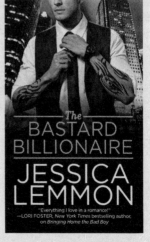

Fall in Love with Forever Romance

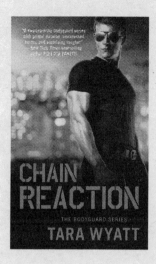

CHAIN REACTION
By Tara Wyatt

Alexa Fairfax is practically Hollywood royalty, but after she discovers a plot more deadly than any movie script, Alexa desperately needs a bodyguard. So she accepts the help of Zack De Luca, a true friend with a protective nature—and chiseled muscles to back it up. Zack is training to be an MMA fighter, but his biggest battle will be to resist his feelings for the woman who is way out of his league...

IF THE DUKE DEMANDS
By Anna Harrington

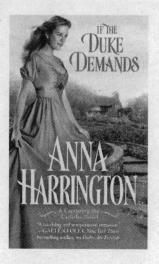

In the *New York Times* bestselling tradition of Elizabeth Hoyt, Grace Burrowes, and Madeline Hunter comes the first in a sexy new series from Anna Harrington. Sebastian Carlisle, the new Duke of Trent, needs a respectable wife befitting his station. But when he begins to fall for the reckless, flighty Miranda Hodgkins, he must decide between his title and his heart.